The Resident Murder

The Resident Murder

by

Jessi Kroft

Disclaimer

This is a work of fiction.

Names, characters, places and incidents are products of the author's imagination or are used fictitiously and are not to be construed as real.

Any resemblance to actual events, locales, organizations, or persons, living or dead, is entirely coincidental.

To Rio,
the boy who inherited my love of reading
and all things Halloween

Prologue

I may not survive the night. I never imagined it would end this way. I'm no stranger to seeing blood, but seeing my own spout out of an orifice in my body is a surreal feeling. My eyes search as my hands feel around to locate where the blood is coming from. Hopefully the knife hasn't seared through a vital organ. The serrated edge comes towards me again, and I maneuver to avoid it, twisting my torso like a contortionist. I gasp as it misses my heart by two inches, slightly grazing my stomach. My heart, which must be going at a million beats per minute, the way it pounds in my chest, the thump-thump deafening in my ears. My instinct to survive, kicking in to protect my heart and my head, the control centers of the body.

Blood continues to spill onto the pleated rug beneath me as I'm pushed down hard and my head makes contact with the floor, sending tremors through the walls. I let out an anguished wail and come to terms with who is trying to hurt me, to kill me. Wincing in pain, I grab the back of my head, hoping it's not cracked open. A breath, trapped in my lungs, escapes my lips as I force myself to confront my attacker. How is this happening right now? How did I get here? I try to scream again, but my voice gets caught in my throat. I am paralyzed with fear. Willing myself to fight back, to escape, I bang my feet hard on the floor beneath me, my body thrashing as my movements reverberate through the floor. I hope someone below us will hear me and call the police. The knife hovers above me, threatening to strike again, but I manage to grab my attacker's wrist and twist it away from me.

Attempting to scramble to my feet, struggling to push my assailant off of me, I'm once again confronted by brute force, and my body slams into the coffee table. A glass vase falls to the floor, shattering, the broken pieces dispersing around us. I feel for my phone, but it's not on me. My eyes scan the room, and I think I see it by the doorway—likely tossed across the room amid the scuffle. I try to crawl my way towards it when I feel another swipe of the knife at my arm. I look fervently around the room for any object I can use to shield me from the blows and stabs.

But it's too late.

My vision is fading.

I hear…

And then darkness…

Chapter 1

Kylie

I roll over in bed and look at the time: 6:15 a.m.

The monotony of my morning routine begins. Sit up. Brush teeth. Wash face. Scrubs on. Grab mug. Walk to subway. The procedure brings me a sense of comfort as I embark on another day of a grueling training program.

Barely two years into my neurology residency, and it feels like I've been walking these streets forever with no end in sight. Passing the same bodegas on the way to the train, greeted by the same eccentrics hanging out around the station, hearing the same quintessential voices saying, "It's showtime," while clutching my bag and white coat closer to my body. Performers jump from subway pole to pole, kicking in the air, doing acrobatics as if we are spectators at the Cirque du Soleil. Except at 6:45 a.m., I assure you, nobody is ready for the show. I watch as the usual passengers roll their eyes, stick in their AirPods, and bury their noses deeper into their books, cementing the sentiment that they have no time for shenanigans and are unfazed by the scene unfolding around them. Tuning into my true crime podcast, *Crime and Conviction*, I close my eyes and join the masses, blocking out the cacophony of the train.

When we stop at Union Square, I hop off the subway, push through the turnstile, fend off the morning crowds, and climb the stairs to street level. The air feels muggy this morning, but refreshing after sitting on the cramped train for the last fifteen minutes. On my way to the hospital, I pass food trucks and coffee stands with lines of people waiting to kickstart their mornings. One great thing about Manhattan is knowing that others are also up at this hour about to start the daily grind. Misery loves company, I guess.

The flashing sign outside the hospital entrance illuminates the block. I loop around the back entrance of the hospital, swipe my ID, and traipse toward the resident work room to relieve the overnight resident. The stench of overworked residents, a mixture of body odor and acrid sweat, coalesces with pungent food and collides with my nostrils. I think about the last time someone thoroughly cleaned out our resident room. Sure, housekeeping probably does a quick vacuum once a night, but what about the food rotting in the fridge from weeks ago that no one has bothered to throw out? When I last opened the refrigerator, a box of noodles remained, a remnant of Chinese takeout from two weeks prior.

Before I can even step through the doorway, the overnight resident, Bailey, shouts at me, "Hey, Kylie, it was a doozy of a night. Twelve consults, one pending. Let's run the list." His hair is tousled, and dark circles are visible under his eyes. Candy and granola bar wrappers litter the desk in front of him—a diet fit for a medical resident.

"Hello to you too, Bailey," I say, my tone laced with annoyance.

"Sorry, I'm tired," he retorts as he buries his face in his hands.

The room feels hot and stuffy, but a portable fan is blowing towards him. His reflex hammer rests on the patient list, serving as a paperweight. As I pull on my white coat, I look over the list:

Robinson—65-year-old man who presents with 5 days of headache, MRI of the brain: unrevealing, diagnosis: status migrainosus;

Barker—48-year-old woman with hypertension and diabetes presents with right facial droop and right arm weakness, diagnosis: middle cerebral artery stroke;

Zhou—38-year-old man who presents with tingling of bilateral arms, cervical spine MRI pending.

Bailey walks me through all the patients he was called about last night and catches me up to speed on what we're doing for them. Before we can finish the patient sign-out process, the pager at my hip goes off and reads, *ER—stroke alert.* I haven't even been here for ten minutes and already there's a stroke alert.

"Sorry, Bailey, gotta go, just leave the list here for me and text me if there's anything urgent," I shout. Bailey packs up his stuff to leave, and I rush out of the resident room, heading down to the emergency room.

Walking past rows of stretchers, I'm surrounded by a sea of paramedics and nurses leading me to the patient while barking out observations and pertinent pieces of information: "Sixty-eight-year-old man," "woke up with right arm weakness," "last normal at 5 a.m. this morning."

I sidle up to the stretcher at the far end of the emergency room where a man with peppered grey hair and deep blue eyes is lying. He gazes up at me, a beseeching look on his face. Placing my hand on his, I explain that I'm a neurologist and will be examining him. I do a perfunctory exam, asking the patient to lift his arms, lift each leg, and smile for me. Observing that his smile is asymmetrical and his right arm drifts down while his left arm stays steady, it's clear he has weakness of his right face and right arm. He's going to need a brain scan to confirm what is most probably a stroke of the left middle cerebral artery. Hovering over my shoulder is presumably his wife, who appears scared.

I turn to her and offer what reassurance I can at the moment. "I'm sorry, but it looks like he may be having a stroke. We will have to get a scan of his head to confirm this, and then we will discuss next steps. You can wait out here for us."

She nods. As I push my way through the hordes of nurses and emergency room staff to get the patient to the scanner, I almost collide with someone exiting the radiology suite. He turns around. *Oh, crap*, I think. Standing face-to-face with me is Blake Weathers.

"Hey, Kylie, is this a stroke code?" he asks casually. He towers over me as he flashes that pearlescent smile. That smile that makes me weak in my knees. His brown hair is slightly disheveled, indicative of an already hectic morning on the neurosurgery wards, and a blue ink stain is visible over the breast pocket of his white coat where his ID badge is clinging precariously. Feeling like a deer in headlights, I quickly adjust my demeanor to appear unperturbed.

"Hey," I respond with an apprehensive tone. "We need to get a CT head and then a CT angiogram. He will probably need a thrombectomy." Pushing past Blake to wheel the patient into the scanner, the discordant sounds of the emergency room fade behind me. Once the patient is safely strapped into the scanner, I go back to the radiology office to view the images as they come in. I can feel Blake's presence behind me, looming over my shoulder to see whether the brain shows any sign of a bleed. If there's blood, we won't be able to administer the necessary treatment. If there's a clot in a major artery, a neurosurgeon will be asked to help remove it, which is why Blake is here. The radiologist clicks through the images of the brain, and thankfully, there's no bleed. There is, however, a brightness in the left middle cerebral artery. And bingo! Just what I suspected. He has a clot in the middle cerebral artery. Time to get this guy some clot-busting treatment and a thrombectomy to pull it out. It's always gratifying when you can identify the cause of a stroke and know that there is something that can be done to potentially treat the patient. As a second-year resident, it's especially rewarding when what you suspected is correct. It's common for most residents to deal with imposter syndrome on a regular basis so it's moments like this one that make me feel like a competent neurologist or at least on my way to becoming one. I excitedly turn to Blake and ask him to alert his attending. Blake is a fifth-year neurosurgery resident, and apparently currently rotating on the neurovascular service.

We met about two months ago, when we bumped into each other at a bar and spent the rest of the night talking. I thought we had chemistry, and we exchanged numbers at the end of the night, intending to meet again, but then he ghosted me. I later heard through the grapevine that he had an on-again, off-again girlfriend. Typical neurosurgeon behavior, I guess. I shouldn't have been surprised as I have a habit of picking the wrong guy, which sometimes makes it hard to trust my instincts around people. Since that night, I've run into him at the hospital a few times, and there's always an awkward silence followed by meaningless small talk. I haven't had much dating luck since moving to Manhattan as the dating scene is intimidating, and at times, I wonder whether I'm the problem.

Blake calls his attending and notifies her that the patient will need a procedure to remove his clot. His attending, Dr. Casey Lane is one of the few female neurosurgery attendings in the department. Surgery is a male-dominated field, but that is changing, and it always fills me with a sense of pride when she is on call. While he's speaking to Dr. Lane, I slip out of the room and go update the patient's wife.

She's standing in the corner of the emergency room with a somber look on her face. As I walk over to her, she lifts her eyes to meet mine, scrutinizing my face for answers.

"Hi, Mrs. Emerson," I start just as another page interrupts. I quiet the piercing sound coming from my hip and continue, "Your husband appears to have a clot in one of the major arteries in his brain, which is causing the stroke. We will give him some medication to break up the clot and then do a procedure that will take it out." I go over the potential risks of the procedure with her, and she agrees to move forward with it.

As I walk back into the radiology room to use the phone and return the page, Blake is still standing there, and now we are both alone in the room. He speaks as he moves a hand through his messy hair. "Hey, I've been meaning to reach out, but I've been so busy."

My eyes dart away from him. "Yeah, I figured," I respond coolly, attempting to mask my disappointment. I'm not sure whether to believe him. After all, we're all busy, but we find ways to prioritize the things we want. I tend to give more grace to his kind, however, as I know neurosurgeons work arduous hours that leave little room for socialization and dating. Plus, the rigors of the field turn so many of them into desensitized robots.

"If you're still up for it, I'd like to take you out sometime," he says sheepishly. My eyes scan the monitors in the room. Incoming images of the nervous system are displayed across them, each waiting to be deciphered by a radiologist. Patients and their families anticipating news, whether good or bad. News that will determine their fates. The days can be grueling, but what we all collectively do, putting puzzle pieces together to take care of people, leaves me in awe. I'm reminded again why I chose this profession.

"Sure, text me and we'll see," I reply, once again trying to come off like I don't care, which is hard to do as I meet his intense dark eyes again, which are currently penetrating my soul, making me want to collapse right there outside the scanner. But since I don't want to become a stroke code myself, I gather myself and tell him I have to go.

I think back to the night I formally met Blake, at a bar on 85th and 2nd where my co-residents and I were decompressing after work one day. I grabbed a drink at the bar and felt a brush against my shoulder. "Hey, you're one of the neuro residents, right?" The first thing I noticed were his deep, enigmatic, brown eyes that hinted at a complexity I would soon learn about.

"Yeah, I'm Kylie," I replied. I brought my vodka tonic to my lips and took a sip, the liquid burning as it traveled down my esophagus.

"I'm Blake, neurosurgery," he asserted. "I've seen you around the hospital." He swirled his drink in his hand, a whiff of whiskey hanging in the air.

As he gazed at me, a warm sensation spread throughout my body, into my chest, making me feel like I was on fire. There was something mysterious and potentially dark about him, but there was also a veil of kindness that made his aura all the more confusing. Slight creases formed at the corners of his eyes as he smiled, giving away the many sleepless nights he endured and stressors of being a cog in the wheel of the neurosurgery department.

We locked eyes for about five seconds before I said, "So what's it like getting yelled at all day long? I heard the neurosurgery group is pretty toxic." He motioned for me to follow him to a table for two near the bar.

"I think that's the norm everywhere, but thankfully we are all masochists, so it's not that jarring," he said with a sinister smile. "But for real, we break away when we can. I still wouldn't trade it for anything else. Being privy to the complexity of a living, breathing brain and all its functions working synchronously to keep a person alive. The rush of putting a scalpel to someone's head and taking that first cut. The confidence that patients have in you. It's all pretty intoxicating." He looked completely enraptured as he spoke.

"Yeah, I can see that, but I prefer the view outside of people's bodies." He chuckled at that.

We spent the rest of the night talking, mostly about our respective residencies and our upbringings. Blake told me he grew up as an only child in a small town in upstate New York called Seaway. Neither of his parents were in medicine, but his interest in the field was engendered early on. He talked about neurosurgery as if it was the most magnificent thing imaginable. The thrill he got when he identified a tumor, knowing he could help someone, the immense satisfaction attained from predicting the outcome of a case but simultaneously from not knowing what to expect when he opened somebody's skull. I was enthralled by his fascination with the field of neurosurgery. It was like he woke up every morning prepared to conquer another day in the operating room. I envisioned him entering the operating room and echoing Dr. Shepherd from *Grey's Anatomy*: "It's a beautiful day to save lives." I didn't know many people who were five years into training and had such a positive outlook on medicine. Hell, I was only in my second year of residency and already felt myself separating from that part of me that was intrigued and bewildered by the brain. It was nice to be in the presence of someone so passionate.

Our conversation flowed so easily, I didn't notice that about three hours had passed since we started talking. Looking around the bar, I no longer saw his friends or my co-residents. I figured they had seen us talking and left us to be alone. I looked at my phone, and Lisa had texted me: *Saw you were busy* (a winky face inserted), *come meet us at Dorian's if you want.* My mind immediately conjured up the "preppy murder" case from the 1980s where a young high school student, Jennifer Levin, was murdered in Central Park by one of her classmates, Robert Chambers, after they had been spotted at Dorian's.

Dorian's, a hub for well-connected young people, was often frequented by Chambers and became a symbol of elitism and privilege that contrasted with Jennifer Levin's more modest background. I've often thought about her when passing by that signature red awning and how scary it must have been to think she was in the presence of someone she could trust only to find out they were dangerous. It's easy to always think about the possibilities for danger at every turn, especially when living in a big city, but in my time in NYC so far, I've never really felt as if I was in danger. The city always seems to be wide awake and bustling with people, so it feels like the odds of being murdered out in the middle of the street in front of hundreds of gaping eyes are low.

But being the true-crime enthusiast that I am, I can't help but think of the many murders that have occurred right out in the open. For example, the 1960s Kitty Genovese case. In that case, a young woman was raped and murdered right inside the apartment building she lived in while neighbors and onlookers who heard her cries did not call the police. This is referred to as the "bystander effect" or "Genovese syndrome," the idea that bystanders are less likely to intervene or call for help when others are present. Presumably, each witness probably thought someone else called for help and went about their business, passing on the responsibility to others. Whenever I feel my guard go down, I think back to Kitty Genovese and remind myself that's when I need to start worrying.

Despite my tendency to think of worst-case scenarios, even though I had just met Blake, I felt at ease with him. Don't get me wrong, there was something mysterious and maybe even frightening about him, but as our conversation ensued, I felt it was more of an exciting mystery rather than a dark one. Plus, he saves lives for a living, so how dangerous could he be? At this point in the night, I was about three drinks in on an empty stomach, so I already felt drunk, and the idea of meeting up with my co-residents at Dorian's and potentially abandoning Blake did not appeal to me.

Blake suggested we take the short walk back to his apartment and continue our conversation there. He gripped my hand tightly as we walked, as if he feared letting go and losing me. It felt good to have someone who wanted to protect me, even if for a moment. We stepped out onto the street, and the evening air felt crisp. It was my favorite time of year—the fall—and something about walking hand in hand with a strikingly handsome man I just met on the streets of Manhattan at midnight felt ethereal. While the city is always alive and in constant motion, at night, there's a serenity that emerges, creating a unique ambiance. The tall buildings seem to lean in and whisper the secrets of the tenants inside. Restaurants and bars buzz with activity along the sidewalks. The taxis rev through the streets carrying some passengers home from a wild night out, and others home from work (more times than not, an overworked medical resident or investment banker).

Blake lives in a high-rise building that houses several units subsidized by the hospital. It's much nicer than the building I inhabit and makes me wonder whether the surgical residents get special treatment, at least when it comes to housing.

As we entered, the doorman gave him a nod, and we took the elevator to the eighth floor. A doorman building with an elevator on the Upper East Side of Manhattan is definitely a luxury as a resident. Most of my co-residents live in walk-up buildings with virtually no security.

"Here we are," Blake said as he opened the door to his apartment. Eager to see what it looked like, I hurried inside, but it was dark, and I felt my head spin a little.

Noticing my disoriented state, Blake led me towards the couch, steadying me on his arm. "Are you okay? Can I get you some water?" He asked with concern.

"Yes, that would be great."

When he turned on the lights, I ogled the sizeable living area, which included a newly finished kitchen and modern furniture. The design and placement of the furniture was sophisticated, giving notes of a woman's touch. The couch, a vivid burgundy hue, looked expensive and felt inviting, the perfect place to curl up with a book after a long day. My hand stroked the plush cushions that were neatly placed in the crooks, admiring the soft fabric. Two cream-colored loveseats sat on either side of the couch, providing a sharp but tasteful contrast. The apartment was also noticeably clean and organized; perhaps the sterility of the operating room transcended to his living spaces. Although his apartment was a studio and his "bedroom" was visibly next to the kitchen, there was a wall that blocked off the view of the side his bed was on. Nonetheless, I was impressed by the digs.

I took a seat on the couch and felt myself sink into the cushions as Blake plopped down right next to me, our knees touching. As I took a few sips of my water, he recounted a riveting surgical case he assisted with earlier that day. A patient had come in with a headache, dizziness and vomiting. An MRI of the brain showed a high-grade glioma in the posterior fossa, and there was some swelling in the surrounding brain structures. His attending took the patient to the operating room and performed a craniotomy.

As he went on about the case, I noted a change in his affect, his serious demeanor transforming into an animated one. His eyes widened as he described the surgical technique his attending used and the way he maneuvered around the patient's brainstem, avoiding any catastrophic complications. He waved his hands exuberantly as he described all the steps taken to save the patient.

Suddenly, he stopped mid-sentence. "Sorry, am I boring you? I can get carried away sometimes," he said abashedly.

"Not at all, I think it's cute how excited you get about neurosurgery," I replied, tucking a strand of hair behind my ear.

He grinned back at me and moved closer. "Well I think you're very cute," he said, and I felt my heart race. He reached his hands out, and as he cradled my face in his hands, he delicately kissed me on the lips, lightly biting my lower lip. I melted into his grasp as I moved closer to him. Our bodies were now touching, and his hands were moving swiftly through my hair as his mouth continued to move along with mine. He dropped one of his hands to my thigh, his fingers delicately marching upwards until they reached the hem of my shirt and landed on my bare skin, sending chills across my body. After a few seconds, he slowly pulled away. "I should get you home. I have an early case tomorrow."

A feeling of disappointment rushed up inside of me, but I also admired that he was being a gentleman, and that he was clearly so dedicated to his training. "Sounds good," I conceded.

"I'll order you an Uber. I don't want you walking home late at night. You never know what crazies could be lurking in the dark," he said. If he only knew how much I know about the "crazies."

He walked me down to the lobby of his building. "I'd love to see you again, Kylie. I'll call you to get dinner soon," he said as he gently kissed me on the lips again. We exchanged phone numbers, and he said he would reach out later this week.

When I got home, Blake texted me to make sure I made it. It was definitely a green flag that he was so concerned about me getting home safely. I felt giddy, especially when I got another text the next morning indicating he had a great time and wanted to see me again soon. But then, after that, I didn't hear from him again. Obviously a red flag, canceling out that earlier green flag.

The last few weeks have been torturous as I've replayed that night over and over in my head. Reflexively looking at my phone every time I get a text message to see if it's from him or analyzing our last few text messages to each other, I feel pathetic. At times I feel silly, as it was just one night, but then I feel justified in my confusion that he led me on only to disappear. I've even wondered if I had imagined the chemistry between us or maybe I was more drunk than I thought I was and misinterpreted the whole night.

As I leave the emergency room, I spot my co-resident, Chloe, down the hallway. She walks towards me, a measured sense of confidence palpable in every step she takes. Her aura exudes a radiance and warmth that can be felt from several feet away, contrasting with the sterility of the hospital hallway. The lights overhead bounce off her blond hair, which loosely rests on her shoulders, and her blue eyes meet mine as we get closer. "Hey, Kylie, what's going on?" she asks, a warm smile taking hold on her face. "Oh, you know, just walking back from a stroke alert. What are you up to?"

"Just checking in on a patient I saw yesterday who came in with acute memory loss. It was strange. His daughter brought him in and said he suddenly forgot where he was and what he was doing. His labs were sent off, and we are still waiting for those to come back, but I just thought I'd check in on him and see how he's doing. He should be on your patient list."

"Yeah, I didn't get a chance to finish hearing about all the patients from Bailey," I say, with a hint of irritation. "Aren't you rotating on an elective?" I ask, confused as to why she's checking in on a patient on my list. Chloe covered a late afternoon consult shift yesterday, but she is not on our consult team.

"Yeah, I'm on outpatient psychiatry, but clinic doesn't start until 9 a.m. so I have some time to kill." So like Chloe. Getting here early, before she needs to be here to go check on a patient she is no longer caring for. It's admirable, but I also find myself a bit annoyed that she's such an overachiever.

"You're such an all-star," I say as I playfully roll my eyes at her.

When I get back to the resident room, Lisa is sitting at a computer, typing up a note, and looks at me quizzically. Her auburn hair is neatly pulled back into a low ponytail, which is draped down her back. She tilts her head to the side and narrows her hazel eyes. "You look flushed, you okay?" she asks as she swivels her chair towards me.

"Yeah. I'm fine. Just had another awkward run-in with CNS."

CNS stands for "cocky neurosurgeon," a play off the acronym for "central nervous system." (I know, we are dorky). Lisa keeps tabs on my awkward encounters. As someone who has been in a stable relationship since we started residency, she relishes dissecting my personal life and tracking all my dating tragedies. Blake has been branded "CNS," as there are multiple cocky characters currently circulating in my dating pool.

"Well, you know what they say about neurosurgeons? They are basically sociopaths," she says as she turns her attention back to the computer and starts hammering at the keyboard. I have never known anyone to type so forcefully and intently, as if she's writing a declaration of war. Her keyboard clacks can often be heard from the next room, perhaps a reflection of her intense personality. "Everyone knows that, Kylie," she adds, glancing back at me as she continues to type.

I take a sip of my coffee, my reward for a top-of-the-hour stroke alert. Residency has turned me into a regular coffee drinker. Coffee was never a vice before, but there seems to be some association in my mind now that connects coffee drinking to going to the hospital, as if it's my lifeline or security blanket. It's probably a placebo effect, but when that sharp, bitter taste softened by creamy milk hits my taste buds, I instantly feel revived.

"Let's not generalize. I'm sure there are some good ones out there," I respond, sounding more peeved than I intend to. Regrettably, I know exactly what she's talking about, as I recently read a book about psychopaths where the author dedicated an entire chapter to the sociopathy associated with being a neurosurgeon. Turns out, they are more likely to be sociopaths than psychopaths, so that's good, I guess, but the lack of emotional availability the book associates with being a neurosurgeon is not a good sign for personal relationships. Some argue that to an extent, being a sociopath is an advantage when performing neurosurgery because it allows neurosurgeons to disassociate from the emotions that can cloud their judgment when it comes to patient care and put their energy into the technical skills required to operate effectively, which can lead to better outcomes. In essence, good for patients, bad for lovers. Still though, it's not like this is fact, just stereotypes and theories.

"Maybe so, but the evidence is pretty damning," Lisa quips. "They have the highest rate of divorce and the most sociopathic tendencies of all specialties." She suddenly stops typing and turns to give me a knowing look. The distinctive heart-shaped mole on her chin, the one she tries to conceal underneath cover-up, falls within my line of sight. "Kylie, it's okay to have a little fun once in a while, but we need to find you a solid guy."

I give her an annoyed glance and sit down at the computer across from her to write my consult note for the patient I just saw. It must be nice to be in a solid relationship and just pass judgement on other peoples' dating lives, but I know Lisa's heart is in the right place. In the time I've known her, she's always been a supportive friend, but sometimes her honesty stings. She can be rather blunt and critical, which makes me wonder whether I should divulge every aspect of my dating life to her. But maybe I just can't handle the truth. It's good to have a friend who doesn't always tell you what you want to hear. A few weeks ago, we went shopping, and I tried on a pair of black leather pants, thinking they'd be a great addition to my fall wardrobe. Lisa casually told me they looked cheap. I remember being dismayed by her honesty, but she was probably right.

My phone, which I forgot to take off sleep mode this morning, lights up with a text message. *Hey, it was nice seeing you in action. Will keep you posted on how the thrombectomy goes. Does Friday work for a date?*

…and there it is. The text I've been yearning to get the last few weeks suddenly appearing out of thin air. An intense feeling of anxiety rushes up into my chest and triggers a subtle fluttering of my heart. Something tells me this guy is trouble, but perhaps I should give people the benefit of the doubt once in a while. One thing is for sure, though: he enjoys sending mixed messages.

Chapter 2

Blake

I roll over in bed and look at the alarm clock on my nightstand: 5:30 a.m. *Here we go again.* It might seem archaic to have an actual alarm clock these days, as everyone just relies on the alarms on their phones, but I need to make sure I have a backup alarm just in case the one on my phone doesn't wake me up. After all, my role is pretty important. Another day of boring holes into people's brains and spines awaits. In other words, kicking ass and saving lives.

As I sink back into the bed, I am confronted by the warm body lying next to me. There's a blond woman sprawled out naked on the bed with the covers pulled up over her body, lightly draped over her hip bone. The vertebrae of her spine are visible, and I imagine making an incision at T1, perhaps to do a laminectomy. She is softly snoring, and her back rises with each snore. Amber, I think? Or maybe Amanda? I'm ashamed I don't even remember her name or really anything about her. Racking my brain for details from the night before, I recall she said she works as a nurse somewhere. Hopefully not at my hospital.

We met last night at Legacy Hall downtown where I was attending a benefit for pediatric brain cancer. It seemed the entire neurosurgery department was there. Drinks were flowing, and shots were being taken, and I may have gotten a little too drunk. It's unusual for me to drink a lot, especially when I have to work the next day, which is most of the days, but the peer pressure from colleagues was too strong last night. Typically, I'm not one to succumb to peer pressure as I like to maintain a sense of control, but I've been feeling off and making questionable choices lately, specifically when it comes to my love life. I've felt torn between wanting to find a partner, someone on my wavelength to commit to, and wanting to wreak havoc and partake in a series of one-night stands. It's been getting hard juggling all these women, though, and then having to ghost them when I can't commit, but I'm still pretty messed up after losing *her*.

I slip quietly out of bed and throw on a pair of shorts, tiptoeing to the bathroom so I don't wake the woman next to me. I'd like to avoid the awkward morning-after small talk. Things used to be easier when I had her in my life. They were more effortless. No matter how hard I try to get out there and meet different girls, no one really measures up, and I find it harder to fill the void. Sometimes, I feel like it's much easier to be hyper-focused on neurosurgery and come to terms with the fact that no one will fill the void. It feels wrong to lead all these women on when I know it will all end the same. It's almost like a sickness, though, trying to feed my soul with attention, with sex, with human touch, not being sure if any of those elements will ever fulfill me. I wish it could have worked out with her, though, but I didn't realize at the time what I was losing. I tried to get her back, but she deserved better than me.

On my way to the bathroom, I admire the layout of my apartment. It's nice to have a woman in my life who has an eye for interior decorating. Someone who is a constant no matter who comes and goes. Someone I can trust with my life.

While brushing my teeth, I glance at myself in the mirror and think, *Yep, still pretty good-looking.* Moving my eyebrows up and down, I observe the creases that form on my forehead. I dread the day when those creases deepen and become visible to the naked eye. Neurosurgery can be challenging, but thus far, I don't think it's aged me. In fact, it feels like the work has rejuvenated me.

I throw on a clean pair of scrubs and consider leaving a note for Amber or Amanda, whatever her name is, but then decide I'll just text her later. As I gently close the door to my apartment, I realize I don't even think I have her number. Gosh, I'm an ass sometimes.

Passing by my doorman, Ben, I give him a little wave and walk out to the street and towards the subway at 86th and Lexington. This walk is getting old, but I love this neighborhood. The hospital where I work operates out of two locations, one on the Upper East Side and one downtown, so it's a pleasant change of scenery to be able to experience both neighborhoods—it carves up the monotony a little. After five years of training, I still don't know what to expect when I arrive at the hospital. Some days, there's a shitstorm already awaiting me. Other days, I get to operate all day, which is really when I'm at my best. The less patient interaction, the better.

I've wanted to be a neurosurgeon since I was a little kid because it was the one job I could think of that competed with God. After all the awful things that have happened in my life, it's made me question whether there is a benevolent God out there, and I figured if I could do something that made me feel powerful, it would make up for the powerlessness of my childhood. At least, that's how therapists have explained it to me. I've always been doubtful that there is a God, though, and often wondered whether, if there is one, is he or she or they really benevolent? How could God be benevolent when there's so much destruction, famine, abuse, hardship everywhere we look?

As a child, I'd often get dragged to church on Sundays. I'd watch as dutiful and pious people strutted into the church and filled the pews, their noses pointed towards the sky as if they were being ordained. The air of superiority emanating from the churchgoers made me feel sullied. I wondered how invested some people could be in this ideology of a higher power that they had never laid eyes on. How could they follow so many rules without asking questions? How could they just accept that an entity, whomever he, she, they may be, is watching us from above and determining the course of our lives? At least in the world of medicine and surgery, we are doing things with our hands, building with them and witnessing real miracles take place right before our eyes. Constructing a limb, mending a heart, removing a cancer. I know neurosurgeons stereotypically have God complexes, but how can we not? We are determining whether people live or die, whether they will speak again, see again, walk again, love again…

Chapter 3

The boy

The boy is awoken by the noise. Someone is banging a hard object against the ground, or maybe against the wall. It's hard to tell, but the sound is deafening. His room is pitch black, but through the crack beneath the door, there's a sliver of light coming through. The commotion is coming from downstairs. He hears a grunting and then a moaning and then an eerie silence. He places one foot on the floor and slowly brings the other down. Every move feels glacial. Unsure of what he will find, he moves with trepidation. He feels paralyzed, as if his limbs are immovable, frozen in a sea of ice. He halts to listen for any noise, but there's nothing, just an uncomfortable silence.

It is a common occurrence that he is awakened in the night by the sound of his father shouting, his mother crying, and on the worst nights, objects being hurled or someone being pushed (usually his mother). He has witnessed both his parents behave violently towards one another, but his father is usually the aggressor. He has often seen the results of their fights—his mother holding ice to her face the next morning as he gets ready for school, a purple shadow developing over one eye, dark marks on her arms, avoiding eye contact with him as she pours his cereal. His mother often makes excuses for his father, blaming the alcoholism that runs in his family, blaming the stress he is under at work. The boy doesn't think those are excuses for behaving badly.

There's been times when he's tried to intervene on behalf of his mother, but that just seemed to make his father even angrier. Once, in a fit of rage, his father threw him against the wall, and his mother shrieked so loud that the neighbors called the police. When the police arrived, his mother said he accidentally fell and covered up what his father did because she was worried they would take him away to a foster home. When he went to school the next day, the teacher noticed he was holding his arm a lot and sent him to the school nurse. She questioned him about why his arm was hurting, but he was too worried to tell her, also fearing he would be taken from his parents. There were days when he hated his father for what he did to him and his mother, but then there were days when he hated his mother for not leaving and for putting them in harm's way. Then there were still days when his father seemed almost loving, when he only had one or two drinks before coming home and they would eat dinner together like a normal family. He knew his father also had a rough childhood, as his grandfather was an alcoholic and abused his grandmother. The cycle of abuse and alcoholism continued, and unfortunately, he was going to be collateral damage.

Lately, the only way he's known how to escape is to lose himself in a book. Reading about the adventures of Tom Sawyer and Huckleberry Finn always brings him a sense of solace. He was a precocious child and learned how to read at a young age. Ever since he could read, he started spending hours after school trying to fill his head with as much knowledge and stories as he could. He often stays late at school and goes to the school library while he waits for his mother to pick him up after her shift at the local grocery store, where she works as a cashier. The librarian, an elderly woman with silver hair, strands of it often falling in front of her face, always sets aside a stack of books for him that she thinks he'll like. When he arrives at the library, she summons him to the stack and whispers, "I think you'll appreciate these" or "Let me know which one is your favorite." Sometimes he thinks she knows what his home life is like. As if she can read his thoughts. Or maybe she just knows that many children use the library as a refuge, a sanctuary where they can lose themselves in another world for a few hours a day. He always watches the clock, savoring each minute he has with his books before his mother shows up and forces him back to reality. Often when she arrives, she has a nervous smile on her face, trying to mask her own sadness at the circumstances that await them at home. But he can see the sadness in her eyes. She's never been good at pretending. In the car, there's a tension that hangs in the air between them, neither of them knowing what state his father will be in when he walks through the door, but both silently hoping for the best.

That night, standing in his room, he thinks things sounded different. The lack of noise now is the most terrifying of all. He thinks about walking downstairs and getting involved but is pulled back by some magnetic force. His mother's voice echoes in his head, beseeching him not to budge. He creeps towards the door and opens it a crack. It is still completely silent. He tries to step forward, one slow step at a time until he gets to the top of the stairs. The step creaks as he places his foot on the first one, making him abruptly pull back.

A shuffling sound, like someone moving downstairs, someone moving with a sense of urgency, makes him freeze again. The shuffling gets louder and seems to move towards the stairs. The boy carefully steps back again, inching back closer to his room. He returns safely to his room, lightly closing the door, being careful not to make a sound. This time, his instincts tell him to call the police.

He knows in his heart what he doesn't allow his mind to acknowledge. His worst nightmare has already happened, and he knows he can't stop it. He considers walking to the guest room across the hall from his bedroom, where his mother usually spends the night to escape his father's wrath. Hoping her cell phone is plugged into the charger in the guest room, he attempts to walk gingerly across the hall again. Telling himself that he's brave and capable, he moves towards the door. He listens from the top of the stairs and hears more movement than before, like a body hitting the ground and then a dragging sound over the linoleum kitchen floor. Terror strikes him in his chest. When he gets to the guest room, he is relieved to see the cell phone plugged into the wall charger. He closes the bedroom door behind him, crouches down on the floor, and calls 911.

Chapter 4

Kylie

I wake up in Blake's bed Saturday morning. My head feels like a sledgehammer is pounding into it. The morning light gleams through the shutters at the window across from me. Blake's already left to go to the hospital, as he told me last night he had an early case. Lying there in the quiet of the room, I play back what happened the night before in my mind.

Blake and I met at a nearby wine bar, Leila's, and ordered a few appetizers and way too much wine, apparently. When I arrived at the wine bar, Blake was standing outside, leaning casually against the wall, and texting on his phone. As I walked up to him, my stomach in knots, he looked up from his phone, his posture abruptly straightening as if he were a child caught with his hand in the cookie jar. A slow smile spread across his face as I approached, and he leaned in to give me a hug, a waft of a woodsy, pine-scented cologne enveloping me. "Hey, Kylie," he said. He placed a hand on my shoulder, and the warmth of his breath on my ear made the hairs on the back of my neck stand up. "I hope you like tapas." He embodied textbook chivalry—holding the door open, pulling out the chair for me to sit. These gestures may seem like basic etiquette rules of dating, but I've been on enough dates to know that men rarely follow these rules.

While he's a man of few words via text messaging, he was effortlessly engaging in person. "Do you prefer red or white wine?" he asked, his gaze steady on mine as if he wanted to register the answer, depositing it in his "all about Kylie" compartment. "Typically, I like white wine. A solid pinot grigio, but I'm easy." He smiled at that and glanced back at the wine menu before calling the server over to order their best pinot grigio. "So, tell me about your day. Anything interesting happen?" He sat up straighter in his chair and leaned in, the candle in the center of the table setting his face aglow.

"You really want to hear about my boring day at work?" I asked, incredulous.

"If it tells me more about you than yes," he replied, the corners of his mouth curling upward. This guy really knows what he's doing, I thought. The conversation moved from small-talk to lighthearted banter to philosophical dilemmas to more formal questions that made me feel like I was being interviewed. Yet, I appreciated the depth of his line of questioning as an attempt to forge a deeper connection. Watching me intently as if hanging on my every word, he asked, "What's been the biggest challenge you've faced in residency?"

I answered, "Meeting the expectations I have for myself without being too hard on myself when I fall short." He nodded in agreement with that sentiment, although something told me he rarely fell short, at least when it came to neurosurgery. As the night wore on, the tightening ball of anxiety in my stomach loosened, and I felt more at peace in his presence. It occurred to me that when we are together, just the two of us, without the barrier of technology, the conversation flows naturally. As we sat and talked, the spark between us, ever present and undeniable, I started to wonder what a future with Blake could look like.

We left the bar around 1 a.m. and took a cab to his place. I remember little about the cab ride, but a few salient moments stick out to me, like how Blake wove his fingers through mine, clasping my hand as we rode in the back of the cab. The way he periodically glanced in my direction with a look of endearment and how his fingertips grazed my knee as we exited the cab, making my body tingle with electricity.

Of course, we made out when we got back to the apartment, but I don't think much more happened since I look down and still have my clothes on from last night—a blue spaghetti strap top and dark skinny jeans. To my dismay, I even have socks on. Ever since moving to NYC, I've gotten into the unattractive habit of wearing socks to bed, initially to keep warm since it's cold most of the year, but now it's just habit.

As I sit up, the sledgehammer turns into an icepick, and I wince and grab my head. I never used to get intense headaches, but since starting residency, I've had them more regularly. Now that I know what a migraine is, I'm pretty sure I get migraine headaches, and this headache feels like it's gearing up to turn into one. Shielding my eyes from the sunlight as I roll out of the bed, I get up and amble to the bathroom.

Blake's apartment is as orderly and clean as I remember it from the last time I was here except for my shoes and jacket, which are strewn on the floor. That exquisite burgundy couch still sits in its grandeur with the fluffed pillows exactly where they were the last time I was here. Walking past the washer and dryer unit, I gawk for a few minutes, as it's a luxury to have one of those in a Manhattan apartment. I didn't even think apartments like that were accessible to those of us living on resident salaries. Okay, the surgical residents definitely have it better. I remind myself to bring this up to our program director without giving away the fact that I was in this man's apartment. Normally, I have to lug my clothing across five blocks to the nearest laundromat and wait there for at least an hour until my clothes are fully washed and dried, but that's Manhattan living for most, I guess.

Staring at myself in the bathroom mirror, I'm horrified to see that my hair looks like a rat's nest and my mascara is smudged, darkening my under eyes, as if I need my dark circles to be any more accentuated. Apparently, I didn't even think to wash my face last night. Gosh, I hope Blake didn't catch a glimpse of me this morning before he left for work. Splashing water on my face, taking care to wipe off as much makeup as I can from the night before, I try to mitigate the inevitable walk of shame out of here. I wonder if the doorman from last night will still be there this morning.

Attempting to pull my hair back into a ponytail, I realize my scrunchie is no longer around my wrist. It likely fell off at some point last night. Retracing my steps from the doorway to the bed, I crawl onto the floor and start scouring the carpet, then the bedsheets, and then under the bed. There's an elastic scrunchie, one of those plastic spiral ones underneath Blake's bed, but it's not mine. I'm pretty sure I wore a silky black one last night. A few strands of blond hair are woven within the spiral pleats. Obviously, some other girl has been here recently, but I have no right to be jealous, as this is only the second time we've hung out. Nevertheless, it does sting a little.

Searching the bed again, I flip over the pillow, and there it is. Pulling my hair back into a ponytail, I try to get it as tidy as I can get it without a brush, and pat down the flyaways. Grabbing my sweater and kneeling down to put my shoes on—stylish black boots I recently purchased from Bloomingdale's, I am drawn to a bookcase in the corner of the room.

I look more closely at the bookcase, as it looks like it was picked up at an antique store. It doesn't fit in with the rest of the furniture in his apartment, which is more modern, but it looks like a special piece. It has a mahogany finish reminiscent of the Victorian era, delicately stenciled patterns line the edges, and there are several glass compartments housing books. Given my dad is a carpenter, I grew up knowing way too much about putting furniture together and the various materials used to build furniture. I remember my dad marveling at an antique table he had remodeled to use as our kitchen table, treating it like it was a piece of history or art. As I approach the bookcase, I can smell the woody scent, and it makes me nostalgic for home. I swipe the top of the bookcase with my hand, admiring the finish, and sure enough, there's no dirt on it. Either Blake has OCD or he has a great housekeeper. There's a skull on top of the bookcase that looks like it came from an anatomy lab. So predictable. Opening one of the glass compartments, I marvel at all the books stored inside. Most of the books are medical books—the neurosurgeon's atlas, a comprehensive guide to neurosurgery, a handbook of neurosurgery, but there are a few novels as well. I flip through the handbook of neurosurgery, and it's replete with highlighted marks, notes scribbled in red ink in the margins, and markings within the anatomical figures on the pages. It's clear he is dedicated to his craft. I return the handbook to its spot and keep browsing.

When I spot a Stephen King book, I feel a rush of adoration. There's nothing more attractive than a man who reads actual books. Nowadays, men seem to be sucked into the manosphere vortex of podcasting bros. I'm starting to think they don't accept information as truth unless it's being dictated to them by an angry man yelling into a microphone. Don't get me wrong, I love my true crime podcasts, but nothing quite compares to a good book. As a voracious reader, it's probably a top five requirement for me to be dating someone who values the written word as much as I do. Reading specific authors I respect is a bonus, and Stephen King is definitely one of them.

Perusing the other texts, I spot Malcolm Gladwell, Fredrik Backman, Zadie Smith—all authors I revere. Snooping further, I find a stack of envelopes buried in the corner of the bookcase. Pulling them out one by one, I notice there are several envelopes from the alumni office at Dartmouth University. Smart cookie. I don't think we talked about where we went to college. Apparently, you can learn a lot about someone just by going through their furniture. Before I get too carried away, I push the envelopes back in their place and gather my things to head out.

Thankfully, it's Saturday, and I'm post-call, so I don't have to be at work, but I'm meeting Lisa for a Pilates class at 9 a.m. In retrospect, I should have known I'd be sluggish and possibly hungover the next morning when I booked this class, but our studio requires at least a twenty-four-hour cancellation notice and it's too late now. Plus, I'm looking forward to telling her about my night with the hot neurosurgeon.

As I wait for the elevator, I hear the door opposite to where I'm standing open, and out walks a woman dressed in a bright orange pullover and leopard print yoga pants. She has a short brown bob that frames her pale complexion, giving her a severe look.

Aggressively tugging at the leash of her white mini poodle, she pulls the dog away from me as if I'm diseased. Her stern, judgmental glare moves up and down my body, surveying my appearance. Feeling self-conscious, I pull out my phone and check myself out in the camera. *Okay, I don't look that bad.* She steps onto the elevator on the opposite side of where I step on. Trying to distract myself from the awkward silence penetrating the space between us, I continue to scroll through my phone. *Sheesh, tough crowd,* I think. As if the walk of shame on its own isn't enough, I now have to endure the patronizing looks of neighbors and the doorman.

On the next floor down, a man dressed in a navy suit appears, nods at both of us and gets on right in between us. After an uncomfortable thirty seconds in the elevator, we get to the lobby, where I quickly swing my eyes to the doorman and, yep, he's the same one from last night. Just my luck. Ducking out past him, I pull the hood of my jacket over my head, hoping it provides some cover, and exit the building.

On the ride home, the Uber driver is silent. I've learned after living in Manhattan for the last year that it's best not to engage with rideshare drivers. In fact, most don't really care to talk. The first few times I got in a cab here, I tried to make small talk with the driver and was met with a series of grunts and curt responses to my questions. Another time, a cab driver rudely turned up the volume on the radio so as to obviously tune me out. He wasn't even subtle about it.

The ride only takes about five minutes, and we arrive at my building. I probably could have just walked back to my apartment but did not want to subject myself to more shame-walking.

I've lived in my apartment for over a year now and have never seen a single person leave or enter the building. It's like every tenant waits until they don't hear anyone in the hallway before they leave their apartment. I was taken aback by this obvious avoidance of human contact at first, but now I have a new appreciation for this, as I, too, would like to avoid judgmental stares as I return from a night out. I know people in my building must do this because as I enter the building, I often catch a neighbor in the act of watching me through the slit in the doorway. Odd. But I've learned that most things in this city are odd. New York has an unmatched peculiarity that is at times disturbing and at times endearing. I revel in all of it. The strange characters in my building, the circus acts on the subway, the people who like to act "NY tough" but are actually the kindest of anywhere you will meet, and the tourists who are totally clueless to the fact that this city hates tourists but tolerates them.

I recall my own initiation to NYC. After spending most of my life living in the suburbs of Florida, I arrived in NYC with a feeling of astonishment and gratitude. Being swallowed up by this city with open arms, soaking in the stench of the streets and absorbing the energy of the people, I felt a thrill at the opportunity to become a neurologist at the center of the universe.

Growing up in a large family as one of five siblings, it was difficult to venture out and travel much. The only trips my family took were to Disney World, which they'd often save up a few years for. Until I moved, I hadn't been on a plane except for one time when we went to visit cousins in South Carolina. I didn't know what to expect when I got here, but I knew I wanted to try something different. When I arrived, I was quickly embraced by my co-residents, but it seemed all of them were more seasoned than I was, more accustomed to the fast ways of the city, more experienced when it came to riding subways and using public transport or even when ordering a bagel at a pushy bagel shop where the workers scream at the customers to move along quickly. I was a fledgling being released into the harsh, mean city and having to carve out a place for myself with the limited resources I had—resources like street smarts, refinement, and an eclectic palette for ethnic foods. The small town I grew up in had limited options for ethnic cuisine, and we often found ourselves eating out at the local pizza place. Feeling like an outsider was normal for me, though. It was probably the most normal feeling I had ever experienced. As one of five siblings, I often felt alone. Our parents had to divvy up their attention, and inevitably, some of us would get the short end of the stick.

I consider myself lucky, though, because I was and still am an avid reader, so that's how I spent all my free time. Getting lost in the stories of Dickens and immersing myself in Stephen King, I had an outlet, a way to create an alternate reality through my books. Reading everything from the classics to thrillers to history books, I learned to enjoy my company and the company of a good book. It was through reading that I also became interested in becoming a physician. Books like *Mountains Beyond Mountains* and *Cutting for Stone* inspired me to seek greater meaning and pushed me down the path of helping others. In high school, I started volunteering at a local clinic where I'd perform simple tasks like taking blood pressure for patients or monitoring their glucose, and even those seemingly minute tasks seemed to engender so much appreciation in patients that it just felt right.

I also value the moments around medicine that brought me

closer to my mom. My mother and I, both fascinated with medicine, would binge all the medical shows like *Grey's Anatomy* and *House*. We were both in awe of the diagnostic process and the outcomes. My mother is a schoolteacher, and my father is a carpenter, so neither of them had much medical knowledge, but I could tell that my mother was enamored with the medical profession. She would always comment on the cases we watched on television and say things like, "This sounds like it could be a heart problem." She was often wrong, but the experience of figuring medical mysteries out together was special. When I told my parents I wanted to go to medical school, my mother got teary-eyed, and I could tell that part of her wished she could be on the journey with me.

My fascination with the brain was piqued when I took neuroscience in the first year of medical school. There is so much about neurologic disorders we still don't know about and many diseases that are considered incurable like Parkinson's, Multiple Sclerosis, Migraine. The levels of disability vary across neurologic disease, and while there may be some mitigating treatments, there's still a lot left to discover. It's exciting to be immersed in a field where there's ongoing growth and innovation aimed at giving patients a better quality of life. I feel privileged to be able to make my dream a reality even if some days I question my choices.

I meet Lisa at the corner of 86th and 3rd so we can walk over to the Pilates studio together. She's wearing a matching evergreen ALO set with a black zip-up sweater. She's chipper and looks wide awake while I'm trudging along restlessly.

"Okay, girl, tell me everything," she demands, wide-eyed. Her high ponytail bounces from side to side as we cross the street.

"It was an amazing date. He's kind and attractive, of course, and the conversation was effortless."

She interrupts me, "So that's it? You just had a conversation?" She has a smirk on her face.

My cheeks burn. "We went back to his apartment and made out, but that's it. I spent the night there, and he was gone when I woke up. He had to go into work early." I pause, waiting for her reaction, but she's watching me with a look of quiet suspicion. "I really enjoy talking to him. He's smart and interesting, and he seems to really care about what I have to say." She nods her head in approval, but continues to watch me, her gaze pointed. I hesitate to keep gushing about our date as somewhere deep down I fear he won't live up to my expectations. I add, "I also admire how dedicated he is to neurosurgery. It's refreshing to see a fifth-year resident who still loves his job," hoping his commitment to neurosurgery will redeem him in Lisa's eyes.

"What was his excuse for being a jerk and not reaching out sooner?" she asks, raising an eyebrow. I glance at my phone screen and quicken my pace, realizing class starts in five minutes and we are still several blocks away. Lisa follows suit.

"He said he's been really busy and was super apologetic for not being consistent, chalking it up to a crazy neurosurgery schedule, but who knows if that's really what's going on." Once again, Lisa goes quiet, perhaps trying to withhold judgment, and I'm grateful for that. I continue, "I think they deal with a lot more crap than we do, and maybe we just don't understand the extent of it." I'm making excuses for him, which makes me feel icky. The thought of finding another girl's scrunchie underneath the bed pops into my head, but I decide not to tell Lisa. After all, he and I hardly know each other, having hung out a total of two times. I don't have the right to feel jilted.

"Well, we can give him another chance and see, I guess," Lisa says, resigned.

When we arrive at our class, the instructor, Zach, an eccentric and bubbly guy, greets us at the door. He's wearing a white cut-off tank top that reads *Free Britney* in big block letters across the chest with spandex shorts, and his hair is pushed back with a white headband. Zach teaches the Saturday morning classes and is popular. His classes are always booked, so we have to sign up weeks in advance. "Hey, ladies, ready to work hard today? Hopefully you didn't get smashed last night," he says with a sly grin on his face.

"We are," we answer wearily. Unfortunately, I probably did get smashed but now have no choice but to be here. We take our usual reformers when they're available, the two closest to the wall to avoid being the centers of attention. The class is filled with the usual Saturday morning crew, which I suspect is also the usual weekday morning crew judging by the appearance of all the women filing in. Lithe and athletic women in ALO and Lululemon sets occupy the reformers closest to the front of the room and the instructor, perhaps wanting to showcase their perfected planks and arabesques, going through the movements with aplomb. I imagine they don't have real jobs or have less demanding ones that allow for 9 a.m. daily Pilates classes, which give them multiple chances to hone their skills.

Zach turns on a new Britney Spears and Beyoncé compilation

he's excited about, exclaiming, "Okay, ladies, let's get started. Hands on the reformers, feet on the foam pads, and give me a blue and yellow spring." The clacking sounds of metal springs being adjusted rivals the booming music as we get into position. Thankfully, we are not usually the targets of Zach's adjustments, as he favors the "regulars." "Get it, Layla, stand straighter, Paige, I want to see higher lifts, Annie," he yells, his voice reverberating through my head, compounding the headache I already have. I probably should have taken an Advil before coming. Also, I should probably see someone for my migraine headaches, I remind myself, knowing all too well how doctors make terrible patients.

After a painstaking fifty minutes, we jump off the reformers and head to the locker room. "That was intense," Lisa says as she pulls her damp hair out of her ponytail and reties it into a tight bun.

"Wouldn't expect anything less from Zach," I respond, slipping out of my grip socks. I look around the room at all the women and wonder what the rest of the day holds for them. Maybe a manicure and pedicure or massage followed by a shopping spree and dinner with friends while their nannies watch their children. A group of the regulars congregate and start chatting about their plans for the night. Surreptitiously eavesdropping on these conversations is my favorite pastime.

"We have reservations at Per Se tonight, so Marie is coming over to watch the kids," I overhear a woman declare. She looks like the ringleader of the pack. The other women bow their heads in agreement. As if it's perfectly normal to visit a Michelin-rated restaurant that probably costs $1,000 a person on a random

Saturday. Part of me envies the effortless lives that many of them seem to live, but the other part of me also thinks I could never live that way, being content with the comfort of luxury. I'm sure even that gets monotonous after a while. I need adrenaline rushes, brain teasers, triumphant saves because that's what makes me fulfilled, but to each her own.

"Do you want to go grab a smoothie?" Lisa suggests, interrupting my eavesdropping.

"Sure," I respond as I chug my water bottle.

"Thank you, ladies," Zach hollers at us as we walk out.

We walk to the nearest smoothie shop and go to the counter. I order my usual, a banana berry smoothie with almond milk, and Lisa orders the same. Once again, we retreat to a corner table, out of reach from the other customers.

"So, what did you guys end up doing last night?" I ask her.

"Well, after work, Marta, Hassan, and I met up for drinks and dinner. Bailey was supposed to come too, but he conveniently forgot that Omar's parents were in town and he was supposed to meet them for dinner."

"Sounds like things are getting pretty serious between the two of them." Bailey and Omar met during our intern year, on a dating app. It felt like everyone had coupled up over the last year, which was our busiest year of residency, so it made me wonder if there was something I was missing. Intern year is mostly about survival. Wake up, go to work, get yelled at, come home, feel bad about oneself, second guess all the decisions you made that day, cry, go to sleep and do it all over again the next day. The fact that several of my co-residents managed to find partners during that crazy year is baffling.

"What's Jeff up to?" I ask.

"He's working on a new case that's been so time-consuming, I hardly get to see him these days." Lisa leans back in her chair and sighs. Jeff and Lisa met at the beginning of our intern year, also on a dating app. They have what appears to be a stable relationship—one I could only hope for. I've only met him a handful of times, but he has always been gracious and affable. He's a good-looking guy—tall with shaggy blond hair that falls below his forehead, but he doesn't give off an unkempt appearance. He is noticeably smart and hardworking, which is why we don't see him out much. His personality is a little bland and sharply contrasts with Lisa's vivacious personality, but Lisa is hard to measure up to. She is bold, charismatic, witty, and brilliant. In fact, I think she's out of his league.

Jeff's a corporate lawyer and has been working at the same law firm for a few years now. Lisa recently moved into his apartment, which looks like the apartment of someone who has been adulting for a long time. They seem to be getting serious, as I often catch Lisa scrolling through engagement ring websites at work. Pursuing medicine is such a long, arduous path that I always feel like we are still students while everyone else is growing up. A lot of my friends have been working real jobs for years while I've been in training. It can be isolating, but that's why it's nice having friends in residency that understand the stage of life you're in.

"What is corporate law, anyway?" I ask.

Lisa takes a long slurp of her smoothie. "Beats me, honestly." She snickers. I watch over Lisa's shoulder as a few of the women from our Pilates class line up to order smoothies.

Prior to meeting Jeff, Lisa had a boyfriend in medical school. Things were pretty serious from what she told me. They were even supposed to couples match together, aiming for both of them to end up at residencies in the city. A few weeks before they had to submit their match list, she found out he had been cheating on her when she stumbled upon text messages between him and his college girlfriend. Apparently, he had gone home to New Jersey for the holidays and rekindled his relationship with her. Lisa was devastated, of course. They had so many mutual friends in medical school, and she felt like she ended up alone while they all rallied around him. Medical school can be so lonely, since you're stuck with the same people for all four years, and if you don't find your people, you're basically on your own. She ended up spending her last year as a pariah. When she told me that story, I really felt for her. I was lucky to have a tight-knit group of friends who kept me sane throughout those years. I didn't really date in medical school, though, which allowed me to focus on building solid friendships—friendships I hope will continue to grow over the years.

I've really only had one serious relationship, with a boy in college. It was a pretty stable relationship, but our ambitions ended up getting the best of us. Jared also applied to medical school, ending up in a different part of the country because he got into a "top ten" and didn't want to give that up to "settle" for the school I got into. We tried the long distance thing for a while, mainly seeing each other back in Florida when we'd go home for holidays, but we were just too busy and focused on our own experiences at our respective schools to make things work. At that time, I remember thinking it was probably not meant to be. I often wonder if I've missed my chance, and I'm meant to watch everyone else's happy relationships while I pick up the scraps from the Manhattan dating pool. I really like Blake, but I don't want to allow myself to get my hopes up. There's something mysterious about him, something I can't quite put my finger on.

Chapter 5

Kylie

I'm waiting for Chloe to show up for patient sign-out, the highly anticipated ritual of the passing off of patient care from one provider to the next. As I drum my fingers on the desk, impatiently waiting for the patient list to print out, I count down the minutes until she arrives. I imagine her torpedoing into the resident room as she often does with a grocery bag full of snacks, the scent of herbal tea emanating from her mug, ready to conquer another night on her night shift rotation.

Giving sign-out to Chloe is always pleasant because it's efficient and quick. She doesn't need long-winded details about a patient case or much instruction about what to do overnight for each patient. She just hunkers down, absorbs the information like a sponge, and sends you on your way home. It's been two weeks since I started this rotation, and I've been lucky to have Chloe as the resident on night shift during this time. It's also been two weeks since I saw Blake, but I try to push that thought out of my mind because it just makes me angry that he hasn't reached out recently.

After spending so much time with your co-residents, you become a family, albeit a dysfunctional one. Yet, while we are connected by this shared experience of residency, none of us know each other that well outside of the hospital, as it is always difficult to find time to get together. During our intern year, this was especially challenging since we were all focused on trying to survive and keep our sanities intact. Plus, our schedules were always conflicting, making it hard to make plans outside of work. Lisa ended up being my closest confidante mostly because we ended up having a lot of the same rotations and schedules. Whenever we did all get together, though, we'd share just enough about our lives that we all became close. The journey of neurology and training on its own creates mutual understanding among us all. We are all part of something meaningful that maybe doesn't feel so big in the day-to-day but collectively makes an impact.

Throughout training, you also get a good glimpse of what kind of doctor each person will be. You have the residents who are super reliable and responsible, the ones who just get by, and the ones who try really hard but somehow come up short. We quickly learn whose assessment of a patient can be trusted and whose assessment may need some clarification or questioning. Some are more thorough than others, but Chloe had proven herself reliable.

We also all have our quirks and idiosyncrasies and play different roles. Marta is the maternal one in the group—always checking in and asking how everyone is feeling, offering up her snacks and bringing an extra coffee to a tired colleague. Bailey is more the troublemaker in that he often makes asinine comments to attendings, cracks inappropriate jokes, and pushes the boundaries of propriety, but most take his transgressions in stride because at the end of the day, he's a really sweet guy. Hassan is a rule follower, often admonishing others for not doing things by the book and easily getting annoyed by perceived laziness. Lisa is a hard worker, a skilled neurologist, but sometimes focuses too much on the details and misses the whole picture. Anaya is the reserved one, saying the most while actually saying the least. She's pensive, calm, and collected. She's also the most fashionable of our crew. While most of us prefer schlepping around in scrubs, she takes care to dress up every day, always wearing a crisp pressed blouse paired with pants or a skirt. Her hair, typically tightly wound into a neat bun or fashioned into a braid, exudes an air of professionalism and class. Chloe, though, is the favorite both with attendings and her colleagues. She's the right amount of detail-oriented, compassionate, hardworking, and reliable. And if I had to pinpoint my style, I'd probably say I'm most like Chloe, or rather I strive to be most like her.

While some of us seem confident, no matter how many patients we see and treat, there are times when questions linger, and we feel a sense of anxiety over whether we made the right call. We often ask ourselves, "Did I make the right decision sending that patient home from the emergency room?" "Did I wait too long to call neurosurgery?" "Should I wait before I call neurosurgery?" In the world of medicine, there are certain rivalries between specialties, and the somewhat tacit rivalry between neurology and neurosurgery is a common one at most hospitals. Neurologists often question whether they will look dumb to the neurosurgeon for calling a certain consult that may be beneath the neurosurgeon's scope of practice, and the neurosurgeons, often dealing with complex cases, look at the neurologists disapprovingly, as if they are idiots. It's common for one of us to call a neurosurgery consult, have an overtired neurosurgery resident answer the page, and be met with a barrage of questions about the case, questioning the necessity for neurosurgical involvement. Unfortunately, I have been on the receiving end of this several times. Thankfully, though, I have never had to speak with Blake on the phone. Given he's a fifth-year resident, he typically isn't answering pages about consults. He primarily spends his time in surgery. Then, of course, sometimes, we contemplate the more existential questions like: "Am I supposed to be here?" "Did I really choose the right profession?" I hope as we embark further into our residency training, the imposter syndrome abates, but sometimes I think we will have more questions than answers the deeper we get.

The clock on the wall reads 8:05 p.m. Chloe's already five minutes late. I decide to give her a few more minutes before I text her. Maybe she's just getting off the subway and hasn't had service to let me know she'd be late. The trains can be quite unreliable at times, and often there are delays in the evenings. Just then, I get a page: *Consult requested: 43-year-old woman with seizure in ED47—please come see.* Knowing I will not have time to see this patient before I sign out, I write down the patient's name and do a quick review of the chart to make sure she's stable. The patient has a history of seizures and was placed on an anti-seizure medication the last time she had a seizure, but it looks like she ran out of her medicine. I figure this can wait, as it's not urgent, and make a note for Chloe to see her when she gets here.

It's now 8:10. I text her, *Hey, are you on your way?*

A few minutes go by, and there's no response. This is unusual for her and, quite frankly, disconcerting. By 8:20, I'm starting to get annoyed. Where could she be? She's been working nights and sleeping during the days, so maybe she slept in. I keep checking my phone, but there are still no messages. I decide to call our chief resident.

Mae picks up her phone on the second ring.

"Hi, Mae, I'm sorry to bother you, but Chloe has not shown up for night float," I tell her nervously. As junior residents, we try not to disturb our chief resident unless something is really wrong, but I think this instance qualifies.

"Did you text her?" she asks.

"Yes, I did, and still no response."

Cutlery and dishes clink together in the background, and I feel a pang of guilt for disturbing her while she is starting dinner. "Okay, give it another fifteen and if she's still not there, let me know and I'll come over. I'll try to call her in the meantime." Mae Lang is an exceptional chief resident. She exemplifies everything a leader should—reliable, capable and compassionate. She also knows everything there is to know about neurology and is always willing to teach. Even though she's almost done with her training and is at the top of the residency hierarchy, she doesn't treat us as if we are morons and actually takes the time to answer our questions. The fact that she didn't even hesitate and offered to come in to relieve me says a lot about her character.

When another fifteen minutes go by, I call Mae back and she tells me she's five minutes away and hasn't been able to reach Chloe either.

Now I'm getting really worried. A knot forms in my stomach, and naturally, my mind goes to worst-case scenarios like something out of my true crime podcasts, even though I know the most likely explanation is that she slept in.

A few minutes later, Mae strolls in to save the day. "Hey, Kylie, I called Chloe's emergency contacts, her parents, and neither had spoken to her the last few hours, but they will let me know when they get in touch with her." She looks me up and down and says, "Looks like you're really tired. You should go home and get some rest." Did I mention Mae is also very blunt? I've been here since 7 a.m., so yes, I bet I look like a hot mess. "I'll let you know if I hear anything," she adds.

I hand her a copy of the patient list and give her a synopsis of each patient, making sure to alert her to the sicker patients on the list who need extra attention. Profusely thanking her for taking over for me so I can go get some rest, I grab my bag and wish Mae good luck.

As I walk out of the resident room, something nags at me. Scrolling through my phone, I pull up my last few text messages with Chloe. There was nothing unusual about our exchange. We had been texting back and forth about our plans for the upcoming weekend, and she knew she was taking over for me tonight. Since she is on the night shift rotation, she didn't make any plans to go out at night or even before her shift starts at 8 p.m. It's hard to make any plans at all on nights since you want to maximize the amount of sleep you can get during the day and be refreshed for the night shift.

When Chloe is not working nights, she is the definition of a "social butterfly." As someone who grew up in Manhattan, Chloe has an extensive network of friends and acquaintances and always seems to have plans when she's off. Like me, she is also on the dating apps. Not that she needs to be, seeing as she probably gets enough date requests just by working at the hospital. Everyone at work loves being around her. She's one of those people who gives off a "no fucks given" attitude, but actually in reality, she gives enough fucks to do her job well. While she is mainly out to do things her way, she manages to somehow be herself in the confines of a hierarchical training program. Her superiors are always impressed by her clinical acumen and the way in which she cares for her patients. She seamlessly straddles the boundary between obstinacy and submission to authority figures. She can turn the charm on for any attending, present her cases with a finesse seen by no other resident, and banter with patients in a playful yet serious way, letting them know she is competent but also compassionate. We all strive as doctors to exude confidence without coming off too cocky and at the same time show empathy and compassion. This can be a hard task to achieve, and given most of us are type A perfectionists by nature, we are often hard on ourselves when we can't quite get there.

There are no perfect humans, yet society expects physicians to be superhuman. Throw in the fact that you're a woman, and the expectations are even greater. While women now represent the majority of medical students, and research has shown that women physicians outperform men on various measures, societal perception has not caught up to the science. We are often objectified, often mistaken for non-doctors, and often questioned in an offensive way. There have been so many times when I have walked into a patient's room only to be referred to as a nurse or asked, "When's the doctor coming in?"

One time, a male medical student was following me around and when we entered a patient room, the patient, also a man, looked directly at him and assumed he was the doctor even though I was wearing the badge and white coat that clearly said *Doctor* on it. Even the medical student felt embarrassed for me. A flush of crimson spread across his face as he gave me a nervous glance.

Playing it off like it was no big deal, I just vehemently said, "I'm Dr. Saunders, nice to meet you," while making sure my ID badge was in his line of sight. The patient's face also matched the resident's as he stumbled over his words to introduce himself. I figured that was enough vindication. While I get really offended and annoyed by these incidents, Chloe often plays them off and makes the awkward incident into a joke. She has a knack for making serious things lighthearted.

Where could Chloe be? I think back to everything I know about her and her background. Chloe grew up on the Upper East Side of Manhattan as one of two children to two successful parents. Her father, the CEO of a Fortune 500 company and her mother, a consultant, are powerhouses in their professions but also really lovely people, just like Chloe. At the beginning of our residency, her parents threw a lavish party at their opulent apartment on York Avenue, the apartment Chloe was raised in, and invited us all. When I think about people growing up in Manhattan, I imagine cramped spaces and shared bedrooms, but when I arrived at Chloe's parents' apartment with Lisa and Bailey, I was completely awed by the sheer elegance and size of their apartment. Bailey, who somehow always knows the tea about everyone's personal life, told us Chloe's parents had bought the two apartments flanking their apartment and turned it into a mega apartment.

We took the elevator to the tenth floor and were greeted by an elegant woman, draped in a floral dress, wearing pink stiletto heels. She had a disarming smile and didn't look a day over forty. I figured it must be a combination of good genes, Botox, and possibly a facelift. She introduced herself as Mrs. King and offered to take our coats.

Chloe came bouncing up behind her with a jubilant expression on her face. "Hey, guys, welcome to our humble abode," she said as she grabbed me by the hand and ushered us inside. The irony of that statement was not lost on me, although I don't think she intended it to come off the way it did. Chloe was wearing a low-cut navy blue dress that clung to her figure like a rubber glove. Pearls lined the hem of her dress, and she wore tasteful nude heels, which made her look about three inches taller. Her blond hair lay on her shoulders, and it looked like she had visited the hairstylist that day as the waves in her hair created a perfect silhouette, not a strand out of place.

Her father sauntered up next—a tall, handsome man with an endearing smile. He was more modestly dressed than his wife and daughter, wearing a wool sweater and jeans, but he had the same icy blue eyes reminiscent of Chloe's and a full head of blond hair that was neatly coiffed. The first thing I noticed when I walked into the apartment was the expansive floor-to-ceiling windows that surrounded their home, offering a breathtaking view of the skyline and East River. I was stunned by the splendor of it all.

One of my personality quirks is the inability to refrain from attaching a place to a story where a crime or catastrophe occurred. When I think of the East River, my mind goes to the body of a woman found in the East River the year before I moved to Manhattan. Brandi Lyle was a college student in the city, and while there wasn't any evidence that there was a crime committed, the circumstances of the case are unnerving. It was eventually ruled a suicide—a young student struggling with her mental health. But her family was adamant that she would never do such a thing. I recall that case because I remember my mother, concerned about me doing my residency in a new city and being in a potentially fragile state of mind, fixated on the case.

Chloe walked us out to the balcony, passing through the immaculate living room that looked like a page out of *Architectural Digest*, and through a hallway lined with sculptures and ancient relics that each probably cost more than my family home. As we stepped out onto the balcony, I took in the view, still captivated by the grandeur. There was an outdoor bar being manned by a bartender adjacent to a long table decorated with an array of hors d'oeuvres. Some of my other co-residents had arrived before us—Marta, Anaya and Hassan. Chloe proceeded to give us all a tour of her parents' home, explaining the art on the walls and talking about their significance as if she was a curator at the Met. I was blown away by how cultured she seemed, how knowledgeable she was about so many different topics, and how confident she came across. As she walked us through the apartment, an attractive guy who shared Chloe's and her father's eyes emerged from the kitchen.

He introduced himself, "Hi, I'm Stratton, Chloe's brother." *Wow, how does everyone in this family look like they stepped out of a J.Crew catalog?* I thought to myself. With a boyish grin plastered on his face and hair that resembled his father's, he came across as a suave guy. I could definitely see why many women would find him attractive, although he wasn't really my type.

He spoke in a soft, melodious voice and exuded confidence, just like Chloe. Unlike Chloe, though, he had followed in his father's and mother's footsteps and pursued a career in finance after graduating from college. Chloe told us that after college, Stratton started out working as an investment banker and then went on to business school, where he met a girl he fell head over heels for. They dated for the length of business school, and then she moved back to the West Coast and broke up with him. He was devastated and was still getting over the breakup.

Stratton was easy to converse with. We all felt a little out of place at this palatial home, but Stratton was gracious and made us feel like we belonged. As we stood around in a circle, trading stories about our first few weeks of residency, Stratton shared the many mishaps and tribulations he endured when he first started his job in investment banking. Working in the world of finance is a lot like working in a residency training program (except for the fact that residents are severely underpaid), in that there's a clear hierarchy, and there's always someone you have to report to. The hours in both professions are often long and unpredictable as well. He explained that he lived downtown in a fancy high-rise building, but that Chloe, who lived a few blocks away from their family home, chose to live in a more unassuming building. According to Stratton, their parents wanted to put Chloe up in a fully furnished doorman building with maximum security, but she, being the modest person she is, chose to live in a three-story walkup building without a doorman, one she could afford on her own. While I thought this was honorable, I would have taken the offer if it were my parents.

As I walk out of the hospital towards the subway station, I suddenly remember that I have Stratton's phone number in my phone. A few months ago, I had been out with Chloe and Anaya, and Stratton met up with us. He had taken a few group photos of us on his phone and texted them to our group chat. Quickly pulling out my phone and scrolling through old text messages from that night, I find his string of texts. Not wanting to bury my face in my phone while I walk through the subway station, I wait until I get onto a train to text him. *Hey, Stratton, how are you doing? It's Kylie, Chloe's co-resident. Do you happen to know what Chloe is up to? She didn't show up for her shift.*

The subway ride from downtown to the Upper East Side takes about ten minutes on the express train, making an evening ride home on the subway less painful, especially after a long shift. When I get off at my stop, I'm met with hordes of people gathering around the subway station entrance. Many of them look like they are getting home from work after a long day, their weary faces looking straight ahead, as they hurriedly walk towards the street, on a mission to get home without any interruptions. Others look like they are headed out to an evening dinner—women wearing dresses underneath long coats and faces caked with makeup rush down the subway stairs in high heels while others stand on the sidewalk hailing a cab.

Periodically checking my phone as I walk up to my apartment building, there's still no response from Stratton. I take off my scrubs and toss them in the hamper. It always feels like I'm shedding a second skin whenever I peel my scrubs off after a busy day of seeing patients. There were fifteen neurology consults during my shift, all different types of neurologic issues—several stroke alerts, a few patients with seizures, a few patients with headaches, and a newly diagnosed multiple sclerosis patient. The shifts can go so fast since we are usually busy, so it's sometimes hard to stay in the moment and think through every case. I often find myself coming home and reviewing the cases I saw in my mind and then sometimes even checking their charts from home to see what the updates have been since I left the hospital. Did the patient with suspected stroke get the MRI of the brain done, and what did it show? Is the patient who came in for seizure still having seizures? Was I right about the multiple sclerosis diagnosis?

I get in the shower and change into some sweats. As soon as I lie down on my bed and close my eyes, I get a ping on my phone. I shoot up to see if it's Stratton, and low and behold, it's CNS. *Hey, I'm on call tonight, but I haven't gotten called in yet. Do you want to come by and hang out for a bit? I've missed you.*

Staring down at the message, I'm in disbelief. The gall of this guy. I haven't heard from him in two weeks, and now, out of the blue, he misses me? After that night where I ended up in his apartment with a migraine the next morning, we went on one more date. He took me to a cozy Italian restaurant downtown where we spent the whole night huddled into a corner booth. The ambiance was intimate with low amber lights, checkered tablecloths and black-and-white photos of celebrities lining the walls, reminiscent of old-school Italian restaurants. When the hostess offered us a booth, Blake jumped at the opportunity to sit next to me, and said something to the effect of "While I like the view sitting across from you, I'd rather sit close to you in the booth." I smiled nervously at him, but the softness in his face put me at ease. It was sweet. The conversation was easy and natural, like it always is when we are alone together. As we spoke, he inched closer to me, placing his hand on my thigh, pushing a strand of my hair out of my face, caressing my hand with his, making me feel like we were a couple even though we hadn't made anything official.

At the end of the night, we shared a cab back to his apartment. Per usual, he had to work early the next morning so I woke up alone in his apartment and let myself out. That day, he texted me: *I had a great time last night. Let's plan another date this week,* ending the text with a heart emoji. We texted back and forth for a few days, our conversations growing more intimate. We actually made plans to see each other again later that week, and then on the day of the date, two hours before we were supposed to meet, he texted me saying an emergency came up and he couldn't meet up. I was annoyed, of course, but couldn't argue with a work-related emergency. The next day, I texted him and asked if everything with the emergency went okay, and he gave me short answers, indicating it was, and he didn't try to continue the conversation. Feeling stupid that I reached out to him only to be met with apathy, I decided I wasn't going to text him again. I haven't heard from him since. I actually thought we were moving toward something more exclusive, but I've started to think he's just playing games.

Trying to decide what my next move should be, I hesitate to immediately text him back. Running the possible scenarios in my mind, I conclude that I'm going to stop by because I want to get a lot off my chest and perhaps cut this off if it's not going anywhere. It's been exhausting running through our dates and trying to figure out whether something went wrong or whether he's just a jerk. I'll wait as long as I can to text him back so I don't seem desperate, but I want to have a face-to-face conversation to set the record straight. Obviously, I need to look cute even if I am going there solely to give him a piece of my mind and potentially end things, so I search through my closet and pull out a flowy pink silk top with a plunging neckline and a pair of dark jeans. Heels may be too much of a statement, so I go with a pair of ballet flats.

As I apply my makeup, I notice that my face does look tired. A whole day of running around seeing patient consults will do that to you. Taking my time, I dab on some foundation, blush, and mascara, trying to look presentable, but not like I tried too hard. Once I'm ready, I sit on my couch and try to watch some trashy reality television, contemplating how long is long enough to wait before texting him back because two can play this game.

The grating sounds of the street are coming through my window. Most nights in Manhattan are loud, but particularly Saturday nights. Sometimes, if I was out late on a weekend night, I still hear the sounds of people laughing and talking on the streets below as I climb into bed at 3 a.m. When I first moved here, I remember thinking, what could they possibly be doing staying out that late? Now, I know there are so many things to do in Manhattan at that hour. It truly is the city that never sleeps.

Figuring that forty-five minutes is probably enough time to make him sweat, I text him back. *Nice to hear from you, stranger…I guess I have some time to spare.* I try to sound unbothered, but witty. It's a delicate balance, trying to maintain interest yet not letting him get away with his bullshit. Deep down, I can't help but feel as if I'm being stupid for letting him lead me on, but I can't deny how strong our chemistry is, and I think having a conversation will clarify some things for me.

He instantaneously texts back, *Perfect, when can I see you?* Now who's the desperate one?

I'll be there in 20 minutes.

When I get to Blake's building, that same doorman is sitting out front. I feel like he is silently judging me. Just my luck. Is he the only doorman this building has? Holding my gaze, he asks, "Who are you here to see?"

I clear my throat and say, "Blake Weathers, please," as I lower my eyes towards the floor.

"Okay, Dr. Weathers. I'll let him know you're here." He says this, and I swear there's a hint of disapproval in his tone. Oh, the things this doorman has probably seen. Surely, there have been plenty of women traipsing in and out of this building asking to see the prodigious "Dr. Weathers." He probably thinks I'm just another groupie.

As I ride the elevator to Blake's floor, I wonder how many girls Blake is seeing and whether that one girl ever got her scrunchie back. As I get off the elevator, I look around skittishly, hoping none of his neighbors will spot me. Before I can knock, Blake opens the door and…whoa…he's wearing a towel.

"Hey, sorry, I was about to get in the shower. I lost track of time and didn't think you'd be here yet."

My mouth agape, I gawk at his chiseled abs. Clearly he's not so busy that he doesn't have time to work out. His lips curl into a devilish grin—he knows he looks good. My gaze darts back to his face. His hair is hanging loose in his face, and his eyes have that subtle mysterious look to them again. Before I lose myself in his eyes, I remind myself of why I'm here and push past him, letting myself into the apartment. "I just need to know what is going on here. It seems like you're interested, but then I don't hear from you when you say you're going to call or text and then we have a date to meet up and you no-show saying you had an emergency. Maybe you did have an emergency, but it just seems like you're too busy to have a fling, let alone a relationship. I normally wouldn't care except you continue to flirt with me and lead me on."

Feeling my voice get elevated, I tell myself to slow it down and wait for him to respond before I continue my tirade. The smell of microwaved food tickles my nostrils. I wonder what he was eating, and that makes me wonder whether he even cooks. There's so much I don't know about this man. The grin on his face slowly devolves into a muted expression. He looks contemplative now, like he's trying to plan what to say next, treading carefully to avoid saying the wrong thing. That might be a red flag. His hand goes to the back of his neck, giving it a slight squeeze as his eyes meet mine again.

"I'm sorry, I've had a rough few weeks and now a rough day. I'm not sure I'm ready for anything serious, but I enjoy hanging out with you. I really do like you. I just haven't been in the best headspace of late." He stands there with the same stoic look on his face, and I wonder if perhaps he *is* a sociopath. Perhaps he is preoccupied with something because this doesn't seem like him. But again, how well do I really know him?

My throat feels dry, and it dawns on me that I've hardly had any water today. Feeling parched, I walk over to the kitchen and ask if I can grab some water. He's still standing in front of me with a robe on, looking completely detached. He opens the cabinet over his sink and hands me a glass. When he opens the refrigerator to grab the filtered water and brings it to my glass, the lid of the filter isn't secured, and the whole jug of water spills all over myself and the floor. My silk blouse is drenched and sticking to my chest.

"Ugh, crap, I'm so sorry," he says, and for a moment his expression actually morphs into one of consternation. He grabs some paper towels and attempts to dab my soaked shirt, but then hands them to me, realizing the futility and awkwardness of the act of drying my blouse while I'm wearing it. I bend down, attempting to dry up the floor, and Blake gets down to help. As we dry the floor, our heads almost collide, and his phone buzzes, startling us both. The scene reminds me of a classic romantic comedy where the date is going wrong in so many ways, and I suppress a chuckle, tightly pressing my lips together, attempting to maintain my serious veneer.

"Hey, sorry, I have to get this. I'll be right back." As he stands, he re-secures the towel around his waist. Grabbing his phone off the kitchen countertop, he retreats into the bedroom area behind the wall. Thanks to my rigorous eavesdropping ability, I can hear bits and pieces of his conversation, but not enough to make out who he's talking to. His voice sounds surprised, and he ends the call with, "No problem, I'll be there as soon as I can." *Great, well, there goes that.*

When he returns, he has a sullen look on his face although he didn't sound so sullen on the phone just now. "Sorry about this, Kylie, but I gotta go into work tonight. I'm going to take a quick shower and bounce." He looks down at my soaked blouse. "Feel free to grab a towel over there by the washer or borrow a shirt if you want," he says, pointing to a shelf over the washer with towels neatly placed on it. Trying hard not to reveal the anger brewing inside of me, I casually nod and go over to the washer. He walks up to me, wraps me in his arms, as I stand there stiff as a board, and plants a kiss on my forehead before he goes into the bathroom. A kiss on the forehead…well, that's never good. "We should talk another time. I'll text you later," he says as he walks away. This has been a strange night. A feeling of unease simmers inside of me. I consider how his disposition wavers between impartial and seemingly disappointed, which is not a state I've seen him in before. Something is going on with him and I don't know what, but I should probably cut my losses.

Once he disappears into the bathroom, I head over to the washer and start sifting through the pile of clothing on top of the machine. The hamper is also filled to the brim, and there's some overflow of clothing onto the floor, which is unusual because every time I've been in Blake's apartment, it's been so tidy, it's unnerving. Come to think of it, even the kitchen looks more disorderly than usual. Dishes are piled up in the sink, and the drying rack is full. There are clothes scattered across the couch in the center of the living room and a few books sprawled over the coffee table. *I guess you can't be perfect all the time,* I think to myself. He's probably having an off day.

Perhaps I can find a sweater to cover up or a towel to dry off, anything to mitigate my walk of shame out of the building. The doorman has already seen enough of my trauma on full display. As I reach for one of the towels sitting on the shelf, I knock over the hamper and several scrub tops and scrub pants spill onto the floor. I quickly start placing them back into the hamper and then—

Hold on, what is this? When I see it, panic flits through me.

Chapter 6

Kylie

At first, I wasn't sure what was staring back at me, but it looked like blood—a white t-shirt completely stained with a dark reddish-brown hue. Dangling the t-shirt in the air, inspecting it, my jaw tenses. My first thought is that this is gross, and my second thought is that he's a surgeon, so seeing blood on clothing is probably not that odd, but we aren't supposed to wear street clothes in the operating room. We usually wear scrubs and then put surgical gowns on top of them. I'm sure Blake abides by protocols for sterilization. In fact, there's no way he'd get past the pedantic operating room nurses if he didn't. My stomach twisting into knots, my eyes land on a pair of crumpled jeans that have the same reddish-brown stains on them. What the heck is this?

I still hear the shower running and suddenly get the urge to flee. Something about today just feels off. First, his strange behavior. Second, the uncharacteristically messy apartment, and finally, finding these bloody clothes. Pushing the clothes back down into the hamper, I grab my purse and decide to forego wearing one of his shirts.

As I step into the elevator, I wrap my arms around my body to shield my soaking shirt from view, and in steps a woman with her dog. I know that dog. I'm pretty sure this is the same woman I saw the last time I was here, although tonight, she's wearing a long suede trench coat and knee-high boots. She looks like she's ready for a night out on the town. She has that same severe look on her face and gives me and my wet shirt a judgmental glance. Lovely. We once again take the uncomfortable thirty-second ride down to the lobby, and as she walks off, she doesn't even acknowledge my presence. Trying to remain as casual as possible to not draw attention to myself, I sulk past the doorman and step out onto the street. There's a chill in the air, but I'm too discombobulated to order an Uber, and I want to get out of this area as fast as I can, so I decide to walk back home. Thankfully, it's only about a ten-minute walk.

As I walk up to my apartment, a million things are swirling in my mind. I'm spooked by the bloody clothing, but I'm even more spooked by Blake's overall demeanor today and behavior over the last few weeks. I'm not surprised he suddenly had to leave to go to work again. He did say he was on call, so I guess that's actually what could have happened, and maybe I'm just reading into it too much. But if he's not ready for anything serious, why does he keep trying to hang out with me other than you-know-what, but we haven't even gotten that far, so what's the point? And a few weeks ago, he told me he really liked me, so why would he lead me on and tell me he liked me if none of it was true? Maybe Lisa is right, and he is a sociopath. He's not capable of having feelings. Maybe I'm just a pawn in this sick game. I start feeling angry at myself for even coming here tonight. I'm glad I said what I needed to say, but I think I need to stop holding out hope that he's a decent person and will come around.

Suddenly remembering I haven't heard back from Chloe or Stratton, I pull out my phone. Crap, I accidentally left my phone on silent, and I have several missed calls from Stratton. I quickly call him back. It only rings once before he picks up.

"Hi, Stratton... I called earlier because we couldn't get a hold of Chloe. I was wondering if you knew—"

And then, with a tremor in his voice, he says, "She's dead, Kylie. We are at her apartment now. She's dead." He goes quiet, and I can hear him sniffling. Trying to process what he just said, I take a seat on my bed to steady myself.

"I'm sorry, I-I don't understand. What do you mean?" I stammer. Dread rises within me.

"She's dead, Kylie," he says again, this time more forcefully, choking back sobs. My mind goes blank. Unable to think of what to say next, I remain speechless. There's several seconds of heavy silence, although a backdrop of commotion and sirens heard on Stratton's side punctuates the silence. Even though my mind had conjured up such a scenario, I hadn't truly believed it would be the reality of what happened.

Mustering the strength to say something, I ask, "Where are you, Stratton?"

"I'm outside her apartment now," he says glumly, more subdued. His voice is hoarse, like he's been crying for some time.

"I'm on my way," I whisper, barely able to get the words out.

Dead? *Dead?* How could this be real life? My whole body feels numb and cold, really cold, partly related to the fact that I'm still wearing my wet shirt, which is now sticking to me and partly due to the chill of terror sliding down my spine. Peeling off my shirt and tossing it in the hamper, I quickly scan my closet and settle on a blue cotton sweater with a green corduroy jacket on top. I feel so out of sorts, I don't even care that my outfit doesn't match. I grab my keys and sprint out the door. When I get outside, I realize I am probably underdressed for the weather, but I'm running on adrenaline, which makes the cold tolerable. The time on my phone reads 11:30 p.m. I don't have to be at the hospital for another eight hours, but work is the furthest thing on my mind. This has been the craziest day.

Chloe lives a few blocks away from me, so I decide I can just sprint there. Running as fast as I can, my heart pounding in my ears, as I approach her street, I see several police cars stationed and blocking the road nearby. Throngs of police officers are circling the apartment building, and loud sirens are wailing. Running up to the police, breathless and shaking, I imagine I look like a madwoman. I yell over the sirens that I'm here to meet Stratton. One officer directs me to where he's standing.

"Oh my God, Stratton, what happened?" I belt out, panting. He looks distressed. His face is red and his eyes look puffy, like he's been crying for days. Strands of his hair are slicked to his forehead. The officer he's talking with, a portly man with a stern expression, turns to me.

"And who are you?" he asks, arching his right eyebrow.

I stutter as I can't catch my breath and blurt out, "Kylie."

"How do you know the victim?" he asks with a leery look.

"I work with her at the hospital," I yell, trying to compete with the sirens. "She was supposed to relieve me from my shift tonight and never showed, so I contacted Stratton after I couldn't get in touch with her," I explain.

He nods his head and scribbles on his pad. "I'm Detective Cranston," he says as he raises his head again. "Do you know what she was doing earlier today?" He studies me.

"I'm sorry, I don't." I pull out my phone and show him the last few text messages I had with Chloe from the day prior. "Nothing seemed out of the ordinary to me based on our conversation, but of course I panicked when she didn't show up for her shift today. She's always punctual and reliable, and I just felt like something had to be wrong."

"I see." Detective Cranston jots down a few lines on his notepad. He puts his hand in his pocket and pulls out a card. "Here's my card. Don't hesitate to call me if you have any information. I'm sure we will have questions for all her coworkers."

I take the card from the detective and place it in the pocket of my jacket. Several officers are going in and out of the apartment building, and residents of the building stand outside as they are questioned by other officers. I look over at Stratton, who looks like he's seen a ghost, his face ashen.

"She was murdered, Kylie," his voice shrieks as he gets this horrific statement out. "There was no sign of forced entry, and she had three stab wounds to her chest. Can you imagine that? To her chest!" he cries out, his hands curling into fists, pounding against his thighs. Detective Cranston lays a hand on his shoulder, attempting to console him. I do the same.

"I'm so sorry, Stratton. Where are your parents?"

"They're upstairs with her—with her body." He has difficulty getting the words out. "They're a mess."

I look back at Detective Cranston, who now has a sympathetic look on his face. "Well, thanks for the information, Kylie. Like I said, we will reach out to you again soon. Please call me if you learn anything else."

"Of course," I reply. I feel myself getting flushed as heat rises in my chest. I try to catch my breath, repeating what Stratton just told me. No forced entry. Three stab wounds to the chest. That assessment echoes in my mind. As a true crime obsessed enthusiast, I know what those words mean. This was someone she knew, perhaps someone she trusted. She let them into her home, and they betrayed her trust. The fact that she was stabbed three times intimates something personal. Who would want to hurt Chloe? I couldn't even begin to come up with a list. She was somewhat elusive about her dating life, as I never got any details about the guys she went out with, but there wasn't anyone in particular who stood out as sketchy.

"You should get out of here, Kylie. I'm sure you have to get up for work in a few hours, but I appreciate you coming by," Stratton says in a low voice, speaking through tears. I feel awful leaving him like this, but I'm not sure what I can even do to help.

"Please reach out to me if you need anything," I say.

He pulls me in and hugs me and through sobs, he whispers, "Thank you" in my ear. I can't imagine what the pain of losing a sibling must be like. Chloe and Stratton are three years apart, and he's the older sibling. I don't know what their relationship was like or whether they were close, but regardless, this must be gut-wrenching. I have four siblings, and while we were not that close growing up, we've become much closer as adults. The pain of losing one of them is too much to imagine.

As I walk home, I feel scattered, my mind foggy. The air feels even colder than when I left my apartment. Putting my hands into my pockets to keep them warm, I feel the edge of the card Detective Cranston gave me. Quickening my pace as gusts of chilly air blow against my face, I think about who I should call. Does our program director, Dr. Mick know? This is going to crush her. Not only was Chloe an amazing person and neurology resident, but she and Dr. Mick got along very well. Dr. Mick is a great leader. She is one of the reasons I chose to do my residency here. Kind, detail-oriented, and compassionate, she represents what a leader and neurologist should be. She also makes it her mission to empower women, encouraging us to speak up more and mentoring us in ways we can enhance our academic careers. She truly cultivates a warm, accepting environment, a difficult thing to do in residency. When she's running the inpatient teams, it's also apparent how much patients adore and trust her. I really don't want to be the one to break the news to her. Plus, it's past midnight, and she's probably asleep. I'm sure she will find out soon enough.

Next, I consider calling Mae, who is now covering the night float, but before I can dial her number, I see that she's texted me first. *I just heard from Chloe's family. They said you stopped by, so I'm assuming you already know. I'm so sorry*, she writes.

I text her back, *I'm sorry too.*

This all feels so surreal. As doctors, we deal with death often, more often than anyone should. In my intern year, I had several patients pass away. The deaths always stick with you. We deal with it so much that we come to expect it and then prepare ourselves for it. We have practice, but no amount of practice can prepare anyone for losing someone unexpectedly and, even more traumatically, to something senseless like murder.

Chapter 7

The boy

After I went to live with my aunt, I started seeing a therapist. During the first few therapy sessions, I didn't utter a word. I would just look down at my fingers, examining my bitten fingernails, and wait for the session to be over. The therapist, Dr. Stern, was perfectly kind. She was around my mom's age with short brown hair and a doe-eyed expression. Her face was pleasant, but she looked at me with such sorrow in her eyes, it actually made me more uncomfortable. I didn't want to be pitied. Pity is for weak people. Everyone said I was in a state of shock regarding what happened to my mom. I wasn't able to have a conversation about what I had heard that night with anyone, not even Aunt Claire. I could still hear those hammering sounds in my head, the barely audible shrieking, the careful footsteps, trying to be as quiet and discreet as possible. The sounds of her last gasps echoed in my head. Then there were the intense emotions. The sense of regret over not waking up a little sooner, over not going downstairs, over not saving my mother's life, which all haunt me still. Otherwise, I remember very little about the events and details of that night.

I remember tiptoeing to the room next door and grabbing the phone off the charger and dialing 9-1-1. The operator asked, "How can I help you?" to which I responded, my voice cracking, "I think my dad just hurt my mom. Please come now."

"Where are you?" she asked me. I answered that I was hiding in the upstairs guest room. "Are you safe?"

"Yes," I responded. After hearing that I was hiding out upstairs while my parents were downstairs, the operator then asked me questions like, "How do you know?" to which I just responded that I knew. Sometimes you just know. When they arrived, I was hiding under my bed, shivering with fear. Too scared to use the restroom and perhaps in a state of shock, I may have even wet my pants. The sensation of something wet trickling down my legs and a puddle pooling beneath me stays with me. I stayed still and remember a light shining through the crack in my doorway.

A woman stepped into my room holding a flashlight. Getting on the floor, she coaxed me from under the bed. She had a kind voice. She kept saying, "It's okay now. You can come out," reassuring me, but I knew that what was waiting for me on the other side was anything but okay. I wanted to stay hidden under that bed for as long as I could. I didn't want to face reality.

When I finally came out, I could see that she had a softness in her eyes, and she looked sad. Someone's eyes can be very telling. She draped a blanket over me and took me downstairs, where I sat at the kitchen table and waited for my aunt to arrive. The clock on the wall of our kitchen read 1:30 a.m., and I remember thinking about the saying that nothing good ever happens after midnight. The kettle was on the stove. Perhaps my mom was making her nightly tea before she was killed. It's incredible how things can change in an instant. One minute, you're doing something you always do like boiling water, and the next, you're fighting for your life. I bet I was the last thing she thought of before her body gave up.

Looking outside the window, I could see my dad's silhouette. He was being handcuffed and put in the police car. He looked back at the house for an instant, his eyes landing on mine, and in that moment, I saw that he was remorseless. That's when I decided that I wished him dead.

When my aunt Claire arrived, she looked like she had been crying all night. As my mom's younger sister, she had always looked up to my mom, but after my mom married my dad, my aunt lost respect for her. She knew there was ongoing abuse and repeatedly urged my mom to leave, but she wouldn't. During those years, my aunt and my mom drifted apart, and we saw less and less of my aunt. In fact, we didn't really see any family members. It was as if my mom was too embarrassed to see family and friends for fear they were judging her for staying with my dad.

While my aunt appeared distraught, she was visibly trying to keep it together so as to not frighten me, but I already knew the worst thing imaginable had happened. I knew it deep in my gut. My aunt ran to me and embraced me. My body stiffened, resisting her embrace because allowing myself to succumb to it would mean I'd have to accept what had happened.

There are still gaps in my memory of that night, but I remember waking up the next morning in my aunt's home, wishing it was all a nightmare, that I had dreamt it all. When I opened my eyes and saw the pastel-colored walls, the checkered bedspread that was hiked up to my chin, the antique bookcase in the corner of the room, I knew it was not a nightmare. My body tensed up, my eyes holding back tears, trying my best to stay composed. I couldn't even cry if I wanted to. Nothing would ever be the same again.

Chapter 8

Kylie

We are called down to Dr. Mick's office where she tells us the police are investigating and are going to question us all about our relationships with Chloe. Bags protruding under her eyes, Dr. Mick looks like she hasn't slept all weekend. Normally dressed in a colorful dress or a pressed pantsuit, today she looks like she grabbed the first shabby sweater she could find and tossed it over a pair of old jeans. She could never look slovenly even if she tried, but there is a clear downgrade from her normal getup. Fighting through yawns, with a muted tone, she speaks to us about potential mental health resources that are available if we need to talk to somebody about what happened.

We all sit there in silence, still stunned by the news and unable to formulate our thoughts. Dr. Mick walks over to where I am sitting, wedged between Lisa and Bailey, and places a heavy hand on my shoulder. "How are you all doing?" she asks, her eyes scanning the three of us. I glance at Lisa and Bailey, their faces frozen, drained of color.

"Shocked," Lisa mutters. I nod my head in agreement as she gets up and excuses herself to the restroom. Bailey looks on. He hasn't said a word all morning, but his expression offers insight enough into how he is feeling. As Dr. Mick hovers over us, seemingly not knowing what to do next or who to check in on, I will myself to speak, wanting to break up the silence.

"It's just hard to believe anyone would want to hurt Chloe," I manage, my eyes meeting hers.

She draws her lips into a taut line and replies, "Yes, it's all so surreal."

Detectives take us to a conference room, and one by one, they pull each of us aside to gather information about Chloe. Detective Cranston shows up with another detective, a woman named Detective Ford. Detective Ford has a kind face, one that exudes sympathy for what we are all going through. She's tall and lean, towering over Detective Cranston by a few inches, and when she looks down at us, her eyes display warmth. Unsurprisingly, several of us were working at one of the hospitals at the time of the murder, and none of us spent an appreciable amount of time with Chloe outside of the hospital to be privy to the details of her personal life. While we were all relatively close, given the nature of residency, our schedules always conflicted. Chloe also had an extensive network of friends and acquaintances outside the hospital with whom she frequently spent her time.

When it's my turn, I tell the detectives I knew she was actively dating and using dating apps, but I'm frank about the fact that Chloe didn't share specifics about her dating life. I recall swiping through a few profiles with her once during a slow workday and picking guys for one another, but beyond that, we didn't keep track of one another's dates. Of course, I had to tell the detectives where I was the night of the murder. Knowing I have to be fully transparent, I say I was at the apartment of a guy I am seeing.

When Detective Cranston asks, "And who is this guy?" I feel my face flush when I answer, "Blake Weathers, a neurosurgery resident at this hospital." I sink into the seat. Probably sensing my discomfort, both detectives smirk and nod their heads, indicating they understand.

After work, I grab a drink with Bailey and Hassan to debrief. We are all unnerved by the police questioning. It's been almost forty-eight hours since Chloe was found, and we don't have an inkling as to who committed the crime. While Chloe's death was treated as a homicide from the start given the way she was stabbed, it is now officially ruled a homicide. The police are obviously looking for someone close to her, and it is clear they are starting with her family, friends, and co-residents. After all, killers are often close to their victims. Bailey's boyfriend, Omar, is meeting us at the bar. Omar works as an investigative journalist and focuses on hunting down true crime stories. My fascination with him and his job borders on fandom. At times, I envision spending a day toting after him and getting a glimpse of what he does. The son of Lebanese immigrants, Omar was raised with the high expectation that he would someday be a doctor, a lawyer, or an engineer. He often speaks about how his parents would remind him that those were the only acceptable professions growing up. After all, his three siblings all went into medicine. The fact that he went into journalism nearly broke his parents, but he's made it pretty big, working for a well-respected newspaper and receiving many accolades early on in his nascent career. That seemed to quell his parents' concerns, at least for the time being.

Omar, with flawless olive skin, gorgeous curly locks that periodically bounce over his eyes, and a fit physique, epitomizes tall, dark, and handsome. He is impeccably dressed all the time without appearing too formal. He has a domineering yet soothing presence and speaks with a measured tone, confident but not arrogant. Interestingly, Bailey is the opposite of measured.

Opposites attract, I guess. I enjoy talking to him, mainly because he is such a smart guy, but also because of his immense insight into crime cases in NYC. I often ask him his thoughts on a particular case. However, we now have a personal case to discuss, which makes the discussion seem tasteless. If anyone can lend it the dignity it deserves, though, it's Omar. He is always working on a groundbreaking piece. Last year, he was an integral part of bringing a serial murderer to justice after he obtained highly coveted security camera tapes that even the police neglected to uncover. It was thought that the security cameras were tampered with, but he was able to somehow uncover their content, displaying another talent of his.

We sit down and order a few drinks and appetizers. I don't think any of us have eaten all day. The pit in my stomach continues to grow, making it hard to distinguish anxiety from hunger, but I know I have to eat something. Bailey, who usually can't contain himself, looks at Omar with fervor in his eyes and blurts out, "So, what did you find out about Chloe?" He shifts forward in his seat, the chair making a screeching sound as it moves across the floor. Given how quiet he's been today, understandably in a state of shock, I'm struck by his sudden enthusiasm.

The server brings our drinks over, and Omar, waiting for her to walk away, lets the question hang in the air. He brings his drink to his lips, locking his gaze with Bailey's, calculating what he should and shouldn't reveal. After a few seconds of contemplation, he responds, "So they have a few suspects." This isn't news to me since it's public information now that the police have deemed Chloe's case a homicide and they are looking into her family and friends.

Bailey inches closer to him. "Like who?" Once again with that look on his face that says he means business and wants to know the tea, but Omar is not giving in. It feels wrong to be out at a bar casually discussing the murder of our colleague like it's salacious gossip, but I also feel the need to be productive and get answers about what happened to her.

Omar's lips press into a thin line, his brows furrowing. "You know I can't say anything."

"Awww, you're no fun," cries Bailey. He genuinely looks disappointed.

"Are we suspects?" I chime in.

"Again, I can't really say, but based on the police questioning today and the fact that you are all perpetually working at the hospital, I'd say the odds are low. Not sure when any of you would have time to commit a crime." He lets out a small chuckle, and then quickly transforms his face back into a stern expression as if the gravity of the situation won't allow him to laugh, even for a moment. "It probably comes as no surprise that the police are looking into the family closely. They also found a few contacts in Chloe's phone she was talking to through dating apps."

"Yeah, well, it's usually someone close to the victim," I add, once again, unable to withhold my true crime knowledge. "I don't know how suspicious her family would be, though. There needs to be a motive."

"Can you give us any hints about family dynamics?" asks Bailey. "It's clear she has a close-knit family, but every family has skeletons." Bailey turns and looks at me with a sideways glance. "Take the brother for example," Bailey offers, his eyes widening as he says this in an accusatory way. "I mean, he has a motive…I'm sure they have lots of family money that will be bequeathed to the siblings, and the brother may be greedy."

I give him an incredulous look. "Stratton? No, I don't think he's capable of murder." I take a chip and scoop up some guacamole, hoping it will quell the gnawing in my stomach. As I bring the chip to my mouth, I feel a tinge of pain developing at the back of my head—another headache gearing up into a full-blown migraine. My headaches have continued to increase over the last few weeks and especially now, with the recent traumatic events coupled with an empty stomach, it's no surprise I'm getting a migraine again. I try to ignore the pain and focus on what my friends are saying.

Bailey has a dubious look on his face. "You never know. It's always the quiet ones."

"I saw him the night she was murdered, and he was completely beside himself," I say, bringing a glass of water to my lips and taking a sip.

"Well, don't you think that someone who just committed murder would behave like the saddest person in the room? They'd obviously want to throw people off," Bailey says.

I glance at Hassan, who is shoveling guacamole in his mouth, as if the faster he eats, the faster his grief will be buried. "He was the one to find her, right?" Hassan interjects. Omar nods his head in confirmation.

"True, but that doesn't automatically make him a murderer. Maybe a suspect, though," says Omar, clearly the voice of reason in this group. He takes a sip of his drink and swivels his glass in his hand before he places it back down on the table. He continues, "It's all just conjecture at this point; we need solid evidence."

As I leave the bar and head home, I think about the accusations. Could Stratton really be a murderer? Hassan is right. He is the one who found Chloe after all.

A few days later, it comes to light that Stratton is indeed one of the suspects, as the police found angry text messages between the two of them the day before she was murdered. One notable text from Stratton even said something to the effect of *I'm going to kill you*, but I don't put too much stock into that, as it's common for siblings to talk that way to one another. I recall all the arguments I would get into with my own siblings where we'd often say things we didn't mean in the heat of the moment, things we'd come to regret later.

Apparently, their dispute was over who was going to use the house in the Hamptons for a particular weekend. Yeah, I know, what a problem to have. It does make me wonder about sibling rivalry, though, and the division of affection by parents. In their case, division of assets and money as well, which rich people tend to get the most heated about. I could see that being a major motive for many family murders.

Although, admittedly, it isn't always about money. There were the Amityville murders where Ronald Defeo, the mass murderer, killed his siblings and parents, but they never did identify a motive for those killings. He was just unhinged and likely fueled by drugs and alcohol. Then there were the two half brothers who murdered their sister and her three young children over property disputes in 2021 in California. But in general, siblings murdering each other is pretty rare. There are more cases of siblings turning on their parents, most notably in the case of the Menendez brothers. Like all murders, though, there should be a clear motive, and as far as I could tell, Chloe and Stratton had an amicable relationship. If not a family member, who else could it be? My mind flicks back to the description of the crime scene and the manner in which she was murdered—three stab wounds to the chest. It has to be someone she knew. A crime of passion or someone with an ax to grind.

Chapter 9

Kylie

About a week later, a few of us are able to make it to Chloe's funeral. Only a few of us, because someone needs to be at the hospital. As residents, we don't get the luxury of all being off at the same time to attend an event, even if the event is a cataclysmic one such as the traumatic murder of our dear colleague. It feels surreal—grieving the death of a young colleague and friend, someone with such a promising future. Someone who was going to make an amazing neurologist and had so much potential. The thought of a young life ending so senselessly overwhelms me whenever I think about it, my chest growing tight, my breath catching in my throat. Tears well up behind my eyes, but I quickly blink them away.

I stop by Lisa's place to pick her up so we can go to the funeral together. Lisa steps out of her apartment building wearing a long shearling coat over a black knee-length dress with matching black pumps. Her hair is tied into a low ponytail, and she's wearing pearl earrings. She looks crestfallen and tired. She must have had a rough night on call last night. "This is all so depressing, girl," she says. I nod in agreement. We walk in silence for the next few blocks.

We are about a block away from the funeral home, and I can see that there's a large group of people wearing black congregating outside, spilling onto the street. It's clear that Chloe had a lot of friends and loved ones. Inside, the foyer is lined with white lilies, and there are multiple tables with photos of Chloe during different stages of her life. There's also a projector in the corner playing a slideshow of Chloe's childhood. I pick up a photo of her where she looks like she's about six years old. Stratton is kneeling next to her and hugging her tight. They are both smiling from ear to ear. It's a sweet photo, and I can feel the love emanating between them.

Chloe's parents and Stratton are huddled together in the corner of the funeral home. They all look like they've aged a decade since the last time I saw them. I can't imagine the pain of losing a child.

The foyer is cramped as more people file in and take their seats on the benches before the eulogies begin. Lisa and I sit somewhere in the middle, not wanting to take closer seats to the casket, which will likely be filled by the family and close friends. As the procession begins and Chloe's casket is carried down the aisle, my eyes tear up. I look to the back of the funeral home near the entrance where the casket is being carried in, and squinting through tears, I can't believe my eyes. Is that who I think it is, standing at the entrance? No, it can't be. What would *he* be doing here? But there he is, a looming presence wearing a black suit jacket that outlines his broad shoulders.

I quickly turn back around before he catches my eye. "Oh my God, Lisa, CNS is here," I whisper.

"What? Why would he be here?" She gives me a skeptical look. She tries to turn her head subtly towards the back, and then slowly looks back at me. "I wonder how he knew her," she says. I now find it hard to focus on the procession. As expected, Blake hasn't attempted to meet up with me again since the last time I saw him. He was acting so strange at his apartment that night and then I found those bloody clothes, which I later convinced myself were just related to an occupational hazard. But something still nags at me about that night and the fact that he didn't even try to reach out to me to explain his behavior. Considering all that, I've decided it's best to stay away. There's a small part of me, though, that wants to hold out hope. He also looks pretty damn good in that suit right now. I keep thinking back to the conversations we've had, the way his eyes light up when he talks about his passion for neurosurgery, the comfort I felt when telling him about my fears for the future, the undeniable physical chemistry between us. Did I imagine all that? Or is he just really good at playing a part?

I watch as each of Chloe's parents take the stage to give their eulogies. Her mother, elegant and poised on the outside, is having a hard time getting her words out. She stops every few seconds to gather herself and periodically grabs a handkerchief to wipe her eyes before continuing. Chloe's father is next, and he is practically wailing while he speaks. His wife stands next to him and rubs his back while he gets his bearings. It's hard to watch the two of them comfort each other during what must be the hardest few days of their lives.

Stratton then takes the stage, and he, too, is visibly bereft, but more composed than his parents. He takes out a piece of paper, his hands trembling, and reads from it. "Chloe was a force to be reckoned with. She had a bright light that nobody could put out and wasn't going to allow anyone to stop her from achieving her dreams. I always admired her drive and ambition. I know she had so much more to offer the world. She was taken from us too soon."

As I'm listening to the speeches, I shift in my seat and try to discreetly look back towards the exit again to see if Blake is still there. This time, he catches my eye, and I quickly face forward again. Crap. He caught me. It takes everything in me to not turn around again.

After the speeches, Lisa and I walk up to Chloe's family and offer our condolences. Stratton reaches out and hugs me. "I really appreciate you coming today, Kylie, and I especially appreciate you showing up at Chloe's apartment that night. I never had the chance to thank you for that," he says with sincerity.

I nod my head in acknowledgement. "I'm sorry for everything your family is going through," I say. I know we don't know each other that well, but I feel connected to him. Perhaps it's because I admired Chloe so much, and her brother feels like an extension of her. Perhaps it's because I was there at probably the lowest point in his life, when he was most vulnerable. "She was an amazing person. We all really miss her," I say solemnly.

Out of the corner of my eye, I see Blake approaching us. "Kylie, this is my friend from Dartmouth, Blake. He's actually a neurosurgery resident at your hospital," Stratton says. Ah, right, they went to Dartmouth together. I'm still not sure Blake told me he went there, but I remember seeing his mail.

"Yes, I know," I reply. "I mean, we know each other." There's an acridity to my voice. My face gets hot, and my eyes are piercing his like daggers. Blake moves closer to me and looks like he's going to hug me but then changes his mind and takes a step back.

"Hey, Kylie, how have you been?" he asks, a sorrowful expression etched across his face.

"Good," I answer, intentionally trying to keep my responses curt.

"So, were you close to Chloe?" he asks.

"Somewhat, I guess." We weren't best friends or anything, but had a mutual respect for each other and worked well as colleagues. My eyes are still pinned on his. Stratton turns away from us to greet other guests. There's now a long line of people waiting to give their condolences to the family. "So, I'm glad you could make it to the funeral since you're so busy usually," I say, my tone brimming with bitterness.

"Yeah, I just happened to be off this morning."

"Oh, how coincidental and timely." At this point, he'd be a dud not to know that I am irritated. I'm not sure why I'm so mad. Maybe it's the fact that he's so hot and cold and hasn't even tried to provide an explanation for ghosting me yet feels the need to make stupid small talk with me whenever he sees me. I'd rather he just drop the pleasantries and keep moving along if he's not interested. We don't need to pretend for anyone else's sake.

"I've been really busy with work, and I'm not that great at texting or calling, but I have been meaning to reach out to you to see you again. We didn't really get to talk last time you came over. Then all this happened with Chloe, and I've just been so focused on making sure her family is doing okay." He looks down at the floor, despair visible on his face.

"So, are you really close to the family?" I ask, softening my tone. I suddenly feel guilty for being so caustic at Chloe's funeral.

"The Kings are my family away from home. I don't know what

I'd do without them. Stratton and I go way back, but over the years, they've taken me in as one of their own." His tone is somber as he speaks, and I feel a tug at my chest, making me feel momentarily sorry for him.

"I didn't realize you knew them so well. You never mentioned knowing Chloe when we'd hang out."

"Yeah, well, I didn't think it was relevant. She's the sister of one of my best friends."

Satisfied with his answer, I feel my shoulders relax, but there's something deeply sad about his eyes when he says this that makes me question his sincerity. I'm not sure what to believe when it comes to Blake, but despite my attraction to him, there are alarm bells going off. Something isn't right here.

Chapter 10

Blake

It's taken me a long time to work through some of the trauma I dealt with as a kid. Years of therapy. Years of initiating and then ditching relationships. Years of thinking I was going to end up like my dad no matter how hard I tried to escape that presumed fate. I still feel like I'm that scared boy at times, still hiding under the bed, wishing I had the courage to act. I can't seem to let go of the feeling that no matter how hard I try to forget the past, it will always be part of my present and future. Sometimes it seems I'll never recover. I don't even think I've properly dealt with the trauma of losing my mother because I've been so busy battling against turning into my father and trying to survive. I won't even allow myself to think about how life was with my mother. While she was always preoccupied with making sure I was well fed, dressed and taken care of, we didn't get to know each other that well. I only knew her for a short time, but most of the time was in the context of trying to protect her from my father and in turn, her trying to protect me from the abuse.

I know all the trauma I've endured has had dire consequences for my personal life. I've been a bad guy. I haven't always treated women well, often using them and then discarding them once I realize I'm not invested. No one has been worth taking down my defenses and committing myself to being the best partner I could be. Well, no one except for her.

Until she came along, I thought I was hopeless. I designated myself to living a life of solitude and pouring myself into neurosurgery—the one thing I'm really good at. I haven't needed many people in my life. People complicate things. They are better when they are unconscious and on my operating table. You don't have to worry about them judging you, you don't need to feign interest in conversations, you can just exist in a space with their bodies as you work on your craft and hope they reap the benefits of your labor. Of course, there are occasionally complications, and then you feel terrible when people die, but eventually the job desensitizes you. You start to detach more and more from the patients and focus on the art of the craft.

Dissecting the brain is like exposing a masterpiece accessible only to the surgeon. The pressure that builds beneath the surface of the scalp, palpable by the scalpel that is resting on it, ready to make the first cut. Pulling back the dura, the toughest layer of the brain, and exposing the delicate contours of the folds. Watching the organ pulsate the way a heart pulsates, revealing a stunning array of vessels. The intricate design of the circle of Willis, the anastomosis of the major arteries converging at the base of the brain, a tapestry of blood flow essential to functioning. The brain, that exquisitely beautiful organ that controls our thoughts, expressions, and actions, that supplies us with the ingredients needed to survive. What could be more scintillating than that? How could anyone find anything more exciting?

Perhaps I find the control element immensely gratifying too. One wrong scalpel swipe and the brain bleeds out, the person bleeds out, losing brain as time disintegrates, losing control, losing consciousness and then eventually culminating in brain death. The power can be intoxicating. What else gives this much power to one human being? As if there is any human part left to us.

Maybe the lack of humanity is what makes us great surgeons. Some would say that's sociopathic, and perhaps it is, but desensitization sets in at some point during the torture of residency, and harnessing that desensitization into something productive may be a superpower. Maybe we need to allow that desensitization process to take place so we can see the body for what it is in its purest form, detached from any emotion or personhood that may complicate our mastery. A conglomeration of organs and vessels and nerve endings all working together in a beautiful symphony to make a person whole. What could be more magnificent than getting to witness those inner workings every day?

It's surely more magnificent than any love connection could ever be. But one person almost measured up. I often thought she could supplant my obsession with neurosurgery. I started looking forward to our rendezvous the same way I'd look forward to an exciting surgical case. She had an immense power to make me forget about the thrill of neurosurgery and focus on her. Focus on getting her, possessing her, truly knowing her. Those celestial eyes—the ones that could summon a million feelings all at once—adoration, optimism, hope. Those eyes that spoke a thousand languages. They bore deep into my soul and reminded me that I indeed had a heart—something I had abandoned the idea of a long time ago. I've been numb to human contact for so long, I didn't know if I'd ever recover my senses, but now I've lost her, and there seems like there isn't a way back. Will I feel anything like that ever again?

Chapter 11

Kylie

I'm waiting in the subway station and feel someone watching me through the dense crowd. Out of the corner of my eye, I spot a lanky guy with curly brown hair wearing thick-rimmed glasses. The jovial grin on his face widens when he catches me looking. Discreetly trying to squint to get a better look, I realize I don't recognize him from anywhere. Feeling somewhat spooked, when my train arrives, I quickly push through the throngs of people and get on. I somehow manage to score a corner seat near the exit in case I have to make a run for it at the next stop. I'm lucky I even got a seat, as rush hour is absolute mayhem.

As I pull out my AirPods, I feel a presence hovering over me. I slowly look up, and there he is, still grinning at me and holding on to the subway pole next to my seat. "Hey, do you work at the hospital? I think I recognize you," he says.

"Yeah, I'm a resident," I answer with hesitation.

"Don't mean to be a creeper, but I just noticed your ID badge hanging out of your backpack and thought you looked familiar. What department are you in?"

Reminder not to leave my ID badge fully exposed to strangers. "Neurology," I answer.

"Cool, neurology is fascinating. I'm a pathologist, so I don't get much patient contact. They try to keep us locked up in the bowels of the hospital." He snickers as he says this, and a curl bounces in front of his face. He gently moves it out of the way. "It's probably best for everyone that we keep to our own devices," he adds.

Pathologists have a reputation for being introverted and obtuse, given they likely chose the field to avoid human contact. Whenever I look at a pathology report, I imagine the pathologist peering into a microscope, analyzing tissue and blood samples to uncover clues about a patient's condition. Of course, the work pathologists do is important, as they can offer insight into a patient's diagnosis and the best course of treatment, but they are definitely more of a behind-the-scenes crew. It takes a certain type of person to enjoy sitting in a sterile room, mostly alone, analyzing biopsies and samples all day.

As he speaks, the pathologist periodically adjusts his tortoiseshell glasses that keep sliding down his nose, all the while keeping his gaze on me. Behind the thick frames, I take note of an innocent baby face. "I'm Sean, by the way." He stumbles a little as the subway train comes to a halt but catches his fall.

"I'm Kylie. Nice to meet you."

"Are you headed home? I live on the Upper East Side."

"Same," I say halfheartedly.

"What are you listening to?" he asks.

"Oh, you know, a true crime podcast." I haven't bothered to take my AirPods out yet, an extra layer of protection signaling that I remain non-committal to continuing our conversation.

"Oh, I see, a true-crime girlie." He laughs louder this time, throwing his head back as if it's the funniest thing he's ever heard.

"Yeah, this one is about John Wayne Gacey. You know, the guy who murdered thirty-three men. He had a really messed up childhood."

"Yeah, I'd expect that's the case with most of these people," he says, eyes wide.

I usually can't stand small talk, but I'll talk true crime with anyone. Thankfully, the subway ride to my stop is quick since I take the express train back uptown to my neighborhood. As we continue our conversation, however, I no longer feel like I'm in a rush to get away. Removing my AirPods from my ears, I feel my face soften and the tension in my shoulders abate. His demeanor is disarming, and he's actually pretty cute. It's hard to know who to trust out there, but I figure a fellow doctor should be mostly harmless.

"Would you like to grab dinner sometime?" he asks with a look of earnestness.

"Sure, here's my phone number," I acquiesce. Sometimes I think I'm too cautious. Maybe that is what has held me back from meeting someone. It's not like I have a cavalry of men waiting in the wings for me.

Upon exiting the subway station, Sean and I walk in opposite directions. I haven't even walked a block when he's already texted me. *Thanks for making my subway ride home enjoyable. Looking forward to seeing you soon.* Followed by three smiley face emojis. That's cute, but one emoji would suffice. He seems like a nice guy, so I reply:

looking forward to it too. It's time I let my guard down a little. After all, how painful could one dinner be?

As I put my phone back in my pocket, it pings again, and I'm surprised to see I have a new message in the Connections app. I haven't used the app regularly since Chloe's murder, but there's one guy I've been talking to. When I open the app, I see a familiar face. Mateo and I had been talking on the app for a few weeks. I figured it wasn't going anywhere since we hadn't yet progressed to text messaging or setting up a time to meet. Like most of these conversations initiated on the dating apps, if a date hasn't been made early on, odds are, the attraction fizzles out. To my surprise, though, Mateo asks me to meet up. Well, I guess it is my lucky day: two date requests in the span of an hour. Maybe my luck is starting to change.

Chapter 12

Kylie

Okay, it turns out a dinner can be pretty painful. As I watch the pathologist shove another heap of lettuce into his mouth, loudly crunching with each bite, I think, *How have I not escaped yet?* This date probably takes the cake as the most unbearable since moving to NYC, or maybe ever.

When I first arrived at the restaurant Sean had pin-dropped me, he was waiting at the bar. There were no seats available, so he opted to have dinner at the bar (clearly he didn't think ahead enough to make a reservation), but from the looks of the place, it didn't seem exclusive. Friday nights in Manhattan are tough anywhere, though, even at the restaurants where reservations aren't highly coveted. Sean had that same silly grin slapped on his face that spread from ear to ear, practically brimming with joy. He looked as harmless as when I met him on the subway, like a puppy dog waiting for his treat.

"I started to think you weren't going to show!" he exclaimed. There was a tinge of irritation in his voice, but his smile was still visible. I couldn't tell if he was joking or serious. It was only two minutes past nine. I laughed nervously. "You know what they say. If you're early, you're on time. If you're on time, you're late," he said with a reproachful look.

Oh boy, this is going to be fun.

"I ordered you a glass of Pinot. I also got us an appetizer." He pointed down to a plate of half-eaten salad. "Hopefully you like salad." I don't know how I feel about someone I just met ordering for me. I know some women think it's attractive when a man orders for them as if he's taking charge, but I tend to think it's presumptuous. While I do love white wine, the fact that he ordered without knowing that is also a little creepy. The appetizer, the salad, looked like it had been single-handedly demolished before I even arrived. At least the wine was not here yet when I arrived, because I'd have to send it back and ask for another. I know better than to leave my drink unattended with someone I just met.

Okay, Kylie, just be gracious, I kept telling myself. I'm sure his gesture came from a good place. "Thanks, have you been here long?" I asked.

"Nah, got here about ten minutes ago, but thought I'd snag us a good spot at the bar." I looked around, and nearly every table was full. "So, tell me about yourself!"

Before I could answer, he started talking. "So, a little fun fact about me. My grandfather was one of the chemists involved in inventing adhesive, which is now used for things like post-it notes and such."

"So he invented post-its?" I asked incredulously.

"Well, not exactly, more so the materials needed to create post-its." He flashed me a goofy smile as he stuck his fork in another chunk of lettuce.

"But the post-it is literally just adhesive and paper, right?"

"Yeah, so he was an integral part of the adhesive part," he asserted.

"I see. So your family now sits on an adhesive empire," I said somewhat sarcastically.

"Yeah, I guess we do! Well, I guess my mom and I do since my dad is dead and I'm an only child."

"Oh, I'm sorry about your dad."

"It was a long time ago, but thanks." Before I could utter another word, he got a phone call. "Oh, I'm sorry, it's my mom. I have to answer—I don't like to leave her hanging." I watched him get up and walk to the corner of the restaurant. Just then, my glass of wine appeared—perfect timing. I sat there sipping, thinking this was not going the way I hoped it would, but he was nice enough. Nonetheless, I needed an exit strategy so I wasn't stuck here all night. When he got back to the table about twenty minutes later, I motioned to the bartender that we were ready to order, but he seemed to be occupied with other patrons.

"Are you in a rush?" Sean asked.

"Umm, no, it's just that I need to stop by a friend's on my way home. She's having a small birthday party and I don't want to drop by too late," I lied. I quickly changed the subject. "So, everything okay with your mom?"

"Yeah, she just has to check in with me every night at the same time before her favorite show starts. I usually talk to her three times a day—on my way to work in the morning, during my lunch break, and at once before bed. We are super close. I always say if your mom is not your best friend, then who is? I mean, she literally housed me in her body for almost ten months." He chuckled to himself. "Are you close to your parents?"

"Somewhat. We talk probably once a week. You know, it's hard with residency finding the time to call every day—"

"Well, if it's a priority, you'll make it a priority," he interrupted with a hint of judgement in his tone.

And now here I am, starting to feel like I'm a child being chided by a parent. He takes in another mouthful of salad and motions to the plate. "You want to get in here? There isn't much left."

"I'm good. Thanks." *No, I don't want to get into the salad that you've been stuffing your face with for the last thirty minutes.* I'm getting impatient, and the bartender hasn't been back to check on us. Wishing he would get here, I glance over Sean's shoulder, this time more discreetly, furtively searching for him.

Finally, Sean catches the bartender's eye and summons him over to us. A tall guy with wispy strands of dark hair sweeping across his forehead approaches us. "Excuse me, can we please have two orders of the steak?" Sean squawks.

"Umm, actually I'd like salmon," I say, my tone becoming more aggressive as the night goes on.

"Oh, you should really have the steak. It's pretty great here," he says back to me. The bartender's eyes dart back and forth between us, puzzled by the exchange.

"No, I'd like the salmon," I say more firmly this time. "Whoa, okay, slow down, tiger. I see you're a feisty one," he almost growls. I feel my face cringe a little. I'm officially over this date. I'd like to just pack up my food and leave, but I don't want to be rude.

I excuse myself from the bar and go to the restroom. I actually don't have to use the bathroom, but I figure any time spent away from him is time well spent. At least I can wait it out in the bathroom until our food arrives. When I walk in, there's a woman wearing a short denim dress and black stiletto heels bent over the sink. She looks distressed, like she's been crying. I hesitate, but ask, "Are you okay, ma'am?"

"Thanks, I'm fine. Just dealing with a personal issue," she says. Perhaps she, too, is on a date that is going poorly. I can relate.

When I walk back to the bar, Sean gives me an accusatory look and says, "You were in there forever." I think it was only about ten minutes, but this guy is drama.

"Someone was upset in the bathroom. I was trying to calm her down," I say although I don't need any justification for taking my time in the bathroom. He seems to accept this.

"Oh, so you never told me about yourself," he says, flashing a smile again. I think, *Well, if you'd let me get a word in edgewise, I would have.* "So, I grew up in a small town in Florida. I have four siblings—"

"Wow, that's a full house. See, I've always wanted siblings. They're like built-in best friends, right? It was pretty lonely growing up as an only child. Sometimes I would get teased at school, and I would imagine that I had an older sibling who could protect me from the bullies. At the same time, though, it was nice to have my mom's attention all to myself. Maybe that's why we're best friends, ya know?"

As he talks, I'm getting more and more antsy. A cold sweat is breaking out on my neck, and my body feels like it's overheating. A dull throb starts up at my right temple, signaling the start of a migraine. The lighting in the restaurant is now dim, which I'm thankful for, but the music is getting louder, and I envision my temporal artery pulsating with each beat. I consider how much time I have before the nausea sets in. As my migraine headaches have increased, the associated symptoms of nausea, light sensitivity and sound sensitivity have gotten worse with time. I can barely hear Sean, but I don't think it matters at this point as he appears to just like hearing the sound of his own voice. Out of the corner of my eye, I watch as the woman who was in the bathroom walks out and goes to a table near where we are sitting. A man is already seated there, a glum expression on his face. She sticks her finger in the guy's face and looks like she's scolding him. She then grabs her purse and walks out.

"Are you listening?" asks Sean, scrunching up his face into a dissatisfied expression.

"Yes, I'm sorry, I was just seeing what happened with this woman I saw crying in the bathroom." This time, he does not seem appeased by my answer, but that doesn't stop him from continuing to talk.

After another twenty minutes of him rambling about every minutia in his life, our food finally comes. I am eager to eat and get out as soon as possible, and then, just as I cut into my salmon—

"Wait a minute, this is not well done. I asked for well done." Can this date get any worse? I watch Sean's face change into a grimace as he berates the bartender. "It's not that hard to take instructions, you know. I know you have a notepad on you, so maybe it makes sense to write things down." Okay, I need to get out of here. Panic courses through me, catching in my throat as my migraine intensifies. I stare at him dumbfounded. "Take this back to the kitchen and get it right this time," he scolds the bartender. I flash the bartender an apologetic look, wanting to crawl out of my skin. Sean then turns and looks at me, throwing his hands up in exasperation as if his behavior is completely acceptable. "Sheesh, that was unbelievable. I clearly asked for well done," he harrumphs.

"Umm, that was kind of rude of you," I point out, which seems to only make him more angry.

"Well, he got my order wrong," he says defensively.

"Yeah, but you didn't need to speak to him that way. The people who work here probably don't even make minimum wage, and they are all doing their best. They deserve more respect than that. Everybody does." Sean stares at me. His glasses slide down his nose while he maintains his gaze. For the first time since we got here, he is speechless.

"I think we got off on the wrong foot," he finally says. A surge of courage rushes through me, and I stand up, but as I stand, I wince in pain and grab the side of my head, which is now throbbing so badly, it hurts to move.

"I think it's time for me to go."

"No, please don't leave. Sorry if I was rude, but it's just been a long day. Are you okay?"

"No, I should really get going. My friend is waiting, and I have a migraine." He looks at me, a hint of concern visible on his face.

"Okay, let's do this again sometime," he yells as I hurriedly walk to the exit. Another date gone horribly wrong. I start to think this city will eventually kill me.

Chapter 13

Blake

When I first saw her, I couldn't stop staring. She had a radiance about her that shone through every room she walked into. Her deep-set eyes, an ocean blue color, twinkled and spoke to me in a way no one else had before. Her long hair flowed in waves, catching the light at the right angles. When she smiled, it was a soft, sensuous smile, which held secrets known only by her. That day, she was wearing a white linen dress that stopped at her mid-thigh and a jean jacket, shielding her from the cool breeze in the air. I had accompanied Stratton and their family on a weekend trip to their home in the Hamptons. As the weekend wore on, I tried my best to maintain my distance from her, being careful not to fall too hard. It was a difficult task, though, as her personality was as bright and captivating as her appearance. She had a quick-witted nature and sense of humor that spawned many belly laughs on my part. She was noticeably smart, always preaching about the injustices of society, and when she wasn't preaching, she was reading. Trying my best not to exemplify the trope of falling for one's friend's sister, I banished the thought of something romantic with her from my mind. Yet as I spent more and more time with Stratton's family and her, I couldn't stop thinking about the possibility.

When I heard she was starting residency at our hospital, I took it as a sign. Maybe we were meant to be after all. The first time we kissed was at Stratton's birthday party. His parents had rented out a rooftop in the city overlooking the Brooklyn Bridge, and it felt like a magical night. She walked in wearing a tight red dress that grabbed her in all the right places, and her hair cascaded down her bare shoulders. A glimmer in her eye—the same glimmer that always signaled she was ready for a good time, but that she also had immense depth to her. She walked up to me, balancing on her toes, and threw her arms around my neck to give me a hug. "I'm so happy to see you," I remember her saying as she looked into my eyes, and her gaze lingered a little too long.

We later met at the bar and started talking about how the end of medical school went for her. She was glad to be done and ready to embark on the next chapter of her life. She had such a resplendent glow about her, and her face lit up when talking about neurology as if it was her favorite thing in the world. I could relate to that feeling. While I was a few years into my neurosurgery residency, I still felt the same wonderment and admiration for the field as if it was the first day of my intern year. My studies were always the constant in my life. Other things changed, my family dynamics, my school, my friends, my living situation, but my love of neurosurgery never wavered. It was the one thing that kept me going and the one thing I still look forward to doing every day. I feel lucky that I love my job so much. So many seem to be miserable at their jobs. Stratton seems pretty happy in his position but often complains when he has to work long hours. When I work longer than expected on a case or get called into the hospital unexpectedly, I just think of it as another opportunity to hone my skills and be the best neurosurgeon I can be, all while making people whole again.

Chloe and I had hung out many times before, but it was always in the context of my being Stratton's friend and her being his sister. Something was different about this night, though. She was her own woman, untethered to her family unit. She seemed more carefree and unburdened. As we talked, I could feel the chemistry build between us. She leaned in and touched my arm. Her glossy lips laden with pink lipstick parted as she took small sips of her drink. Watching her as she turned her head to ask the bartender for a napkin, the carotid artery pulsated at her neck, and I found myself imagining what it would be like to reach out and touch it, feel the pulsations under my fingertips, perhaps even slice through it. I had seen the inside of carotid arteries many times— the vital blood supply to the face, brain, and neck, but somehow I felt that hers would look different, more magnificent, more delicate, more aberrant than others. My eyes moved down her neck to her clavicle where a diamond heart pendant rested and envisioned the pulsating subclavian artery that lay beneath it. As she turned back towards me, she once again placed a hand on my wrist. She moved a strand of hair out of her face and smiled at me. Her body language seemed to signal that she, too, was interested in something more than friendship.

I was hesitant to make a move in front of Stratton and others, of course, so I asked her to take a walk with me under the pretense that I could fill her in on some hospital secrets. As a newbie, she was aching to know more about the inner workings of residency. We walked on the street and towards the direction of the Brooklyn Bridge, and she inched closer to me. She brushed up against my arm, and my whole body tingled. Neither of us had much to drink, but it was probably enough so that our defenses were down. The night was quiet, and the air was thick with possibilities. Midway through our walk, I took a risk and kissed her softly. She looked up at me and moved in again for another kiss. I knew that night that things would never be the same again.

For several weeks, we talked and met up in secrecy. We had agreed not to tell anyone, as we weren't sure how her brother would take it, and Chloe still wanted the freedom to date around before she committed to one person. I was okay with this because I knew how busy intern year would be, and it would be hard to sustain a relationship anyway. In the back of my mind, though, I knew she was the one I wanted to be with. I had never fully committed to any girl, always preferring brief dalliances and one-night stands over solid connections. I figured it was better that way with my history. I feared becoming too engrossed and entwined with someone to where I couldn't discern reality from some ethereal love, which could make some people do crazy things.

She was so beautiful that sometimes I felt this urgent need to wholly possess her. Despite our agreement that we would keep things casual, I felt this magnetic pull towards her and wanted her all to myself. I imagined what it would be like to encase her in a glass vessel so I could watch her every move, feel her every whim, and know her every thought. The feeling scared me. What would I do if I finally had her? I didn't want to think about it. Eventually, the feeling became so overwhelming that a few months into our burgeoning relationship, I had the urge to make things official with Chloe. The day I asked her to be my girlfriend, I showed up at her apartment right before we were supposed to go out to dinner and got her a bouquet of lilies. She once told me she loved lilies.

Her face lit up when she saw the flowers, and she said something to the effect of "Aww, you remembered." We sat down on the couch, and I poured my heart out to her. I told her she was all I could think about and that was a sign to me that I needed to make things official. Her head cocked to the side, eyes smiling back at me as I spoke, she looked genuinely touched, but in the end, she rejected me. She said she was still trying to figure out what she wanted and was focused on her intern year of residency. She wasn't sure she was ready to be in a committed relationship.

It felt like I got hit in the face with a ton of bricks. I couldn't believe she would turn me down. Had I been wrong all this time to think we had a concrete connection? How could she not want to commit to me? I started to think that maybe there was something wrong with me. I knew that Chloe had boyfriends before, so she was capable of commitment. I, on the other hand, had actually never had a stable relationship, so my desire to pursue one with her should have been proof enough that I was committed. I was so hurt (or maybe my ego was so hurt) that I told her I didn't want to go to dinner anymore and went home instead. As I walked home that night, I felt a surge of anger bubble up inside me. Warmth traveled up my body, and my ears were burning hot. Feeling vulnerable and cheated, I decided I wasn't going to wait around for her. In fact, I was going to show her what it felt like to be used and discarded.

The following week, at a family event that Stratton invited me to, I made out with a friend of Chloe's, hoping she would see and get jealous. Well, I was right, and she did get jealous, but she decided then that she didn't want to see me at all anymore. Deep down, I thought it would make her change her mind and pursue me, but it just pushed her away even further. Out of stubbornness, I also stopped talking to her for a few months. In the meantime, I started seeing other women again. I met Kylie, and of course I never let on that I knew Chloe because it only would have led to issues.

I couldn't quit Chloe, though. I really tried, but she still had a hold on me. Thoughts of her were like a continuous stream of opium that kept seeping into my brain, coercing me to fuel the addiction. I had to have her back no matter the cost. For weeks, I tried to get her back, texting her and asking her to meet me, but I had a hunch there was someone else. Someone I was in competition with for her affection. It felt as if she was moving further and further away from me, our bond becoming more untenable with time. I just couldn't live with the notion of losing her forever.

Chapter 14

Kylie

I made plans to meet up with Stratton at a café near the hospital to catch up. It had been three weeks since Chloe's murder, and we had kept in touch, texting back and forth about any new information that had come to light. We had forged a close connection, and I found him easy to talk to. Omar was still working on his investigative piece, and it was set to be published soon. He was also remaining tight-lipped about a lot of details he was privy to. Earlier that week, Stratton had met with detectives to verify the details of his alibi. Stratton was shattered by his sister's murder, and being considered a suspect was making the grieving process more difficult. We hadn't discussed the night he found Chloe and the state he found her in, but he seemed to be ready to talk about it now.

"I feel so guilty that my last text messages to her were mean and petty. If those ever get out to the public, I will look like the biggest entitled jerk. Fighting over who was going to use the Hamptons house seems so ridiculous in retrospect." He pulls his hand through his hair and rests it on the back of his neck.

"Yeah, I agree it's not a great look, but you had no way of knowing that would be the last conversation you guys had," I say with a conciliatory tone. "All siblings fight, and it just so happened that after one of your fights, she was killed. I know it's hard, but try not to beat yourself up about it." As he looks up at me, there's a deep sadness behind his eyes.

"I guess. I just wish I could take it back," he says. He rests his forearms on the table, burying his face between them.

When he lifts his head, he begins to tell me about the night he found Chloe. He tells me that his parents were at a fundraising event for a children's hospital the night of the murder and there were many witnesses who had attested to their whereabouts, so the police seemed to mark them off the list of suspects early on. Stratton's alibi was that he was at work late that night, and when he didn't get a response to his text from Chloe, he decided to go over to her apartment himself.

"I figured she wasn't responding to my text messages because she was still mad at me about the argument we had, but I also had a bad feeling." Pulling his chair closer to the table, he looks at me with intensity, his eyebrows furrowing. "She's not one to hold grudges for too long, and this was twenty-four hours after our fight. We had plans to go see this art exhibit at the Whitney and needed to buy tickets in advance. Chloe is really reliable, so even if she was mad at me, she would have answered me to get those tickets." Stratton had a spare key to her apartment since he sometimes crashed there if he had to be at an early meeting uptown or had a late night and didn't want to make the trip back downtown to his place. Chloe had a pull-out couch, and it was common knowledge that he would stay there from time to time. Since she was usually at work, she gave him a key. Tenants had seen him around before and had also verified that.

Unfortunately, it turned out that someone had covered the security camera outside Chloe's building for some time, so it didn't catch Stratton going into the building; thus, the time he arrived couldn't be verified. That's what the police were really focused on—what time he got there. He thinks he got there around 10:30 p.m., which was presumed to be about two to three hours after she was killed. He was careful not to touch anything, knowing he might mess up the crime scene, but when he saw her, he couldn't resist grabbing her and holding her, getting blood onto his clothing.

"It was just so surreal, Kylie. I didn't know what to do but cradle her close to me. Then I saw the bloody knife on the ground next to her and took extra care not to touch it."

I rest my hand on his arm. "Well, that was smart. Did they find fingerprints on the knife?" I ask.

"They did actually, but they don't know who they belong to."

"But they didn't match yours, so shouldn't that absolve you?"

"Yeah, I hope so. I understand how it looks with me being the one to find her and all and no witnesses to verify my alibi."

"Is there anyone at work who could vouch that you were there?" I ask.

"Given I was there late that night, no one was physically there to see what time I left the office, but police have obtained the records of when everyone who entered the building that day swiped their badges in and out. I'm hoping the system will prove my innocence. Plus, they have security cameras that likely show me leaving the building." He runs his fingers through his hair and rests his hand on the nape of his neck. "But I think they have a prime suspect." He looks down at the cup of coffee he's nursing in his hand.

"So who else are they looking at?"

"Well, I think you guys can breathe, as they aren't really interested in any of her co-residents and colleagues. It seems everybody's alibi checked out and no one had a clear motive for harming her, but Chloe was talking to several people on this dating app, and they've honed in on one guy, a Clay Johnson. They asked my parents if they ever heard of him."

It's unnerving to think that someone on one of these dating apps could possibly have killed her. I take a sip of my water and contemplate whether I should also get a latte. It's now 6 p.m., though, and I don't want to be up tossing and turning all night. Stratton is apparently unaffected by caffeine, as he's sitting there gulping down a black coffee, probably preparing for a late night of work.

"Have you heard of him?" Stratton asks, looking hopeful.

"No, I'm sorry. That name doesn't sound familiar, but I really didn't know the names of any of the guys she was seeing. How long was Chloe seeing him?"

"The messages between them go back several months. I haven't actually seen the messages myself, but the police told my parents they are somewhat damning."

"That's good news. Sounds like they have a lead," I say.

"Yeah, so it seems she was communicating with him the most in the weeks leading up to the murder," Stratton adds.

"Were they able to catch anyone else on the security tapes?" I ask.

"That's the disappointing part. The security footage the police have shows several people enter the building that night. They only had a camera at the entrance of the building, so it was hard to know which of those people went specifically to Chloe's apartment. She lived on the second floor. There were many people coming in and out of the building that night, as there was a party on one of the floors. A few of the people had hoodies or coats on, given it was cold that night. Some even had hats and scarves. According to police, it was difficult to discern their faces."

"I see." I think about how Chloe chose to live in a building with low security despite her parents offering to house her somewhere in a doorman building. It makes me sad to think that her life could have been saved if the circumstances were different, or at least we'd have more identifying information about the murderer.

Stratton continues, "Based on the state the body was in and the circumstances, the police estimate she was murdered around 8:00 p.m."

I reeled at the new bit of information. That meant she was murdered at the exact time that she was supposed to start her night shift at the hospital. I shudder to think I was texting her just as it was happening. I imagine her getting ready to leave and someone surprising her at the door. She was already dressed in her scrubs, likely having just taken a shower.

"Did any of the people attending the party hear anything? It's hard to imagine there were so many people there that night and no one heard her screams."

"The police spoke to many of the partygoers, and no one heard any suspicious noises from Chloe's apartment, but they also admit the music was loud."

"What about the security camera? What time was it covered?"

"The security camera was covered right at 7 p.m. They don't know who covered the camera, but it could have been anyone. Apparently, that building is strict and has a quiet policy after 10 p.m., so it's common for people having parties to cover the camera so they can't be identified as the culprits. It's also possible that the murderer did it, perhaps to throw off the police."

"And that would certainly point to this being premeditated," I chime in.

"Right. The landlord was out of town and didn't get any noise complaints either. The party ended up dying out around 10:30 or 11 p.m., which is when the partygoers left to go to a nearby bar. That's about all the information the police have right now."

All the evidence seems to point to this being someone Chloe knew. I think back to that night and how I was waiting for her to relieve me from the hospital. Guilt rises in my chest as I recall feeling annoyed that she was late. Never would I have thought that something so awful was happening to her at the same time she was supposed to start her shift.

Stratton then explains that he got to Chloe's apartment sometime around 10:30 p.m. At that point, she had presumably been dead for at least two hours. He banged on the door and nobody answered, but luckily, he had brought the spare key with him and was able to enter. That's when he saw her lifeless body sprawled out on the middle of the floor.

Chapter 15

The boy

My aunt moved to my hometown for a few years so I could finish up elementary school there, as she didn't want me to have to deal with too many transitions. She sold the house my parents raised me in, and we moved into a new home on the opposite side of town. After some time, though, she realized that being in the town my mother was murdered in was actually making things harder for me. Everyone at school knew what happened, and it felt like the students and teachers all pitied me. Our neighbors, while intending to be kind, often came off intrusive when they'd offer to drive me places or watch after me. Aunt Claire decided it would be better for me to start fresh elsewhere, so we moved a few towns over.

When I first got to my new school, I was alone and scared. I still had a lot of built up anger but was looking forward to a fresh start. During my first week, a group of kids started following me around and making fun of me. They didn't know what I had been through, of course, but it was a nuisance at the least. I hadn't made any friends yet either, but the loneliness didn't bother me. My books always provided all the comfort and entertainment I needed.

We had a science fair one of the first weeks of school, and I was psyched to show off a solar system I had made with Aunt Claire. On the day of the fair, I took the solar system model to school, and all my classmates and teachers gathered around it in awe of how professional it looked. My aunt had gone above and beyond, searching for 3D models of the planets that we could copy and researching the best materials to use to make the solar system. The planets even moved in orbit and looked realistic. I had read so many books on the details of each planet so I could get the models perfect.

The day of the science fair, the bleachers in the school gym were packed with hopeful parents emanating joy while watching their science nerds present their projects. When I was announced as the winner, my aunt was in the crowd cheering me on. The smile on her face was exhilarating, and I think I even saw a few tears as she waved to me from the bleachers. With my first-place medal around my neck, I picked up my model and headed to my locker so I could keep it safe. I felt proud that day.

The group of bullies who had been tormenting me were walking behind me. I could hear them snickering and cracking jokes at my expense. Suddenly, one of them, a callous boy named Stewart, pushed me in the hall, and the solar system I had created crashed to the floor. He started cackling, and all his friends joined in. Tears pooled behind my eyes, but I wasn't going to let them see me cry. I had barely cried since my mother was murdered, and I wasn't going to waste my tears on these fools. Amidst a sea of laughing students who had crowded behind us, I bent down and started frantically gathering the broken pieces to see if I could salvage the model. Anger rising up within me, I grabbed one of the spokes of the planets, and in a swift movement, I turned around and stabbed Stewart in the eye. His eye started gushing blood. As Stewart wailed for his mom, I felt a sense of satisfaction but also regret that I couldn't cry for mine. The teachers ran over and tried to cover his eye with paper towels, while I just stood there glaring at him. My insides went warm as I tried to mask the small smile forming on my face. All that blood gushing out was one of the most magnificent things I had seen. That was probably when my fascination with the human body began.

I went home that night and, understandably, my aunt grounded me, and I was suspended from school. It was recommended by the school that my aunt put me in counseling given my history, but unbeknownst to the school, I was already seeing someone. That night, I got on the computer and researched the anatomy of the eye. Intrigued by the connection between the eye and what later became my favorite organ, the brain, I pulled up a diagram that illustrated this relationship. How the central retinal artery pierces the optic nerve, the ophthalmic artery comes off the internal carotid artery, how the optic nerves meet at the base of the brain, coalescing in the optic chiasm. What I saw with Stewart's eye may be gross to some, but to me it was a thing of beauty—an affirmation of how complex, intricate, and perfectly designed the human body is and how one assault can sever the whole system.

When I returned to school after my suspension, the bullying stopped. On my second day back, I passed Stewart in the hallway. He was still wearing a bandage over his eye. As soon as he saw me, his face twisted into a fear-stricken expression, like he had just seen a ghost. He put his hands up as if shielding his face and ran away in the opposite direction. It felt empowering to know that my very presence struck him with fear. That's when I learned that sometimes it's better to be feared than loved.

Middle school was uneventful. I was at the top of my class, and

I didn't have to try that hard. School just came naturally to me. I didn't have that many friends, but I didn't care because the only person I really trusted was my aunt Claire. My aunt had stepped up, and it felt like we had a real mother-son relationship. No one could replace my mother, of course, but she was the closest thing I had to a mother. Aunt Claire never got married again and never had any children of her own, so she treated me like I was the center of her universe. She had been married once when she was younger but had never talked to me about her marriage or why they separated.

When I told Aunt Claire I wanted to be a neurosurgeon, she set out to help me make that dream a reality. When I was in high school, she contacted a neurosurgeon in our town and asked if I could shadow him. Dr. Bryce was an incredible neurosurgeon. He was stern and blunt, so his bedside manner wasn't the best, but patients loved him because he was a surgical prodigy. His outcomes were the best of any neurosurgeon's in the area, and everyone wanted to be on his surgical team. I spent several weeks fawning over his surgical technique and, more specifically, over the complexities of the human brain. The experience was thrilling and only solidified my desire to pursue that path. Everything else became a means to an end.

When I got to Dartmouth, I had only one thing in mind—get grades good enough to get into medical school. I was lucky to meet a solid group of people, and Stratton was one of them, but it seemed I didn't have the connections to powerful people in various professions that everyone else had. Many of my friends glided through college, got the internships they wanted in the summers, and forged relationships with other well-connected people. I didn't feel envious, just sad that there were lots of kids out there like me coming to these places where they were outsiders.

One summer, between my sophomore and junior year of college, Stratton offered to help me find a prestigious research position in Manhattan so we could live together. I was hesitant to leave my aunt on her own, but she encouraged me to take the opportunity. Stratton's family was involved in philanthropy with various hospitals in NYC, so they connected me with some surgeons at a major academic hospital, and I was able to get a great research gig. Stratton and I lived in an apartment in the financial district, which we sublet for the summer. Thankfully, the research position covered my housing and transportation costs. Stratton could have lived with his parents on the Upper East Side, but since he was doing a grueling internship in the financial district that his mom set up for him, he wanted to be close to the office. Part of me thinks he was also looking out for me, worrying about me being on my own. That summer, we spent a lot of time with his family, and they treated me like one of their own. It was nice to finally have people to depend on besides my aunt.

After some time, I felt like I had gotten to a good place. I could finally sleep through the night without having constant nightmares and waking up screaming. When I was living with my aunt, she got me in to see a therapist regularly, and we worked on a lot of techniques to get a good night's sleep, but whatever we tried didn't help. I even tried hypnosis, which seemed to work temporarily, but then the feelings would creep up again and haunt me. However, since starting college, the nightmares occurred less and less frequently. I continued to see a therapist, though, for fear they would come back and interfere with my studies.

While my mental state was better, the trauma of my past still haunted me, and it kept me from seriously dating anyone. In college, I'd have the occasional fling, but they'd never last more than a few months. Whenever someone asked why I didn't have a girlfriend, I just said I was too focused on my goals, but part of it was also that I was too scared. There was a darkness inside of me that made me feel like I was capable of really hurting people. I was scared that the part of me that was my father would break through and end up hurting someone.

Chapter 16

Kylie

"When did you first notice you couldn't walk?" I ask the patient, Mr. Henderson, projecting my voice to drown out the sounds of the emergency room.

"Three days ago. My legs felt weak, and I felt like I was going to fall."

"Do you have any numbness, or is it just weakness?"

Mr. Henderson ponders the question for a few seconds.

"It's mostly weakness, but I haven't been able to feel my feet in a long time. I take this medicine called gabapentin for neuropathy. This is different, though. I just feel like I'm going to fall all the time," he says with a frustrated tone. "In fact, I fell yesterday and felt like I was in one of those Life Alert commercials. I'm falling and I can't get up." His frown transforms into a rueful smile.

"Have you had any other falls or any sort of trauma recently?" I ask.

"Nope, just that one."

"Are you having any other symptoms like back pain or difficulty urinating?"

"I have some back pain, and I have a prostate issue, so difficulty with going to the bathroom is not new for me."

"Okay, Mr. Henderson, I'm going to examine you, and then we will see if you need any imaging."

As I kneel to examine him, I hear a familiar voice on the other side of the curtain, the one that separates one patient room from the next. That measured yet commanding voice stops me in my tracks, and anxiety tugs at my chest. *Oh boy, it's CNS.* I am not in the mood to run into him today. I've already had a rough morning. It's not even 11 a.m., and I'm six consults in, the ER is overflowing with patients, and the stroke pager has been buzzing to no end. The last thing I need is to run into Blake.

I move through my neurologic exam, focusing on the patient's legs, which are hanging off the side of the stretcher. As I'm testing the strength in his legs, isolating each muscle to localize where he is weakest, he lets out a howl.

"Ouch, that hurts my back." He grabs his lower back with his right hand and winces in pain.

"I'm sorry. It seems we will need to get some spine imaging."

I take out my reflex hammer to check his reflexes. "I'm just going to lightly tap on your knees and ankles with this tool." Mr. Henderson nods, but a trace of worry lingers on his face. Patients always look at me with concern when I pull out a tool that looks like a hammer. I move on to the sensory exam. Removing a pin from my white coat pocket, I gently start moving in an upward direction from his feet up his legs, asking if he feels the sensation of the pin. It's clear he has some long-standing neuropathy as he can't feel much in his feet, which justifies the fact that he was prescribed gabapentin. I think about all the possibilities, and my biggest concern is an issue with the spinal cord. I still hear remnants of Blake's conversation through the curtain with the patient next to us. Yes, NYC hospital ERs are cramped and always overwhelmed, so being in earshot of other patients is a regular occurrence. It sounds like Blake is talking to a patient's family member about a potential surgery. I imagine him charming the pants off the family as I hear giggles on the other side of the curtain. I roll my eyes internally, knowing how they must see him.

I finish up with Mr. Henderson and walk back towards the nurse's station to look for the ER physician who called me. Quickly pulling out my phone camera, I flip it towards me to make sure I don't look like a complete disaster in case Blake comes out and sees me. There are a few strands of hair out of place. I pin those back into my tight bun and pull out my lip gloss from my white coat pocket, slathering it on my lips, then pressing them together.

There are a few nurses gathered around the station, and one of the nurse practitioners from neurosurgery is standing with them. She recognizes me and gives me a wave. Racking my brain to remember her name, I wave back. She's a petite blond who is always twirling the front strands of her hair and loudly chewing gum. There are quite a few attractive young nurses on the neurosurgery side. I often wonder how many of the young nurses, students, physician assistants, or nurse practitioners Blake has hooked up with. I overhear them chuckling and looking at Blake while he's talking to the family of the patient he was seeing.

"Yeah, he's definitely hot, but a total player," the cute blond says.

"Yeah, I used to live in his building last year, and there was always a different girl coming out," one of the nurses chuckles.

I roll my eyes, more aggressively this time. I'm aware he probably goes on a lot of dates and brings back a lot of girls, but I somehow convinced myself I was different. I think back to meeting his rude neighbor at the elevator and my multiple run-ins with the doorman. It makes total sense that I felt judged because I probably was being judged!

I find the emergency room physician who called me down to see Mr. Henderson and tell her the plan. Dr. Fan is a middle-aged woman with greying hair who looks like she is on the verge of quitting her job every time I see her. She looks up at me from her desk, weariness in her eyes.

"Can I help you?" she asks.

"Hi, I'm from neurology. Can we please get an MRI of the spine for Mr. Henderson? I'm worried he may have a spinal injury."

She nods and says, "Thanks for seeing him. I'm probably going to call you about another person later." Trying hard to mask my annoyance, I flash her an insincere smile. Pushing through the emergency room nurses and staff, I walk past hordes of patients waiting to be seen, wondering which ones I'll be consulted on. I somehow make it out of the ER without bumping into Blake, and as I'm walking out, I get another page about a consult in the ICU.

After a stressful day at work, I FaceTime my mom. I haven't spoken to her all week, and I've just had one of those days, which makes me yearn for home and her delicious meatloaf. After one ring, she answers the phone. "Hi, honey. How's it going?" Her face is beaming on the other end. She has curlers in her hair, a spatula in her hand, probably in the midst of making dinner.

"Hi, Mom. It's going okay. Just another busy day at work." She moves to the stove and adjusts the dial. I imagine sitting in that kitchen, taking in the smell of spices and herbs emanating from the simmering pans. It's been so long since I've had a home-cooked meal.

"Aww, well, just remember you are doing something really important. Those patients are lucky to have you."

"Thanks, Mom. How's everybody doing at home?" Almost all of my siblings are still in Florida. Two of them, Jenny and Mark, are twins and still in high school. My older brother lives in Orlando, and my older sister lives a few streets away from my parents' house. When my sister moved back home after graduate school, she was intent on having my parents as close as possible to help with childcare. My baby niece is a year old, but given my schedule, I've only met her once since she was born.

"So when do you think you can come home? Will you be home for Christmas?" my mom asks earnestly. It always pains me to remind her that we can't really take vacation when we want in residency. It's sort of just assigned to us. We get two weeks during the first half of the year and two weeks during the second half of the year. Unfortunately, this year I am working during the holidays. While being a second-year resident is not as bad as being an intern, we are still towards the bottom of the totem pole.

"I'm sorry, Mom, I'm working over the holidays. Hopefully, I can visit in the spring, though."

"I understand, Kylie. It would have been nice to have you here with all the kids." I sense the disappointment in her voice. But then, her tone lightens, and she asks, "Anyway, how's your dating life? Any prospects?" I think about my tragic dating prospects and decide whether I should even give her a glimpse or refrain from saying anything at all. I worry she will worry more if I tell her how hopeless things are on that front.

"Nope, nothing to report. Just busy with work."

"Well, I'm sure the right person will come around when you least expect it. Don't get so busy, though, that you forget about building a life."

I let out an exaggerated sigh, and then immediately feel bad that she could sense my annoyance. There are many people who build a life without a partner or children, but I decide I'm not going to explain that to my mom right now, and she does have a point. Yes, it would be nice to meet someone I could build a life with. After all, isn't that why I'm putting myself out there and subjecting myself to uncomfortable situations?

After I get off the phone with her, I pull up my Connections app and start looking through potential candidates. Swipe right. Swipe left. Swipe right. Swipe left. I stare at the face on the screen. Olive skin. Brown hair. Chiseled jaw. Big brown eyes. Height 5'10". Occupation: lawyer. Location: Upper West Side. *Not bad*, I think. Of course, he could still turn out to be a serial killer. Feeling discouraged, I decide not to engage and put away my phone.

Chapter 17

Kylie

I walk into clinic and open the chart of the patient on my roster. *85-year-old man referred for memory concerns.* I feel exhausted since I didn't sleep much last night. I was up late thinking about Chloe's case and how it had been weeks and still, we were no closer to finding out who murdered her. It's a strange feeling, being expected to continue on with work and life as if nothing happened. I know all my co-residents are grieving in their own ways, but it's not like we can all take bereavement leave. The expectation is that we show up no matter what because patients don't stop getting sick, so we have to put our personal issues aside and focus on healing others. That's the irony of all this— we need to stay healthy to be able to take care of others, but how can we do that when we are struggling to stay afloat? On the other hand, I'll admit that taking care of others also provides a distraction from dealing with the horror of what happened to Chloe. Then, when I get home from work and finally have a few moments to reflect on the last few weeks, thoughts of Chloe and the case rush my mind, preventing me from being able to fall asleep.

I enter the exam room to see a smiling man with a cane resting against the wall. A woman is accompanying him. I presume it's his wife, although I never make assumptions like that anymore considering the times I've gotten in trouble. Once, during my intern year, when a male patient looked much older than his companion, I referred to her as his daughter and he said, "Umm, that's my wife." So, best not to make assumptions.

"Hi, Mr. Geller, I'm Dr. Saunders," I say as I take a seat on the black swivel chair at the computer in the room. "And who is accompanying you today?"

The patient confirms, "This is my wife."

I take a history, asking him questions about why he's here, what is bothering him, and going over his list of medications. His wife chimes in, "He's been losing things around the house. Last week, he forgot how to get home. He occasionally forgets the names of our grandchildren. He often forgets conversations we had the day before. I'll ask him if he remembered to call the internet company, and he acts as if we never had that conversation. I mean, I know sometimes men like to pretend they don't remember something so they can just not do it, but I am worried he's developing Alzheimer's." She continues, "You know, his father was the same way, and they told him he had Alzheimer's."

Mr. Geller shrugs his shoulders but doesn't refute her concerns.

"I see. Yes, memory problems can run in families. We can get some standard blood tests to check for any deficiencies and then an image of the brain and go from there. He may need to do some neurocognitive testing to figure out what's going on," I explain. I move over to where the patient is sitting and start doing an exam. "Please look at my finger and follow it with your eyes," I instruct.

He is able to follow my instructions well but seems to lose his train of thought whenever he starts to have a conversation with me, his voice drifting off as if he's forgotten what comes next.

As I finish the exam, the patient looks up at me from the exam table and asks, "Doctor, are you married?"

"No." I laugh politely. I find that the older patients get, the more disinhibited they are in their line of questioning. It's not usually pathological but a sign that they really don't care anymore what people think, and being blunt is just a consequence of aging or life experience.

"Well, you're a pretty girl and you're a doctor, so I'm not sure who wouldn't want to settle down with you!" he says.

"Mitch!" His wife gives him a threatening look and lightly slaps him on the thigh. "I'm sure Dr. Saunders doesn't want to discuss her love life with you." She looks at me, her cheeks tinged with a flush of pink, an apologetic expression on her face.

I smile at them both. "That's okay. Thanks for your concern, Mr. Geller."

"Well, if you need any potential options, we have a grandson that's right about your age. He's not the sharpest tool in the shed, but he's a kind boy. Actually, I'm not sure what your age is, Doctor, as you look like you just graduated high school."

I look over at his wife, who is now bright red. "Mitch, it's inappropriate to ask how old the doctor is, and our grandson is a teenager."

"I'm older than you think I am, Mr. Geller," I say. It's not unusual for me to be questioned about my age. Many patients think we look too young to be delivering their care. I'll take it while I can get it, though. I hand them the referral for his MRI of the brain and lab work and send them on their way.

When I step out of the exam room, a few of my co-residents are hovering over Anaya, snickering with their eyes wide. "That is so creepy, girl," exclaims Marta.

"Yeah, you almost got fireballed," says Bailey. "I'm coining that term, 'fireballed.'"

Intrigued by this reference to the popular podcast episode we had all recently talked about, I lean over to see what the fuss is about. "Kylie, you would die. This is right up your alley. Tell her the story," Bailey demands.

Anaya turns to face me, her long braid swinging as she moves. "So I was talking to this guy on Connections, and we moved our conversation to text messaging. We had plans to meet at a bar downtown last night. I get there and he texts me that he's running late. I sit at the bar, and he says, quote, I kid you not, 'order us two fireball shots.'"

I audibly gasp, bringing a hand to my mouth. Bailey looks at me and raises an eyebrow. I know where this is going, and it immediately sets off alarm bells. There have been a series of incidents throughout the country where a woman and man meet on a dating site. The man says he's running late and asks the woman to order two Fireball shots at the bar and wait for him there. While the woman is waiting for him to show up, another man approaches her and offers to buy her a drink and dinner. In a few cases where this has happened, the woman goes to the bathroom and is followed by one of the wait staff, who then tells her in the bathroom that the man sitting at the bar has been coming to the bar and meeting different women on various nights. The women are typically instructed to order Fireball shots, and when they go to the bathroom, the man presumably spikes their drink. When they come back, they take sips of their drink and get drunk way too fast. In a few instances, the woman ends up leaving with the man.

"Then, another man who is at the bar starts chatting me up. He's pretty good-looking, and I think, well, maybe this is just a coincidence. I obviously didn't accept any drinks from the guy. Once it was thirty minutes past the time we were supposed to meet, I just texted my supposed date and told him I was leaving. The man I met at the bar tried to get me to stay and was quite obstinate about it, but I left anyway. The whole thing creeped me out, so as soon as I got outside, I got in a cab and left."

"Wow, that is nuts," I respond.

"Oh, there's more," says Bailey, placing his hand on my shoulder as if to brace me.

Anaya continues, "This morning, I texted the guy who stood me up just to see what happened to him. Well, the text didn't go through. I then looked on the Connections app and his profile had been deleted!" She looks at me, waiting for a response.

"Terrifying," I say.

"You could have been sex trafficked, Anaya," says Bailey. The theory is that these incidents could be tied to a sex-trafficking ring.

"Good thing Kylie made us listen to that podcast episode. The whole situation was so uncanny." I sent our group chat the podcast episode because I found it to be so intriguing, but also as a warning to be careful when meeting strangers.

"Yeah, there's a chance some guys are messing with people too. Like maybe they heard about these incidents and are trying to 'copycat' to mess with people," says Marta.

"Well, either way, it's creepy. I'm glad you stayed on the safe side and didn't fall into a potential trap. You can never be too careful." As I say those words, my mind flicks back to Chloe.

As I ride the subway back home, I think about what happened with Anaya. The dating world is scary. You never know who is sitting behind these dating profiles and whether there's a killer waiting to strike. Even in Chloe's case, the leading suspect is a guy she met on Connections. It's hard enough meeting someone organically, and now we have to worry about people on the internet with ulterior motives. It definitely makes me more cautious going on these dates. I look at my own Connections app and the profiles of the guys I've matched with. The only one I've been consistently speaking with is Mateo. So far, no major red flags, but Chloe was a smart girl, and I'm sure she would have done her due diligence in getting to know a date before having him come to her apartment. She clearly knew who the murderer was since she let the person in. This was someone she trusted and likely vetted. This could have happened to any of us.

Freaked out by the prospect of another one of us getting murdered through a dating app, I close out Connections and transition to Instagram. I occasionally look through Chloe's social media pages, searching for clues or anything suspicious that could point me in the direction of her killer. Chloe was just as private online, though, as she was in real life. Flipping through her posts, I see selfies and group photos taken in NYC with friends. I zoom in on one photo of our class of residents taken at her parents' house the night of the welcome party at the start of our intern year. I'm sandwiched between Lisa and Bailey, looking like a picture of health. My face, once glowing and brimming with promise and hope, has become more dull, more ragged as residency drags on. I'm wearing a blue mini-dress that shows off my toned legs and black kitten heels. After more than a year of residency, I'm pretty sure that dress would hang loosely on my overworked frame, and those heels would exacerbate the constant ache in my feet. Running around the hospital all day has made me averse to wearing uncomfortable shoes. I also look like I've aged at least five years. I rub a hand over my right temple, where a mild ache is growing, perhaps another migraine coming on. Residency has done a number on all of us.

As I click through more posts, I suddenly feel fixated on one photo she took. The photo is a selfie, but I'm more interested in the background. She's at a home or an apartment that isn't her own. I've been to her apartment a few times—once to pregame before going out and one other time when I had to pick up a sweater I accidentally left behind at a bar that she took home for me. This doesn't look like the inside of her apartment, but it looks familiar. A piece of furniture in the corner of the photo catches my eye. As I zoom in, I realize it's a bookcase. A very familiar bookcase. I swear I've seen that somewhere. When I zoom in even more to get a closer look, I gasp aloud. I can't believe what I am seeing...

Chapter 18

Kylie

Chloe is inside Blake's apartment. I have no doubt about it. I look down at the caption of the photo. *When you find good lightning, you gotta take a selfie for the gram.* Her endearing smile, her wavy, lustrous hair spilling over her shoulders, her captivating eyes looking straight on into the camera. Suddenly, I feel my head spinning. I'm going to be sick. My fingers feel like lead, and I nearly drop my phone just as the subway pulls into my stop, letting out a high-pitched screech as it halts. As I'm propelled forward, my legs, which feel like molasses, resist, keeping me glued in place. Feeling weighed down by this discovery, it takes all my energy to extract my body from the subway seat and make it out the doors of the train. As I climb the subway stairs, each step feels like a Herculean effort. I keep telling myself not to pass out until I can get out of here. I emerge from the subway station, and the air hits my face and fills my lungs, prompting me to release a breath. My mind is running wild as I walk back to my apartment, my feet moving more quickly as if seeking the safety of my space. What was Chloe doing in Blake's apartment? I look at the date on the post, and it indicates it was posted about eight months ago, during our intern year. That was before I had started seeing Blake, and I now know that Stratton and Blake were friends, but I had no idea that he was that close to Chloe. From the angle of the photo, and the way the bookcase is framed in the background, I work out that she must be sitting on the bed. But if their relationship was platonic, why would she ever be on his bed? Does that mean they had a sexual relationship? I feel myself go hot with envy. Envy, but also fear.

I hope I am imagining this and that I'm wrong for finding this questionable, but I can't get rid of the nagging feeling that this is all connected to her murder. A sexual relationship would give Blake a motive. And why would he lie about his relationship with her? While I'm disturbed by the potential of Blake being involved with her murder, I'm also ashamed that I feel jealous that there was seemingly something going on between them. Yes, it was likely before I started seeing Blake, but how can I even be sure? Well, it doesn't really matter anymore, I guess.

Panic flits through me as I think back to the bloody shirt and jeans I found in Blake's hamper and—oh my God, wait a minute. Was that the night of her murder? I open my text messages and quickly scroll through to verify that it was indeed the same night I was at Blake's apartment. I had gone there in a fit to essentially tell him off and then left without saying goodbye. When I saw him a week and a half later at the funeral, he seemed distressed, more distressed than I'd expect for someone who just knew Chloe peripherally. I recall thinking at the time that there was something deeper there. Something he was trying to hide. I think back to what he said, and he was clear that he was Stratton's friend and not close to Chloe, but he was obviously lying.

Blake has been MIA once again, which at this point I should be used to, but what if this is just not typical behavior for him? What if he's actually hiding something? My mind turns to the bloody shirt and pair of jeans I discovered at his apartment. Though I don't want to jump the gun, I know what I have to do. I go to my closet and rummage through the pockets of all my coats, trying to remember the coat I wore to Chloe's apartment the night of her murder. Reaching into my olive-green corduroy jacket, I feel for the detective's card. I'm about to dial Detective Cranston's number when I halt. Should I call Stratton first? Maybe he knew about their relationship or can shed some light on this. But maybe he's also involved somehow? Why wouldn't he tell me if he knew that Chloe and Blake had a relationship? We've gotten pretty close over the last few weeks, so I'd expect him to keep me in the loop. Plus, Stratton was the one who found her and was considered a suspect early on, so it's best I go straight to the police. Okay, it's settled. I'm just going to call Detective Cranston and deal with whatever fallout there may be.

When he picks up the phone, I'm hesitant, but try to speak up anyway. "Hi, Detective Cranston, this is Kylie Saunders. You questioned me about the Chloe King case a few weeks ago." I wait for him to recognize me.

"Yes, I remember you." There's a brief silence followed by commotion in the background.

I clear my throat. "I have something to tell you. It may be important information regarding Chloe's murderer." There's a pause on the other end of the line.

"I see," he says sounding incredulous. He lets out a deep sigh. "Okay, well, I'm at the precinct on 78th and 2nd. I'll be here for the next hour if you want to come down and meet me," he replies.

"Perfect, see you soon." I hang up, and a sense of doom builds inside me.

What if I have this all wrong? Am I going crazy? A few weeks ago, when we were all questioned about our whereabouts the night of Chloe's murder, I had told Detective Cranston that I had stopped by Blake's place. Of course, at the time, I didn't think he could have anything to do with this, but the more I think about the circumstances of that night, the more suspicious I am. He answered the door wearing a towel and was acting strange. At times, he seemed downtrodden, and then at other points in our conversation, he seemed apathetic. I remember being put off by his demeanor. Is it possible he already knew Chloe was dead at that point? Maybe that's why he seemed so aloof. Or is it possible he was the murderer and was showering to get rid of any evidence?

When I get to the police station, I am out of breath. My heart thumps in my chest; every thump gets louder and louder, and I question what I'm doing here again. Have the long hours and crazy demands of residency finally made me lose my mind?

Before I can finish my thought, Detective Cranston emerges from a corner room. An inquisitive look on his face, he walks towards me, searching my face for any clues as to what information I might have. When he gets closer to me, he motions for me to follow him back into his office. The desk in his office is cluttered with thick files, and two Styrofoam cups containing a brown liquid are placed at the edge of the desk, the smell of stale coffee emanating from them. As I take a seat in the wooden chair opposite his chair, I take out my phone and reach across his desk to show him the photo of Chloe. I recognize that my voice is now two octaves higher than it normally is. "There's a guy I've sort of been seeing. His name is Blake Weathers. I don't know if you remember, but I mentioned I was at his apartment the night Chloe was murdered." Detective Cranston nods as if he recognizes the name. "He's also connected to the King family, as he's friends with Stratton King. I had no idea that he had any relationship with Chloe, but I was scrolling through her photos on Instagram and came across this one, which was clearly taken at Blake's apartment. I know because I've been there." I feel myself getting out of breath and try to slow down. My voice is quivering and my hands tremble as I hold the phone for him to see, passing it slowly into his hands. Detective Cranston calmly accepts it from me. "This here is Blake's apartment. I recognize that bookcase in the corner. Something was going on between the two of them."

I stop as he looks up at me and then back down at the photo again. "Also, a few weeks ago, the night of Chloe's murder, I was at Blake's place, and I found a bloody shirt and a pair of blood-stained jeans." I pause, waiting to see his response, but his facial expression remains unmoved. "When he answered the door, he seemed out of it, not himself. He was wearing a towel as if he were about to take a shower. I thought that was odd since he knew I was coming over but brushed it off at the time." Now that I think about it, why would he ask me to come hang out if he had potentially killed Chloe right before? Was he going to use me as his alibi? Detective Cranston picks up one of the Styrofoam cups, peers into it and then places it back on the desk without taking a sip. "I had spilled some water on myself, and he told me to go grab a towel or shirt to wear, just before he got in the shower. When I went to grab a towel off a shelf above the washer, I accidentally knocked over the hamper and all his clothes fell out. That's when I stumbled upon the bloody clothing." Detective Cranston raises his left eyebrow, and I see that I've gotten his attention.

He looks down at the photo with a look of consternation, and a crinkle develops across his forehead. I feel embarrassed, as if I'm giving away a secret about myself. As if somehow he knows I've been fawning over this guy who is clearly unavailable and maybe even psychotic, and I have terrible judgment. Maybe he even thinks I'm doing this out of jealousy. I can feel the blood draining from my face. My legs go weak beneath me, and they start to shake. He looks up at me with a worried expression.

Detective Cranston hands me back my phone. He sighs and says, "Thanks for bringing this to my attention, but we've already looked into Blake Weathers. Turns out he had a romantic relationship with Chloe King for some time." My whole body goes numb. I stare back at him in disbelief. How did Blake not tell me he was romantically involved with my dead co-resident? Chloe was private when it came to the details of her love life, but she always shared the big picture with us while omitting specific names. She never mentioned seeing a neurosurgeon. I'm sure of it. He continues, "We went through Chloe's phone and found a text message from Blake asking to see her the night she was murdered. Her brother told us he suspected a relationship between them for a while, but Blake and Chloe tried to keep it from him. We brought Blake in for questioning a few weeks ago, and he showed us his phone. He confirmed that he had texted Chloe asking her to talk the day she was murdered."

I can't believe what I'm hearing. He was trying to get together with Chloe the same day he texted me to hang out? Detective Cranston continues, "Based on their last few text messages, he had been trying to resolve things with her, and she was hesitant. He was actually the last person to see her alive besides the killer. The security camera shows him going to her apartment around

5:30 p.m. She lets him in and they presumably talk for a while, and then he leaves. We verified based on the security tape that he was in her apartment for about thirty minutes." Detective Cranston pauses, allowing me to take in what he's just told me. "I don't know how well you know Blake Weathers, but it seems he's a popular guy," he says with a smirk.

Well, I clearly don't know him at all.

"Anyway, his story added up with the timing caught on camera and the text messages between the two of them. Blake Weathers said he was disappointed because Chloe King didn't want to have anything to do with him anymore. You know, a lover's quarrel." My stomach churns and a wave of nausea overcomes me. While I'm relieved to hear that Blake's been questioned and apparently cleared, I'm disgusted that he called me to come see him a few hours after this took place. What, was I his consolation prize? Was I the backup plan? His shoulder to cry on when Chloe rejected him? I'm so embarrassed that Detective Cranston is aware that I was hanging out with Blake a few hours after he was hanging out with Chloe. I feel pathetic.

"We then confirmed that after Blake Weathers saw you, he went into work, as he was on call, and there was a surgery he needed to perform. Although, as you probably already know, we think Chloe King was murdered around 8 p.m., so that would have been a few hours beforehand." Well, at least he wasn't lying about having to go into work that night. "Now, this is somewhat confidential information, but you may be able to help us. Another gentleman entered the building whom we identified as someone Chloe King was talking to on a dating app. He entered the apartment building around 7 p.m., which aligned with the text messages that were sent to her phone right before his arrival. Several others entered the building right after him, but were verified as partygoers. After that, the security camera was covered, so we have no more footage."

"Is this the Clay Johnson guy she was talking to?" I ask.

"Yes, do you know him?"

I start to regain my composure. "No, Stratton had told me Chloe was talking to a guy named Clay Johnson who she met on the Connections app. He said they were talking for several months."

"Yep, that's correct. She never mentioned him to you?"

"No, she never mentioned the guys she was seeing by name. Sometimes, she would identify them by occupation like 'the finance guy' or 'the lawyer guy,' but that's about it." She definitely never said 'the neurosurgery guy,' I think to myself. "Do you have a picture of Clay Johnson? Typically on those apps, there should be photos."

"Well, the other suspicious thing is that it looks like he erased the photos, likely after they had developed a connection."

That *is* really suspicious, but I'm still not done with the Blake issue. "One more thing—so what about the bloody clothing? The clothing I found in Blake's apartment the night of the murder."

"I'm sure there's an explanation for that given he's a surgeon, but we will look into it."

For a few seconds, I stand there waiting for Detective Cranston to say something and dispel the awkwardness of the situation. I just accused a man I've been seeing of murder while coming to terms with the fact that he was also seeing my murdered co-resident without my knowledge.

"Anyway, call me again if you have any new information," he says, finally breaking the silence. I thank him for his time and head out, feeling defeated, gullible, and blindsided.

Chapter 19

Kylie

Since my date with Sean, the pathologist, I am hypervigilant about surveying the area when leaving work and before getting on the subway. Given the unpredictability of my work schedule, the time I end up waiting in the subway station varies, and some days I work at the uptown hospital location so I avoid potential subway sightings altogether. I'm sure pathologists have more predictable hours given they aren't dealing with emergencies. Thankfully, I haven't seen him around the hospital either, likely because he "works in the bowels." He did text me once, a week after our date, asking to hang out again, and I politely declined. I honestly wanted to just ghost him, but I was worried I'd see him at the hospital or on the street and then it would be awkward, so I told him I was busy and didn't have time. I would think he got the hint given how our first date went, but apparently not.

Feeling triumphant that I had successfully avoided him thus far, I was shopping at the grocery store a few blocks from my apartment when I realized my luck was short-lived. Browsing the various almond milk brands, I suddenly see a bouncing curly head walking towards me. I can almost feel the puppy-dog grin slapped on his face as he inches closer. Dressed in sweats and my hair tied into a top bun, I don't look like my usual work self, but he has no problem spotting me.

"Hey, Kylie," he says as he strolls over to me. He's balancing a shopping basket on his forearm. I steal a glance at its contents, and he has a few essential items—eggs, milk, bread, and popsicles. Whole milk, to be exact. Not sure who drinks whole milk these days, especially in Manhattan, but I've seen stranger things. "Nice running into you here. I mean, we do live in the same part of Manhattan, so I guess it's not that unusual to see you here."

"Hi, Sean," I reply tersely.

"What are you doing here?" he asks.

"Umm, shopping for groceries," I say, my voice dripping with irritation.

"Oh, well, duh, I guess." He cackles, throwing his head back in a fit of laughter. "What are you doing after this is what I meant to say? I can help you take your groceries back to your apartment." An enticing offer for anyone who lives in NYC and has to lug home their groceries on foot, but I'm not willing to pay the price of him tagging along and knowing where I live.

"That's okay, thanks for the offer, though." I take one of the cartons of almond milk off the shelf and throw it in with the other items in my basket. I'm not done with my shopping but act as if I am for fear he is going to follow me around the store for the next twenty minutes. He continues to walk alongside me, that dopey grin lingering on his face. I quicken my pace with each step as I head towards the cash registers, trying to signal that I'm in a rush and don't want to be bothered, but he continues to bounce behind me.

"It's fine. Let me just check out and I'll walk with you. I'm not doing anything else. I owe you after our last date. I acted like a jerk." At least he has some insight.

"That's really okay. Thanks, I'm good." Annoyed that he's not getting the hint, I get into the shortest line and breathe a sigh of relief when another customer gets in line right behind me, cutting him off. Clearly disappointed, Sean trudges over to another short line to pay for his things. Vying to finish first so I can make it out of here without another assault, when I get to the front of the line, I give the cashier an urgent glance, my eyes pleading with her to quickly scan my items. She doesn't seem to get the message as she gingerly swipes each item and places it in the bag, and I get the sensation that time is suddenly standing still. I mean, this is NYC where everyone is always in a rush, but she does not seem to be rushing at all. In fact, I almost feel like she's purposefully going at a snail's pace. I give her an annoyed glance and audibly grunt, trying to communicate the urgency of the situation. She looks up at me, her eyes peering over her spectacles as she hands me my reusable shopping bag. I hurriedly grab the bag and book it to the exit. Sean calls after me, but I pretend I don't hear him and keep going.

As I rush away from the store, I surreptitiously look back every few steps to make sure he isn't behind me, causing me to almost collide with several people on the street. I don't find him scary in a serial killer kind of way, but I get so creeped out by people who can't catch a hint. I imagine there must be some screw loose, and I don't want to be subjected to their crazy. The grocery store is about two blocks from my apartment, so I get back home fast, but the stress of making sure he isn't following me is all-consuming. As I enter my apartment building, my phone pings and I see that he's texted me. *Why were you in such a rush? I was hoping we could catch up*, he writes. I wait a few seconds and see that he is still typing and writes, *Let's try to get together soon.*

What is wrong with this guy? I have given him no indication that I am interested. In fact, I've given him a lot of signs that I am *not* interested. I think about all the trials of being a woman in general. Not only do we have to constantly be fearful for our life—riding the subway alone, walking alone at night, climbing up the stairs to our apartments while having to watch our backs to make sure someone doesn't push their way into our apartment—but everything we do requires concern for our safety. All the while, we are thoughtful about not leading men on and letting them down easily so as to not bruise their fragile egos and avoid getting ourselves killed, but also trying to be direct and opinionated. It can be so taxing, straddling the line of being direct and being offensive. Meanwhile, I've never known a man who worried this much about coming off as disinterested or rude. I think about how to respond to Sean, and I decide on the easy cop-out.

Well…I'm sort of seeing someone so I'm not interested at the moment, I lie. Why is it that we have to resort to lying just to get a man to stop harassing us? I see the bubbles pop up at the bottom of the screen, indicating that he's reading the message and contemplating what to write next. He doesn't immediately text back, but after a few minutes, I see he's texted a sad face. I don't like to lie, but sometimes pulling the boyfriend card is the gentlest way to let someone down. I just wish it was actually true.

The good news is, I do actually have another date tonight. It's with that guy Mateo—the one I've been chatting with on the Connections app. I've been looking forward to meeting someone new. While I love my co-residents and hospital family, it can be so monotonous seeing and talking to the same people every day.

Unlike most of my co-workers, I don't have many friends who live in NYC and are outside the medical field. Most of the friends I made in college still live back home in Florida. They are at totally different stages of life than I'm in. Whenever I go back to visit, it becomes apparent to me how different our lives are. They are mostly married, some with children, and have been working stable jobs since they graduated. The few friends I do have in the city are at other hospitals and also lead busy lives in their respective programs. It can feel quite isolating working in a residency program day and night and not having family or friends from a past life for support. I am lucky I have great co-residents, but it would be nice to have other outlets outside of work.

I step into my apartment and notice the sink is practically overflowing with dishes. I try to stay on top of washing my dishes, but the last few nights have been so busy at work that I haven't had a chance to clean up. I start cleaning up the place when I get a ping on my phone. It's Mateo. *Hey Kylie, looking forward to our date tonight. How does this place look?* He sends me a link to a Mexican restaurant.

I haven't been there, but I could use a margarita, so I respond, *Looks good to me.* I finish washing the dishes and decide to go get a quick run in before I get ready for my date. During intern year, I was ambitious about running and would often try to get up before I had to get ready for work and do an early run. As the mornings got darker, though, I became more hesitant to do those early morning runs. There are so many true crime cases that can be traced back to Central Park, as it provides the perfect environment for a crime. There's the preppy murder that actually occurred in Central Park. After Jennifer Levin left Dorian's with Robert Chambers, they walked to Central Park where he ended up strangling her. Then, of course, there's the infamous Central Park Five case where a runner was raped and attacked, but that case is doubly sad given the egregious wrongful conviction of five children. Racial discrimination played a major role in their wrongful conviction, and while the men are now out of prison, they endured unimaginable trauma and injustice. Nevertheless, people keep running in the early mornings and evenings.

Thinking I was invincible when I first moved to the city, I kept doing the early morning runs, but eventually my mom, who was badgering me about it, wore me down and I stopped. I tried shifting to night runs when I got home, and that was just as disconcerting.

I pull on a pair of black leggings, a tank top and a pullover, tie my sneakers, and get out the door. Still leery about Sean somehow creeping around my apartment, I look out onto the sidewalk and check my surroundings before I walk out of the building.

As my feet hit the pavement, I think about the last week at the hospital and all the cases I saw. I had a patient in her twenties come into the emergency room with numbness in her legs. In the days prior to developing the numbness, she was having vomiting and diarrhea. After examining her, I was suspicious for an autoimmune condition called Guillan-Barre Syndrome that causes weakness and numbness in the arms and legs and can also cause weakness in the diaphragm, affecting the ability to breathe. This disease can progress quickly, so I asked the emergency room physician to order a spinal tap, and the results confirmed my suspicion. We got her on the right treatment before things could progress. A few days later, her symptoms improved, although she's not at her baseline yet. These cases can be quite frightening, though, as I've seen patients quickly decompensate and require ventilation. It dawns on me that I have a job that keeps me stimulated all the time. Some of the days are tough and long, and I reconsider what I'm doing with my life, but other days are rewarding.

I enter the park at the 85th Street entrance. It's still winter, but today is one of those unexpected warmer days that randomly pop up in the middle of winter and remind us that global warming is still rapidly occurring. And by warmer, I mean in the forties instead of the usual freezing temperatures. The trees in the park are bare, as their leaves have been completely shed, and the ground still feels wet from the rain the night before. There's also a musty smell in the air, reminiscent of the rain. There are several people running this afternoon and others biking. After a few loops around the reservoir, I lean on a tree and do some stretches before I head back to the apartment. A flock of pigeons land at my feet and nibble on the remnants of a hot dog bun. A pack of runners come through and force them to abruptly take flight in unison, leaving behind a few particles of bread.

As I turn onto 5th Avenue, I see a recognizable figure in the distance. A tall guy wearing a Yankees baseball cap emerges and, *oh shoot*, I know that chiseled jaw anywhere. I quickly duck into a side street. Ugh, can't I catch a break? You'd think in the largest city in America you wouldn't consistently run into people you know. What is today? The day of date hauntings of the past?

I haven't heard from Blake since I accused him of murder. Frankly, I'm a little embarrassed since that accusation came out. Apparently, Blake was questioned about the bloody shirt and pants, and since I was the one who was at his place that night, he put two and two together and figured I was the accuser.

When Stratton told me this, he said Blake was disappointed but seemed to handle it in stride. When the police asked about the outfit, he told them he had a nosebleed that day, which he's prone to getting. He had already discarded the t-shirt, but he offered to hand over the jeans. Incredibly, there were still traces of blood on the jeans that could be DNA tested, despite the fact that he had washed them, and the blood turned out to match Blake's. Forensic technology is so advanced these days. I felt silly, but I'm glad I said something because clearly the guy is a liar anyway. Turns out Stratton did not know about Blake and Chloe initially, but Blake did clue him in once Chloe was murdered because he knew it would come out after the police went through his text messages. I'm a little peeved at Stratton for not telling me about the Blake and Chloe connection sooner. It could have saved me a lot of heartache and shame. Perhaps he was trying to cover for Blake or protect his privacy, but we've gotten so close recently and have shared information, so it's strange he left that part out. Weirdly though, he hasn't even mentioned Blake to me. I wonder if Blake even told him we were seeing each other. He's so private that I wouldn't put it past him to keep that a secret too.

I crouch down behind a street vendor selling halal meat and watch Blake walk into the park. The smell of Middle Eastern spices and smoky meat fills the air around me. Stretching my neck and almost straining a muscle, I try to see if he's with anyone else, but it looks like he's alone. He seems to be talking to himself, or maybe he's wearing AirPods. It's hard to tell, but man, what a weirdo, albeit a hot one. As I turn to walk back towards my apartment, I get a ping on my phone from Lisa. I had texted her earlier about my run-in with Sean, and she just texted me back.

Wow, just wow. What are you up to right now? she texts.

Heading back to my apartment after a run and guess who I saw on the street moseying around?

The pathologist again?

No, CNS! I write with a nervous face emoji.

She texts back several exclamation points.

Today is your lucky day, I guess. Do you want to get a mani? I desperately need one.

A manicure would be nice before my date with Mateo.

Sure, let's meet up at the nail salon on 87th and 3rd.

Does 4 p.m. work?

Yep.

As I run up the stairs to my apartment, I can feel my tank top chafing my body, drenched with my sweat. I take off my sweaty clothes and hop in the shower. It's been two weeks since I've seen Lisa, as we were on different rotations and opposite schedules. It will be good to catch up. This is my first weekend off in several weeks, and I'm planning on making the most of it. When I get out of the shower, I throw on a pair of black leggings and an oversized cashmere sweater. Moving to NYC, I had to completely upgrade my wardrobe. Most of the clothes I owned were appropriate for warm weather. I had never even owned a cashmere sweater before, but my mom took me to an outlet mall in Florida, and we went on a winter haul shopping spree. I'm so glad I did that because otherwise, I would have been wholly unprepared for the East Coast seasons.

I'm waiting for Lisa outside the nail salon when she walks up wearing a long Sherpa coat and a black beanie. She crinkles her nose as she smiles and waves at me. She looks jubilant. "Well, I'm pretty sure Jeff is going to propose!" she screams. My expression mimics excited shock. "We're going on a trip to Napa next month during my vacation. And lately he's been asking me what kind of rings I like. I try to subtly nudge him towards round-cut diamonds. You know, they are the most expensive ones but also the most desirable, so duh." She lets out a shriek of excitement.

"Wow, that's great!" I wonder if Lisa texted me because she wanted to tell me this news in person. I feel a twinge of jealousy, but I suppress the sentiment because deep down, I'm happy for her. At least one of us is having luck in the dating world. "I'd better be the first to know when it happens. Well, me and your family, of course." We've gotten close over the last few months, and I think Chloe's death solidified our friendship even more, as we needed to lean more on each other.

"So, anyway, what's new with you?" she asks. "Sounds like you had quite an awkward day."

"Yeah, it was so strange seeing Sean randomly pop up at the grocery store and then Blake hanging around Central Park. I mean I know we all live on the Upper East Side, so it's not the weirdest thing in the world, but today it felt like the universe was out to conspire against me. Maybe it was all payback for wrongly accusing someone of murder." I bury my head in my hands.

"Oof, I forgot about that. Well, it was also a really nice day for the dead of winter, so I think many people took advantage of the good weather and got outside," she says. She holds the door open for me, ushering me inside.

When we walk into the nail salon, by a stroke of luck, we spot two seats right next to each other. The woman working motions to us to come pick a nail color and take a seat when we are ready. I scan all the colors and decide on a dark red that gives cozy, winter vibes.

"So, do you really believe the bloody clothing is from a nosebleed?" Lisa asks dubiously. "I mean, he does seem like he could kill someone and enjoy it," she adds. She raises both eyebrows, scrunching her forehead, revealing lines I never noticed before. Residency is definitely aging us all.

"Who knows? I think it's a reasonable explanation. It was definitely a lot of blood. More so than I'd expect from a nosebleed, but the police are pretty convinced he wasn't involved, and the timing just doesn't match up," I explain.

"How sure can they really be of the timing? Can they say with certainty that the body was dead for however long?" Lisa asks.

"Yeah, technology has gotten advanced at being able to decipher how long someone's been dead for, and the autopsy confirmed the findings." She nods her head in acknowledgement. "I am stuck on the fact, though, that when I got to his place, he seemed so bothered, but looking back, maybe he was upset because Chloe rejected him."

I think back to how his demeanor was so off-putting and his apartment was more disorderly than usual. Perhaps he had been moping over Chloe for days.

"Yeah, that makes sense, but maybe he was using you as an alibi," Lisa says, arching an eyebrow. She continues, "I don't know, I still have a lot of questions about him. Like why is he such a psycho in general? He can't just come out and say what he feels? And why did he lie about Chloe?"

Wondering if I should reveal this information to Lisa, I interject, "Stratton told me he actually had a traumatic childhood. Like really traumatic. He didn't give me specifics, and I didn't press him on it, but apparently there was a murder that Blake witnessed." As I get the words out, the nail technician sitting across from me raises her head, a look of unease on her face, and I crack a nervous smile. She averts her gaze and pulls my hand out of the soaking bowl it's been resting in.

"Oh my God." Lisa jerks back in her chair, her mouth gaping open. "Yeah, witnessing murder plus being a neurosurgeon is not a great combo," she adds. Interestingly, the nail technician sitting across from her doesn't even flinch. Probably not a great idea to talk about murder at the nail salon.

I think back to whether Blake and I even discussed his family life. He told me he is an only child, and his parents aren't in medicine. Beyond that, I don't know anything else. A tendril of guilt stirs inside me. Maybe I should have asked more questions about him. What did we even talk about on our first few dates? Looking back, I realize he was always the one asking me questions. He knows everything about my family, my life trajectory, my day-to-day, but I hardly know anything about him. I wonder if that was another manipulation tactic on his part, to keep his life as secretive as possible.

While we wait for our nails to dry, Lisa gets a call from Jeff. She picks up and has a gentle smile on her face. "Hi, hun, how's it going?" She covers the mouthpiece of the phone as she whispers to me, "He's at work right now, poor thing." I nod, knowing all too well how it feels to be working on a Saturday. "Oh, you're close by! We're almost finished here. We can walk back home together." She gets off the phone and says that Jeff is going to meet us at the salon and walk back to the neighborhood with us.

After our appointment, as we stand around outside, we see Jeff strolling towards us. He sticks his hand out and gives a wave. His blond shaggy hair, looking longer than the last time I saw him, falls in his face with each step. "Hey, Kylie, how are you doing? Long time no see." He pulls me in for a one-armed hug. For a guy who has been at work all day, he looks pretty refreshed.

"Good to see you, Jeff! I heard you've been working hard."

"Yep, you know, just been on that grind. I'll be working again tonight while Lisa goes in for her shift. I've got a major case." He puts his arm around Lisa and brings her in for a kiss. They look so happy together. I'm glad she's found the one. The three of us cross the street and make our way back towards our apartments.

"So, Kylie has a hot date tonight," Lisa tells Jeff with a spunky tone.

"Oh, nice, where did you meet him?"

"Oh, you know, on the dating app. Is there another way to meet someone these days?"

"Hah, yeah, it seems everyone is on the apps nowadays. So many success stories out there, though, so the odds of finding a match are pretty good, I'd think," he says, flashing an endearing smile at Lisa.

"Yeah, I guess we'll see. I haven't had the best luck dating recently, so really anyone semi-normal would be great."

Jeff laughs at that. "It is NYC. Normal is relative."

"True."

"Weren't you seeing some neurosurgeon?" he asks.

"Sort of. I think the term 'seeing' is also relative."

"Hah, touché. Well, I hope it works out tonight and he's not a total freak."

"Thanks, wish me luck," I say as I turn the corner and leave them to head towards my apartment.

A few hours later, I'm standing at the hostess stand of the Mexican restaurant where I'm supposed to be meeting Mateo. I'm wearing a black sweater with sequins lining the collar and a heavy black puffer coat. The temperature dropped precipitously over the course of the day, and I wonder whether I should even have worn a hat and gloves. The weather has been so unpredictable, I never feel quite prepared. Mateo hasn't arrived yet, but I'm about ten minutes early. I recall what happened the last time I went on a date and was a few minutes late. I still feel on edge from my crazy day of running into Sean, the pathologist, and nearly running into Blake. At least Mateo's not in medicine, though. He's a professor at a university downtown, so that should be a good change of pace, and the fact that he lives downtown provides enough distance in case I have to avoid running into him in the future. My phone pings, and I see that I have a text from Bailey asking what I'm up to. I respond that I'm on a date.

Ooooo, good luck, he writes back with a smiley face emoji. He goes on to write, *If you want to meet up afterwards, Hassan and I are going to the electric room.*

I give him a thumbs-up. So far, my second year of residency has been much more enjoyable than my intern year. While my dating life is a disaster, at least my friendships with my colleagues have grown.

Scrolling through my phone, I pull up the Connections app and look through photos of Mateo again. He's pretty attractive. The profile says he's six feet, has brown eyes and brown hair, and the photos reflect that. There's one photo of him in hiking gear, standing at the summit of a mountain with a backdrop of evergreen trees. There's another photo where he's dressed in a blue button-down shirt and khaki pants. It looks like he's at a semi-formal dinner. In both photos, he's widely grinning and appears wholesome. Often, though, people put their best photos on their profile, of course, and it can be disappointing when they show up in real life.

As I'm waiting by the hostess stand, I peer out the window, wanting to catch a glimpse of my potential date to see if he measures up to his photos. It's a busy Saturday night, so there are people walking up and down the sidewalk, heading to dinner or drinks. Everyone is bundled up in winter gear, most wearing thick coats, some wearing hats and scarves. I remind myself to invest in a few scarves before it gets too cold out. As I'm peering out the window, I see a familiar man walking with a woman on his arm, but I don't recognize her. Pressing my face into the glass and squinting to get a better look, I recoil in shock. Staggering backwards, I catch myself before I bump into the crowd of people standing behind me, waiting for a table. What the hell am I looking at?

Chapter 20

Blake

Today is the big day. I get to do a solo surgery. Well, solo as in I'm primary lead, but my attending will be supervising. I've prepared for this all week—watching several YouTube videos and reviewing all the patient's images last night, familiarizing myself with the case and the best approach to the tumor. I've scrubbed in on multiple meningioma resections, but this will be my first craniotomy for a frontal convexity meningioma that I take the lead on. While meningiomas are benign tumors, they can be problematic based on their location and whether they grow and put pressure on delicate structures of the brain. It's been a stressful time, especially since I was re-questioned by the police, so channeling my energy into preparing for this surgery has been a welcome distraction.

I pull the jeans in question out of the pile of clothing. I had actually just decided to toss the t-shirt in the trash, as it was pretty bloody, but I kept the jeans, which only had traces of blood. They were still able to test them, though, and eliminate me as a possible suspect...again. I haven't spoken to Kylie since before that. The night she came over, the night Chloe was murdered, I was obviously feeling down. I had gone to Chloe's apartment earlier; I was hoping to convince her to get back together, but she was adamant that she didn't want to see me anymore. I was really bummed about it and didn't want to be alone, so I texted Kylie. Looking back, that was probably a dick move. I don't blame her for being pissed at me, but I can't believe she would try to accuse me of murder. When I saw Kylie at the funeral, I downplayed my relationship with Chloe because I didn't see the point in telling her I was dating her co-resident. Despite how it may seem, I do actually care about Kylie and was trying to avoid hurting her even more. I still feel conflicted about everything.

I think I loved Chloe. I say I think because I have never really loved anyone except my aunt. I often try to remember if I even loved my mom, but I was too young to know what love was or whether I loved her. Love is a strange thing. Sometimes it's instant, and sometimes you grow into it. I think with my aunt, I grew into it. With Chloe, I just knew I had a strong feeling about her, but maybe it wasn't love but infatuation that then turned into love. Or who knows, maybe it wasn't love at all?

I really think Kylie and I have a lot in common, and I enjoy hanging out with her. She's smart, kind and beautiful. Plus, we have great discussions. I even thought about texting her again, but this whole police investigation has thrown me off. I should reach out to her at some point and try to clear the air. For now, though, I'm going to focus on my surgery.

As I walk into the hospital to round on my patients, I anticipate the movements I will make in a few hours. That first scalpel cut is like releasing a symphony into the air—a moment all surgeons anticipate. After that, it becomes like an out-of-body experience. I feel myself floating in the sterile, cold environment of the operating room, the glow of the operating lights above me, guiding my way into the delicate orifices of the brain. Everything I have studied, every video I have watched, every surgery I have been a part of—all that knowledge seeps out of me and translates into scalpel cuts measured in millimeters, making precise incisions with unwavering focus. I think back to a recent complex surgery I assisted Dr. Patel with—probably the most complex surgery I've ever taken part in. Watching Dr. Patel approach the floor of the fourth ventricle engendered a sense of excitement and anticipation within me. A highly delicate area of the brain, the brainstem is the control center of the brain. One wrong move and you could paralyze someone or stop the person from breathing. He was laser-focused, though. With Beethoven's Concerto #3 playing in the background, he wielded his instruments, moving with the beat of the music. With every maneuver, he uncovered more structures, the pons, the medulla, the colliculi, those voluminous structures resembling breasts—the superior ones responsible for our visual reflexes, the inferior ones for our auditory processing. Each structure carries weight in this web of processes.

Suddenly, I'm actually in the operating room. I've scrubbed in, making sure to follow sterile protocol to a T, and I'm wearing a pair of freshly laundered scrubs. I've made the first cut, and my scalpel is gliding across the dura encasing the brain. My attending, Dr. Patel, stands over me, serving as my guide. He's a man of few words, but when he speaks, it's always with purpose. "Nice and easy, Blake…You got it." A few utterances just to guide me along, but nothing more. He's stoic, but he relishes working with competent neurosurgical residents.

I lose myself in the labyrinth of the central nervous system, gently pushing tissue out of the way as I work towards the tumor, my end goal. Several hours go by, but I'm too focused to notice. I'm in my element. Tracing the edges of the tumor with precision, I make sure my margins are clean. My breath, which I feel like I've been holding this whole time, finally releases as I excise the affliction that is ailing my patient. Putting the layers of the brain back together, making it whole again, I continue to work with measured hands.

My task is now complete. I'm grounded again, my mind and body reunited. Classical music is still playing, maybe a Brahms piece. I can tell I have impressed Dr. Patel when he gives me a satisfied nod as we close the scalp and stitch. I step out of the operating room, drained but exhilarated. Our surgery was successful. Jodie, one of the nurses, comes up to me. "Great work, Dr. Weathers." She smiles approvingly.

"Thanks, Jodie." A sensation of warmth rises into my chest, and I feel my shoulders straighten as pride swells up within me. Feeling high off my surgery, when I get back to my apartment, I change out of my scrubs and throw on some jeans, a sweatshirt, and a baseball cap and decide to go for a leisurely walk. After being in the operating room for the last six hours, it's nice to get outside. My face feels hot as the sun beams down on it, reminding me there's a world outside the operating room. I stick in my AirPods and put on a podcast about the opioid epidemic. Yeah, I can't help being nerdy even outside the hospital. Walking up Madison Avenue, I take a right on 85th Street to head towards Central Park. It's a nice day for a run. I try to get out and run when I can, but today I want to take it all in, savor the moment. There's a cold briskness in the air, but not deathly cold. The branches of the trees overhead are dripping with water, perhaps from the rain last night. I've never minded cold weather as long as there's sunshine. Some people hate how cold the inside of an operating room is, but I think the cold helps build stamina, character.

People are walking around aimlessly. Runners pant as they exit the park. Others grasp coffees as they stroll. As if a walk is done better with a coffee in hand. There's a line outside a food truck, one selling halal food. I head into the park for a quick stroll, decompressing from that surgery.

Tonight I'm going to a work event at the home of one of our spine attendings. Stratton is coming with me. His family actually knows our attending well because of all the philanthropy they are involved in. I think about how different our upbringings are, but I'm still lucky to have the life I have. I'm also grateful that Stratton didn't disown me after he found out about me and Chloe. I was honest with him, though, as soon as she was found dead. I told him we had just started seeing each other a few months beforehand and I wanted to make things official, but she wasn't interested. Of course, it helped that the security camera footage absolved me of any wrongdoing. I'm not sure Stratton would have stuck by me if there was a question I could have been involved.

My aunt Claire is coming to visit soon. She tries to make a trip out here once every few months, as I hardly get a chance to break away. She loves going to Broadway, so I bought tickets to a show I think she will like. As I weave around the park, I wonder how simple life would be if I was just like everyone else—ordinary. Sipping an iced coffee, going on a run, having a steady girlfriend. Those are all mundane things that most people seem to get right. Why is it so hard for me to embrace the mundane? I feel like if I'm not living and breathing neurosurgery, if I'm not getting that adrenaline rush, the rush I also got from Chloe, I'm not truly living. I often wonder if the feeling I got from Chloe would have been short-lived if we had made it. Now I'll never know, but it would have been nice to find out.

Chapter 21

Kylie

Right there, across the street from me, is Lisa's boyfriend Jeff, with a long-legged brunette. I'm sure it's him. He's wearing a long grey peacoat that is unbuttoned, and a red scarf hangs loosely around his neck. The woman is leaning into him, giggling, her hair swaying from side to side as she laughs. It looks like she might be intoxicated or maybe just desperate; I can't tell which.

Long-legged brunette has on a beige winter puffer coat, and with bare legs sticking out, it gives the impression she's not wearing anything underneath. She turns towards the street, and I get a good look at her face—she's striking. Jeff blocks my view of her as he motions to her to turn into an Italian restaurant, having almost walked past it. He's smiling at her in a way that screams more than platonic as she leans in and nuzzles his chin. They walk into the restaurant and disappear from view.

I peer so intently through the glass window that the condensation creates an impression of my nose. I contemplate running out onto the street and into the restaurant just to see how he'd react, but I don't want to cause a scene, especially now that I may actually be going on a date with a decent guy. When I saw Jeff earlier today, he said he would be working tonight, while Lisa was also at work. What a liar. Lisa was so ecstatic earlier that he might be proposing, but this is the opposite of proposing. From here, it looks like he's actively cheating.

Trying to give him the benefit of the doubt, I wonder if his plans changed, but either way, what I saw certainly didn't look platonic. Maybe I'll text Lisa and see what she's up to, then casually bring up Jeff and see what she says. As far as I know, he doesn't have any family in the city, no sisters or anything, but Lisa hasn't told me everything about him.

I look at the time; it's 8:00 p.m. My date should be arriving soon. I decide not to text Lisa. Maybe I'll wait until tomorrow and talk to her in person.

As I'm looking at my phone, a voice says, "Kylie?" I look up and meet the gaze of a handsome Mateo.

"Hi! Mateo?"

"Yeah, it's nice to finally meet you." He has that same wholesome look that comes through in the photos. He's wearing a black tweed coat and black suede loafers. His smile is kind, spreading across his face, creating crinkles at the corners of his eyes. They have a tenderness to them—brown eyes rimmed with long, dark eyelashes. I am hopeful that this is going to be a good date.

The hostess motions us to our table. The restaurant is surprisingly warm and quiet for a Saturday night. I wonder if this is the right ambiance for a first date. Mateo pulls out my chair and I take a seat. While I'm trying to stay in the moment and focus on my date, a disquiet simmers inside me, my mind occupied by what I saw back at the window.

Chapter 22

Blake

Stratton and I arrive at a beautiful brownstone on 77th street off Park Avenue. An ode to nineteenth-century architecture, the home retains some historic elements like arched windows yet looks as if it's been updated compared to some of the other homes on the block. I'm dressed in a navy-blue suit, and he's wearing a tuxedo. It's a strange dichotomy, being a resident and living on a meager resident salary and then being expected to "keep up with the Joneses" when you are invited to a fancy formal affair at your rich attending's house. Kenneth Clark is a world-renowned spine surgeon. He's most famous for doing complex surgeries that many other surgeons refuse to take on. He travels all around the world, finding cases that have been deemed inoperable by others. His success rate is incredibly high, and many of us aspire to be just like him. His personality, on the other hand, is polarizing. I find him to be an inspiration, and so it doesn't bother me that he's a level five ass, but for many others in my neurosurgery program ranging from residents to nurses, they would like to avoid being in his path especially, when things are not going well.

Dr. Clark's personal life is also somewhat complicated. He's been married three times and has five children scattered throughout the country. Two of them are in college in California. Two of them live with their mom in New Jersey, and he has one living here in the brownstone with his new, hot, young model wife. Katerina Kassanova is a top model who's signed by an elite modeling agency downtown. Dr. Clark makes a point of bragging about this whenever she comes up in conversation. Last year, she walked in Milan and Paris in prestigious fashion shows, and we never heard the end of it.

Stratton and I walk up the sandy stone steps to the large black double doors. As I reach to ring the doorbell, I hear someone's footsteps approaching the door. The Clarks' house manager, Belinda, opens it. I've met Belinda a few times when I was an intern, and Dr. Clark had me run errands to his home. Once, he had left his laptop at home, and it contained sensitive patient information, which was why he had me leave the hospital to go fetch it. Of course, as an intern, you're on the lowest rung of the ladder, so you are constantly subjected to these menial tasks, but that's how you climb your way to the top. My aunt Claire would always get a kick out of the things I had to do as an intern. She would say, "You went to medical school to fetch someone's coffee?" I assured her that things would get better, and they did. Now I'm doing surgeries that I could only have dreamed of taking part in as an intern, practically without assistance. Not all of our attendings are as exploitative as Dr. Clark, though. Some, like Dr. Matthews are less abrasive and more nurturing. It's rare in neurosurgery to find mentors like Dr. Matthews, though. The unfortunate part is that he's not as well respected by his colleagues, which makes you think, the bigger the ass, the more the respect. It's better to be revered (and feared) than loved, I guess.

"Hello, Doctor, and Mr. King," says Belinda as she opens the door. Stratton also knows Belinda, as he's been here before. We walk in, and I am reminded of the opulence of the home. The foyer is decked out with tall vases filled with flowers, and a stunning chandelier imported from France. Dr. Clark once told me about his trek to get it: he said he saw the chandelier in France and Katerina just "had to have it." The problem was, the chandelier was meant for hotel spaces and unavailable to people who wanted it in their homes. He was so persistent that the designer agreed to send the chandelier as long as he sent the staff who could properly fasten it along with it. Dr. Clark paid for an entire workforce to come out here and properly attach the chandelier. I never understood some people's obsessions with material things. I can't imagine they bring any of them happiness, but perhaps they think if they keep adding things to the pile, to the life, to the repertoire, it will somehow add value. Value that will transcend their hollow spaces and give them life.

Katerina Kassanova is wearing a black, tight, form-fitting dress that accentuates her narrow waist and her slim frame. Her breasts, perfectly molded by a world-renowned plastic surgeon, are bursting out of the top of the dress. She has dark locks of hair spilling over her bare shoulders. She's wearing high-heeled shoes that look like they could poke someone's eye out. Her voice is soft and sensual. "Dr. Weathers, is it?" she says my name seductively.

"Yes, nice to see you again." She leans in and hugs Stratton, her breasts pressing up against his chest. She escorts us into the living area where many of my attendings and co-residents are already gathered. There's a grand piano in the corner of the living room, and someone is playing melodic music on it. Dr. Patel walks up and seems a little tipsy, as he's more congenial than usual.

"Ahhh, Blake, the man of the hour." He pulls me towards the others, and they gather around. "Blake did a phenomenal meningioma resection all on his own. I think he's ready to go into solo practice."

"Well, hopefully he chooses to pursue spine first," yells Dr. Clark from across the room. There's definitely a subtle rivalry between the attendings, who each think their specialty is the best for a variety of reasons. The stereotype is that people who pursue the spine specialization are out to make more money, as spinal surgeries can be more lucrative. I have not yet decided on a specialty for my fellowship, but I need to make a decision soon. I've never been in it for the money, though. Mostly, I've been in it for the thrill—nothing else can provide that adrenaline rush the way neurosurgery does.

Dr. Clark motions me over to the bar. "What can we get you?" He looks to the bartender, a lanky guy dressed in a full suit. Whenever there's a party here, he hires a full staff: a bartender, a chef, and a few waitstaff who walk around serving appetizers.

"An old-fashioned, please," I say. While the bartender gets my drink ready, a server walks up to us with a tray containing what looks like caviar on a little spoon. I am not a food snob by any means and would rather eat a burger than this fine finger food, but I need to fit in, of course, so I watch as Dr. Clark slurps one up, and I follow suit.

"Any plans for your next vacation, Blake?" he asks.

"I haven't really thought about it."

"Ahhh, well, all work and no play makes Blake a dull boy." He playfully wags a finger in my face. "You should get away during your next vacation. You deserve it after that glowing review from

Dr. Patel." A sense of pride consumes me as I relish this moment. "Katerina and I are going to the Maldives in a few weeks. I've been before with previous wives." He lets out a boisterous laugh. "But this will be her first time."

Still buoyed by his praise, I give him a warm smile. He lifts his glass, offering me a toast, and our glasses clink as they come together. "Sounds great."

As we are making small talk, Katerina walks over and whispers something in his ear, pulling him away towards the kitchen. He raises his glass to me as he follows her out. "Duty calls, make yourself at home."

I'm left standing alone and observing the others in the room. It isn't even 10 p.m. yet, and most of the guests already look like they've been overserved. Stratton is engaged in conversation with a few of the big hospital donors whom I'm assuming he knows from other fundraising events. This event is to raise money for brain tumor research. I've been to this sort of thing before. Stratton's parents would invite me to go and network with other physicians before I was applying to residency. It's always a reminder of how far connections get you in this town (and, frankly, money).

Dr. Clark returns from the kitchen and says, "What do you say we go chat for a bit in the study?" Pulling me away from the party, he takes me to what looks like his office. Plaques and various memorabilia pepper the walls, a shrine to himself. A Harvard undergraduate diploma, Harvard Medical school diploma, a diploma for completion of residency at Columbia University, and one for a prestigious spine fellowship at the Hospital for Special Surgery. Books line the dark shelves that stand from floor to ceiling. An armchair sits in the center of the room, tucked under a wooden desk that's piled high with books and papers. There's a leather daybed in the corner of the room, a nice spot for a leisurely afternoon of reading a book or taking a nap.

He pulls a cigar box from his desk and offers me one. I hesitate momentarily, wanting to make sure I do the expected thing. Some people treat cigarettes and cigars differently, as if cigars are more sophisticated and less toxic to one's health, thus, more acceptable. I think cigarettes and cigars are equally disgusting, to be frank, but peer pressure is a thing even as an adult, and fitting in is important in these settings. That's one thing I've learned being around rich, powerful people. Sometimes you have to do things you don't necessarily love to be accepted, to get you closer to the top. I choose a cigar from the box.

There's a doorway that leads to a private balcony outside the study. As we step outside, the night air envelops me. It feels like a special night. It's quiet up here, removed from the city noise. As Dr. Clark takes a long pull on his cigar, the smoke from the cigar curls in the air. "Do you have anyone special in your life, Blake?" he asks. I look at him, pondering the question. In the five years that I've known him, he's never asked me a personal question. In fact, I don't think a single attending of mine has ever asked me a personal question. "You know, like a girlfriend, a boyfriend, a fiancé, somebody?"

"No, I don't," I answer.

He cocks his head to the side. "You're a passionate kid. You remind me of myself. I'm obviously not an expert in love given my track record," he guffaws. Despite the fact that he's in his sixth decade of life, he's really in shape. He looks good for his age. He has that silver fox look, a fit, trim physique and an aura that exudes confidence and power. "You know, it gets old after a while. Hopping from one bed to the next. I know for a lot of us, neurosurgery is the one constant, but it's nice having someone dependable in your corner. I royally screwed things up with my first wife." I can sense the regret in his voice. I hope I never have the same. I take a tentative draw from the cigar; the aroma titillates my nostrils.

"My children grew up in broken homes. I mean, we did our best, but co-parenting is hard. It's not how I intended things to be, but Blake, our kind is unique. We can't be tied down. We live for the thrill. The adventure of it all. The adrenaline rush. When that rush goes to your head, there's nothing that can compete. No amount of pussy, no amount of love. The appetite for more is insatiable. You keep looking in all the wrong places to fill that desire, and nothing comes up. Half my kids hate me, and the younger ones eventually will." There's a darkness in his eyes now as he turns to me and gives me one last ominous look before we are interrupted.

Dr. Patel emerges from behind us. "Ah, here you guys are. What are you saying to this guy, Kenneth? Are you trying to pull him over to the dark side?" They both chuckle.

I excuse myself and walk back into the party, leaving them both standing on the balcony. Everyone looks inebriated, especially Stratton, who has that look on his face that I know all too well from our wild college nights. A little bleary-eyed with a flush across his face, the drink in his hand is spilling over a little each time he brings the glass to his mouth. There's a speaker at the front of the room talking about the impact of fundraising on the research and care of patients with brain cancer, trying to draw in funds, but no one seems to be sober enough to listen.

Katerina is languidly hanging over the edge of the leather sofa in the corner of the room. There's a man by her side whom I don't recognize. He's polished, wearing a tuxedo with a small handkerchief in his breast pocket. She leans into him, whispering and making sultry eyes. He touches her shoulder fleetingly and then moves his hand down to her thigh. Discreetly watching their interaction, I look around the room to see if Dr. Clark is nearby. A sense of embarrassment rushes through me on his behalf. After a few more minutes of canoodling on the couch, Katerina and the mystery man disappear together.

Across the room, Stratton is swaying his hips to the sounds of the piano and still holding a glass with one hand. Looks like he's going to be my problem tonight. Feeling ready to get out of here, I walk down the hallway, trying to find the bathroom. Belinda sees me searching.

"Hey, Belinda, do you know where the bathroom is?" She's holding a stack of coats in her arm, probably preparing to hand them off to guests as they depart.

"Yes, Doctor, the second to last door on the right," she says.

I walk down the hallway and turn the doorknob, suddenly stopping. There's a sound I can't make out coming from inside the bathroom, perhaps giggling.

As I open the door, from the narrow slit in the doorway, I can see Katerina Kassanova up against the wall and that mystery man from earlier pushed up against her, voraciously kissing her neck. They don't seem to even care or hear that I'm right there. I slowly back up out of the room and close the door again, trying to be as inconspicuous as possible. That is not the bathroom. I can hear her moaning even from behind the door.

As I back away, Belinda makes eye contact with me, a smirk on her face. I can't be sure, but she winks at me as if she knew what I would find and then says, "I said the last door on the right." Perhaps I hallucinated the wink, but she definitely said the second to last door on the right.

I quickly use the bathroom and go grab Stratton to tell him we have to leave. This is all just too weird. "Heeeey, Blakey, there you are." His glass is now empty, but he's still holding it and bringing it to his lips as if there's more to drink.

"We gotta leave, Stratton," I say firmly.

"Noooo, the fun's just getting started," he whines.

"It's 1 a.m."

"Oh, relax, you don't have to work tomorrow, right? Come have a drink, be merry." He drunkenly walks up to the bartender to request a refill, but thankfully the bartender looks like he's closing up shop.

"No, we really have to leave now. Things are getting freaky."

"Freaky, you say? Like you getting freaky with my sister?" He lets out an evil laugh this time.

"Come on, man, no time for messing around."

"Oh, like you messing around with my sister?" Clearly, I need to come up with a new word choice here. There's been some underlying tension in our relationship since he found out about me and Chloe. There are times I think he still thinks I killed her. He's assured me that's not the case, but something is still amiss. I understand how he'd be hurt that I didn't tell him about us, but I was trying to protect her as much as I was trying to protect myself. Especially knowing how powerful the Kings are in this city, I didn't want to potentially burn any bridges before I knew what the outcome would be.

The music is now playing as if this is a club. The pianist has taken leave, and this formal soirée has suddenly turned into a rager. Out of the corner of my eye, I see Dr. Clark chatting with some nurses from the hospital. He has one hand on the back of a young operating room nurse as she smiles coquettishly at him. The other women are standing close and leaning into his every word, eating it all up. I wonder if Katerina is still occupied with her "friend." I finally drag Stratton out of there with the promise of a stop at a pizza spot a few blocks away.

As we saunter down the street, I think about what Dr. Clark said. Most of my life, I've been in survival mode. Survive the trauma of my father, survive the murder of my mother, survive the loneliness of being a kid with no parents, survive medical school, survive residency, and now I'm not sure what else there is to survive. I've never thought about getting married one day or whether I want children. Those ideals seemed too far-fetched when I was in the depths of despair and merely trying to make it out. Success is important, of course, but there's a limit to how much success at work can bring into one's life. I reflect on the Harvard happiness study, which followed participants for over eighty years and concluded that only one thing determined happiness—the quality of relationships. As a child, I remember thinking relationships meant heartbreak, trauma, uncertainty. As an adult, I'm not really sure happiness should be the goal— maybe fulfillment, life purpose. I don't think I've fully grieved Chloe's death, but maybe I'm not capable of it. Maybe I'm not someone who is capable of grieving anyone. Loss is so normal for me that I've become desensitized to that too.

I look down at my phone and wonder if I should text Kylie to see if I could make things right with her. Maybe we won't develop a romantic relationship, but at least I could give her some closure. Closure is important to some people. I never got closure from my mom or my dad. After my dad went to prison, I didn't want to see him. A few years after he went to prison, he died of a heart attack, but I had no regrets. In fact, I was more regretful that he got to escape his reality and plunge himself into death. The bastard got away with it

Chapter 23

Kylie

A snowstorm is brewing and slated to start overnight. There's a chance we won't be able to get to work, and the overnight resident will have to stay in the hospital to cover for the day team. I would hate to be them right now. Poor Bailey is actively texting me right now, complaining about how he's likely going to be stuck in the hospital all day. *Cheer up*, I write. *At least it will be a slow day. Maybe you can curl up in the call room and watch some Netflix.* He sends back an eye-roll emoji.

Growing up in Florida, I never had a snow day, but we did have hurricane alerts. Nevertheless, it is sort of exciting thinking about experiencing my first real snow day. At about 6 a.m., it becomes clear we won't be able to go in, as the subways have shut down. The prediction is eleven inches of snow, but typically these predictions are overestimated. I watch excitedly as the flurries start to fall and cover the pavement. They barely have a chance to settle on the street as traffic is still ongoing.

I am about to dial my mom to FaceTime so she could see the snow fall when my FaceTime is intercepted by a text from Lisa. *Hey, Kylie, can I come over and talk? I've had a hell of a night.* She sends several crying-face emojis. I am surprised that she would be willing to make the trek to my apartment, although it is close to where she lives. It must be really important. *Of course*, I answer, wondering if this has anything to do with Jeff and what I saw. After I saw Jeff on what seemed like a date with another woman,

I contemplated telling Lisa the next day, but I didn't want to do it over the phone or by text, so I was hoping we could meet up and talk. When I texted her asking to meet me last night after work, she never responded. Maybe she figured it out on her own. In fact, I hope she did, which would save me the trouble of being the bearer of bad news.

I throw on a pullover and pull my hair into a low bun. A few minutes later, Lisa shows up at my apartment, and I can immediately tell she is distressed.

Her voice cracks as she struggles to get out what she came here to tell me. She is visibly fighting through tears as she walks through my door. I recall in that moment that this is only the second time I have seen her cry—the first was at Chloe's funeral. I, on the other hand, have had many blubbering moments where I was either home sick or tired from call or got chastised by an attending and felt plain stupid, so it was not unusual for me, but this was out of character for Lisa.

"Hey, what's going on? Is everything okay?" I ask as I lead her to the couch and set a box of tissues down next to her.

"Kylie, he's cheating on me!" she screams emphatically. Phew, there it is. "That bastard is cheating on me, and do you know with whom?" Before I can answer, she blurts out, "Chloe! Yes, Chloe who is dead! The audacity! I've given so much of my time and energy to this relationship only to find out he's been playing me all along!"

I stare at her in disbelief and put my hand on her back to try to calm her, but she is beside herself. She struggles to talk through wails and tears. I must have misheard what she said because I can't process what she just confessed to me. I suddenly feel frozen.

"Wait, back up. You're saying Jeff has been cheating on you? With Chloe?"

She nods and hands me her phone. "Look at this! It's a burner phone." I am dumbstruck, not so much about the cheating part, as I already suspected it, but the Chloe part. I'm not sure what to say. I'm not sure anything can be said. I attempt to placate her.

"Oh my God, Lisa, I'm so sorry," I say, feeling genuinely sad for her. I feel guilty that I ever envied her relationship or wished I had a similar one. But wait, did she really say Chloe? "So, you're saying he was seeing Chloe? As in Chloe from our work, who is no longer with us?" I ask tentatively. I wonder if now is the time to tell her what I saw a few nights ago when I went on my date with Mateo.

"Well, based on what I found on the burner phone, he *was* seeing Chloe and still *is* seeing other women, obviously not Chloe anymore. Go on, look," she coaxes me as she motions to the burner phone. Grabbing the phone from her, I nervously scroll through his phone calls, and there it is. He called Chloe on the day she was murdered. My chest feels heavy, and my fingers tingle. What is it with all these guys and Chloe? Sometimes this city feels really small.

"Keep going," says Lisa, prompting me to search further. I open his messages and see several messages between Chloe and him. They date back to almost six months ago, four months before she was found murdered. I can hardly believe what I'm seeing. At first, the messages are flirtatious, and Jeff is doling out compliments. *You have a pretty smile. You look gorgeous in that dress.* Mostly texting her based on the photos she posted in her dating profile. It looks like they met on the Connections app and spent several weeks talking on the app, then transitioned to text messaging on the phone before finally meeting up. The Connections app, however, is no longer on his phone. He must have deleted it. "Were you able to find his Connections profile?" I ask, thinking about all the other potential women he was likely talking to on there.

"No, he must have deleted his profile and gotten rid of the app. Maybe he was nervous I would see him on there, or that one of my friends might. Stupid me, thinking we were getting engaged soon!" She slaps her forehead with her hand and shakes her head in disbelief.

Scrolling through more of the text messages, it's clear to see when things got more physical. There are suggestive texts such as: *I can't wait to kiss you again, Last night was amazing, You're a great kisser,* and then it seems at one point the conversation shifts. Even a little dark and twisted. Jeff wrote, *I want to tie you up and strangle you.* To my surprise, Chloe seemed to play along. It was clear they had a sexual relationship. I look up at Lisa, who still appears to be in a state of shock.

"So how did Chloe not know he was dating you?" I ask cautiously.

"Read the messages from two months ago," she says, looking almost possessed at this point, her eyes nearly bulging out of their sockets.

I scroll further and see that at some point Chloe realized who Jeff was. Prior to this realization, she was referring to him as "Clay." Clay? Why does that name sound familiar? A sinking feeling overtakes me. The messages reflect that Jeff, or "Clay," was planning on breaking things off with Lisa to be with Chloe, but Chloe was horrified by the fact that he was cheating on Lisa with her. Chloe had never met Jeff because they were never in the same room. I think back to the times I had met him, and they were few and far between, so it was quite possible Chloe had never seen him with Lisa. Additionally, Chloe and Lisa weren't close, so there wouldn't be any chance for a run-in.

My stomach knots with anxiety as I scroll further and see that Jeff started sending her desperate texts. *Please, Chloe, talk to me. I'm breaking up with her. I swear. We can be together.* At that point, Chloe stopped responding to his messages. And then I see what I've feared this whole time…

Chapter 24

Kylie

Right there with my own eyes, a message sent on the night Chloe was murdered. *I'm coming over tonight to talk.* My whole body goes numb and frigid, a feeling of dread draining the warmth from my skin. My breath catches in my chest. Could it be? Could Jeff have murdered Chloe? I look back at Lisa, and she looks terrified. Her whole body shivers. I take a blanket and rest it on her shoulders. "Oh my God, Lisa, do you remember what Detective Cranston said? He said Chloe was talking to a guy pretty regularly. Wasn't his name Clay?"

Lisa nods slowly, and the look on her face tells me she's already connected the dots. "Yeah, that's what I'm getting at. Detective Cranston told us they were searching for a guy who was texting her the day of the murder, and Jeff was clearly texting her that day. Also, he specifically said Chloe was not responding to the text messages, so how many other guys could there be? It's obviously him." At that, she grabs a couch pillow and starts crying into it. I scooch a little closer to her on the couch and wrap my arm around her.

"Have you spoken to Jeff about any of this?" I ask, searching her face for answers.

"No, I found this today, and I didn't know who to turn to, so I came straight to you." She looks back at me, her eyes brimming with tears. I know what we have to do.

It's snowing hard out right now, but it doesn't seem to be sticking to the road. One thing about Manhattan, even if the subways stop, the traffic keeps flowing. With all the movement of cars on the road, the snow hardly gets a chance to settle. Given my track record with Detective Cranston and accusing Blake when he was already cleared, I am apprehensive about going to the police with this information, but this seems like a slam dunk.

I call Detective Cranston and tell him I have some new information. Lisa and I take a cab to the precinct, where we are met by another detective, who walks us to Detective Cranston's office. When Detective Cranston sees us enter, he has a look on his face that tells me he's skeptical about what we are here to tell him. I flash back to the last time I was here, accusing a guy who had a solid alibi and feeling like a fool because I was jilted by him. Detective Cranston must think I have no credibility now, and that I just enjoy spending the little free time I have accusing my friends and lovers of murder. Sitting at his desk, holding a cup of coffee, he motions for us to come inside. He puts down the coffee, pushing it aside, and gets up to greet us.

"Good to see you again, Dr. Saunders," he says.

I introduce him to Lisa and let her take the lead.

"Hi, Detective, I have some information to share about the murder of Chloe. I was cleaning out the drawers in my apartment and I happened upon this phone." Detective Cranston looks unmoved, his face remaining expressionless. "After going through its contents, I learned that my boyfriend was on a dating app and had connected with Chloe on there." She pauses as Detective Cranston narrows his eyes.

"Go on," he says. He sits back down in his chair and takes a swig of his coffee.

"I think he was using a fake name on the app. He's since deleted the app and has only been communicating with women over text messaging. At the beginning of his texts with Chloe, she's calling him Clay."

Suddenly, Detective Cranston's face lights up. He interrupts, "Yes, we've been looking for a Clay Johnson actually. We found messages from him on Chloe's phone. There were several others she was talking to, but his messages were the most substantial."

Lisa continues, "He was going to her apartment the night she was murdered." Lisa hands the phone to Detective Cranston, who starts reading the messages. I watch as he scrolls to the most recent message, the one that was sent on the day she died.

"6:45 p.m. That's about an hour before she was presumed to be murdered. The timing is suspicious. It looks like she never responded to his text but that she had been ignoring him for some time before that."

"Yes," Lisa continues, "if you keep reading, there's a point where she stops answering his desperate messages after she realizes he's my boyfriend. I'm sure she felt incredibly guilty for the whole thing." Lisa bursts into tears again. Detective Cranston walks over and lays a hand on her shoulder. He grabs a box of tissues off his desk and hands them to her. "Chloe was a really sweet, honorable person. If she knew that Jeff was connected to me, she never would have started seeing him. I can't believe what a fool I've been." Lisa continues to cry. I rub her back, and she rests her head on my shoulder. I can't believe this is happening.

Detective Cranston sighs. "I'm sorry for the circumstances, ma'am, but we are grateful that you brought this to our attention. It does look like these messages are the same as the ones we found on Chloe King's phone. Her phone is locked up in evidence now, but we will compare the two. We will of course have to bring your boyfriend in for questioning."

Detective Cranston gives me a satisfied look as we leave, hopefully redeeming me from the last time I was here and falsely accused someone of murder. I can imagine the pressure he is under to find Chloe's murderer given how esteemed the King family is. He also looks like he's aged since the beginning of this investigation. He has a more harried appearance since the first time we met. His eyes look glazed over, and his potbelly hangs more robustly over his pants. I hope, for his sake and ours, that we can finally put this case to rest.

We decide that Lisa will spend the night at my apartment because she is in no state to go back home and potentially see Jeff as the police contact him to bring him in for questioning. When we get back to my place, Lisa is still clearly distraught. She admits she hasn't had a bite to eat all day, so I run to the deli while she gets ready for bed and grab her a turkey sandwich. I can't imagine the mental state she is in. When I get back to the apartment, she's sitting on the sofa with a vacant look on her face.

"I feel like a terrible person. Jeff's life is going to be over." She pulls her knees into her chest and rests her head on them.

"No, Lisa, you did the right thing," I reassure her. She looks at me and starts to sob again. "Lisa, I have something else to tell you. Not that it means much at this point and doesn't make a difference now, but I need to get it off my chest." She looks up at me with a questioning look on her face. "The night I went out with Mateo, I was standing inside the restaurant waiting for him and looked across the street. And do you know who I saw?"

"Oh, Kylie, is this another CNS story?" She actually chuckles a little at this, and it's good to see her smile. "No, I wish it was. I saw Jeff with a woman. They were walking into a restaurant and looked a little too cozy to be platonic."

She looks pained by my admission and stares at me wide-eyed. A searing stab goes through my chest, making me wish I had told her sooner. "Wait, what night was this?" she asks.

"Saturday night. I think you were on call overnight at the hospital."

"Yeah…I was." She seems to ponder this.

"I'm sorry, Lisa. I should have told you as soon as I saw them together, but I didn't want to do it over the phone or text, and you were so busy, I never got the chance to tell you face-to-face." She nods, appeased by my excuse.

"That bastard. He told me he was working late that night. I even called him a few times because I was bored since it was a slow night, and he didn't answer. He finally sent me a text at 11 p.m. saying he was swamped at work and would call me when he left. An hour later, I got a goodnight text from him. I was suspicious because he always calls me before he goes to bed, but apparently he's been doing this forever, so he's a mastermind." She looks down at the floor, shoulders slumping into a defeated posture. "What did the woman look like?" she asks, looking up at me, eyes pleading.

"It was hard to tell since I couldn't see her up close, but she was tall and had long brown hair. She was wearing a beige puffer coat, but I could tell she was scantily dressed underneath because her legs were showing, and it was cold that night."

"Did you think she was attractive?" she asks with a pout.

"Like I said, it was hard to see her from up close, but from far away, she looked okay." Trying not to twist the knife in her chest even more, I avoid describing the closeness between Jeff and the woman.

"Why am I so stupid, Kylie? How did I not see this coming? This has happened to me before. I should have been more prepared and less trusting this time around."

"It's not your fault, Lisa. Some guys are just assholes. You can do all the right things and still be swept up by them. It seems this city is crawling with narcissists." While I'm sad about what Lisa is enduring, I feel hopeful for the first time since all this started that we can finally now put to rest what happened to our dear friend and colleague.

The next morning, we both have to go in to work, but Lisa is still acting like a zombie. I tell her she should call out of work, but she refuses to. There's a tacit culture in medicine and especially in residency where no matter how sick we are or how depressed or how bereaved, patient care comes first, and if one of us is out, the workload falls on someone else in our group. This principle makes all of us live by the #nodaysoff motto. It's a sad state of affairs, but that's how the medical world works unfortunately. The people who are supposed to be taking care of your health are often unable to take care of their own.

Last night, Lisa kept her phone on silent, just in case Jeff tried to talk to her. Sure enough, when she checked her phone, she had about thirty-five text messages and fifty missed calls from him. The messages started out mundane, asking where she was and when she would be home and then slowly devolved into more disorganized and angry messages like: *What is wrong with you? What are you doing?* Towards the end of the messages, he was more apologetic, asking for forgiveness and begging her to pick up so he could talk to her.

That night, we learn that Jeff was arrested for the murder of Chloe. News spreads quickly throughout the residency program. Dr. Mick is kind and offers Lisa to take leave, but she says she would prefer working to distract herself. I know she feels immense guilt for what happened to Jeff. I offer to have her continue to stay with me until things die down, but she says she will be okay to be on her own. The police also matched Jeff's fingerprints to the ones found on the bloodied knife at Chloe's apartment. Jeff was adamant that he was not involved, but with the murder weapon found and his fingerprints on the knife, the evidence is irrefutable. The police have their guy.

To my surprise, I get a text from Blake that night. It reads, *I know you probably don't want to see me, and I'm sorry for everything, but I hope you are feeling better knowing Chloe's murderer is behind bars. If you ever feel up for talking, I owe you a better explanation for my actions.* I don't have the emotional bandwidth for this, so I decide to just text back *thanks* and leave it at that. It does feel good, though, that he didn't send me any angry messages about my accusing him of murder. I contemplate thanking him especially for that and apologizing but decide I am being nice enough by responding to his text. At this point, I have told myself that there will never be a future for me and Blake, and if he reaches out again, I will just ignore him or give him a cold reply. It is getting harder to do that, however, as my friendship has grown with Stratton, and they are obviously very close. Despite the fact that Blake was lying to him about Chloe, Stratton seems to love him like a brother. The whole King family treats him as such. I guess there's no getting rid of him anytime soon.

Chapter 25

Kylie

A few weeks have gone by, and slowly, it seems Lisa has gotten back into her normal routine. We've started doing our Pilates classes again whenever we both have a Saturday off. We're attending more happy hours with our co-residents, and we've even talked about getting back to dating.

I had also taken a respite given the string of bad dates I had over the last few months and was feeling defeated. Plus, the whole Jeff situation turned me off of online dating, at least for the time being. Mateo was actually a really nice guy, but he was almost too nice. We went on another date, which went well, but the attraction faded for me. It seemed we didn't have much in common other than the fact that we were both looking to be in serious relationships. I decided I needed a little bit of a thrill sometimes too. With a few months left in our second year of residency and Lisa's last few months in her big apartment, we decide to host a big birthday party for her at her apartment.

The day of Lisa's birthday party, I get a phone call from an unknown number. When I pick up the phone, an automated message says, "You have a call from an inmate. To accept, please press one; to reject, please press two." I momentarily wonder if this is a prank call, but curiosity gets the best of me and I press one. I hear a familiar voice, and my heart skips a beat.

"Hey, Kylie, it's Jeff…I really need to talk to you." His voice sounds hoarse and tired. Why is Jeff calling *me*, of all people? I don't even have his phone number, so why does he have mine? I contemplate whether I should even respond, but he sounds so desperate.

"Umm, hi, Jeff," I mutter. A queasy feeling overtakes me, and I swallow the bile climbing up my throat.

"Oh, thank God. I've been trying to call Lisa, but she won't accept my calls," he says, his voice cracking. "I didn't know who else to call, but you have to talk to her. Ask her to just hear me out." My stomach writhes as I recall the incriminating text messages. "I swear I didn't kill Chloe. Please believe me," he pleads.

My hand feels clammy as it holds the phone to my ear. "Look, Jeff, I don't think it's a good idea for me to be talking to you. I have to go."

"No, please, just come see me, and I can explain everything."

I cringe at the thought of going to see him in prison. He continues to beg, and I panic and abruptly hang up the phone. I do not want to talk to this psychopath. Never would I have imagined that a guy like Jeff could have done this. He always seemed so reliable and loyal. From what Lisa told me, he did not have any problem sharing his feelings or connecting on a deeper level. Obviously murderers come in all shapes and sizes; some even have completely normal upbringings and seamlessly fit into societal norms. Like Ted Bundy. It's often mentioned that he grew up with loving parents and always came across as a helpful and generous guy. Co-workers and friends of his were completely blindsided when it came out that he had murdered all those women. Even the police glossed over him and didn't take

accusations against him seriously because "he didn't fit the part."
I sit and wonder if I should tell Lisa, but I don't want to put her
in a bad state the day of her birthday party.

I call Stratton and fill him in on what just happened. I feel pretty
shaken up about it and can't imagine why Jeff would want to talk
to me of all people. Stratton tries to calm me down and tells me
to just forget about it—that Jeff is probably just desperate to talk
to anyone who will listen.

I take a shower and get dressed, donning a red dress that ends at
my mid-thigh. I pair the dress with some patent leather kitten
heels. I've made an appointment at the blowout bar that Lisa and
I usually go to. One of her friends from high school owns the
salon and gives us a discount.

As I walk over to the salon, I text Stratton and encourage him to
come to the party tonight. His family is relieved that Chloe's
murder has been solved, but the mourning process will probably
never be over for them, so I assume he won't stop by. When I
get to Blow Dry by Kara, I'm greeted by Kara herself. Kara has
lustrous golden curls that fall to her mid-back, and each lock of
hair is perfectly in place, showcasing her hair skills. She's wearing
a cropped sweater exposing her midriff and wide-leg jeans that
accentuate her long legs. She's known Lisa since they were
children. Lisa has always admired her work ethic. She told me
that Kara wanted to be a hairdresser and to own her own salon
for as long as she could remember. As children, they would often
play with Barbies, and Kara would always assign herself the role
of the Barbie's hairdresser. She'd wash all the Barbies' hair with
shampoo and then dry them one by one, and finally style their
hair with hairspray. Since I met her last year, she's become my

regular go-to person for all my hair needs. She is always so welcoming and kind.

Kara puts her arm around me and takes me to the sink to get my hair washed. "It's so good to see you, Kylie," she says with a gentle smile. As she's washing my hair, she treads lightly when asking questions. "How have things been? I know how devastating this has all been for all of you who knew Chloe and now for Lisa with Jeff," she says sympathetically.

"Yeah, it's been a tough time. Residency is hard enough as it is, but add in a murder of a co-resident and now a cheating scandal that's linked to the murder. It just seems surreal."

She nods knowingly. "I always got creep vibes from Jeff to be honest, but Lisa seemed so happy, I didn't want to burst her bubble. The poor girl's been through so much. It wasn't until around Halloween when I saw her and she told me what had been going on with them."

It's interesting to me how people always later claim that the person was "creepy" or they got bad vibes when it comes out that they did something terrible. It makes me wonder whether that was actually the case or they want to make it seem like they had some intuition that others didn't have. "Yeah, it's pretty awful." I pause momentarily, wondering if we are talking about the same thing. "What happened around Halloween?" I ask.

"Oh, you know, when she discovered he was cheating," she says as she aims the blow dryer at another section of my hair. The concentrated heat of the blow dryer burns my scalp as she unclips another section.

"Are you sure that was Halloween?"

"Yeah, I remember it well because we were supposed to go to this Halloween party downtown, but then the whole night got derailed after she discovered the burner phone. I was all ready to go in my Cowboy Carter outfit, channeling Queen Bey when she FaceTime'd me in tears. She was crying, tears streaking down her face and screwing up her vampire makeup. I felt so bad and was of course disappointed we were likely not going out anymore but told her I would come over and talk to her."

I remember that night. Lisa had also invited me to go out with them, but I was working on a busy rotation and couldn't make it in time. I had major FOMO about that since I love Halloween. When I asked Lisa about the party the next day, she said she wasn't feeling well and never went.

Kara continues, "When I went over to her apartment, she was out of her costume and seemed to have calmed down. We talked about her confronting Jeff when he got home. I think he was working late that night, or so he said. Who really knows what he was doing now that I think about it?" She harrumphs, blowing a strand of hair out of her face. "After I left, I assumed she would confront him that night or the next day. I checked in with her a few days later, and she said things had worked out fine, and she sounded better, so I didn't bring it up again. I didn't see her again until after Chloe's death."

This is all news to me. Kara moves in front of me and starts working on the front of my hair. As she pulls strands of hair into my face, she masks the confusion that spreads across my face. Maybe she has her timeline mixed up. Chloe was killed right before Thanksgiving, and Lisa didn't come to me with the burner phone until mid-December. I remember there was that snowstorm, and we were unable to get to the hospital that day for our shifts, so the overnight resident had to stay. That date is burned in my memory. I slowly reach my hand to my pocket to take out my phone, maneuvering my body in a way that would avoid interfering with Kara's craft. I look back at my text messages with Lisa, and sure enough, that was the day she came over. Lisa told me she had just found the burner phone that day and hadn't told anyone else. Did I make that up? Had she known a whole six weeks before? But then why would she seem so distraught that day at my apartment if she had known for six weeks?

I shift back into my seat. "Do you know whether she told Jeff she found the phone?" I ask.

Kara starts smoothing my hair out, putting the final touches on. "I honestly don't know. I assume so because she seemed angry enough that she was ready to confront him and break up with him, but then I called to check on her a few days later and she acted like everything was fine, so I thought maybe they had resolved their issues or there was a misunderstanding. I didn't press her on it because once she makes a decision, she doesn't like others questioning her or making her second-guess herself. I've known her long enough to know when to stop pressing and accept the situation." She hands me a mirror to check out her work. "We're all set. And I must say, you look fabulous. Anyway, I'm glad he's behind bars and can't hurt another person."

I nod in agreement. "Thanks, Kara, this looks great. You're coming tonight, right?" I stand up from the chair and lean in to hug her, my fingers slightly entangled in her curls. We laugh as I try to disentangle them without pulling her hair out.

"Yep, I'll be there!" she responds.

As I walk home from the salon, I have a feeling that something is not right. Why would Lisa lie to me about when she found the phone? I don't know who to call and think this through with, but I figure Stratton might be a good person. Since Chloe's death, Stratton and I have become a lot closer. I feel like he's the only one I can talk to who is as invested as I am in finding out who murdered his sister. I do feel guilty that I ever considered him as someone who would want to hurt his sister, but hey, sometimes sibling rivalry and jealousy are enough motive for murder, especially when there's money involved and you have rich parents. I can probably rattle off at least five true crime cases that centered around those issues. I dial his number.

He texts me back that he's on the other line but will call me later. Perhaps it's for the best. I'm not even sure what I would say. I suspect my best friend in residency is lying to me, but I don't know why. Anyway, I'm sure Lisa will have a good explanation.

Passing store windows on my walk home, I catch a glimpse of my hair in the reflection and am awed by Kara's work. There's nothing like the confidence boost that comes from a fresh blowout in preparation for an epic night. I call my mom to FaceTime her and show her my hair, knowing it's only going to look like this for a short time. When she picks up, she's standing there with my niece, who is sticking her face into the phone and has her thumb in her mouth.

"Hi, Kylie, look who is here?" My heart melts as I see Cecilia's precious face on the other end of the screen. "Awww, hi,

Cecilia." She looks back at me and cocks her head as if she's trying to remember who I am. It makes me sad that I'm missing out on her growing up.

"Wow, Kylie, your hair looks great!" my mom exclaims.

"Thanks! I just got it blown out and wanted to show you." Cecilia tries to grab the phone and then starts to cry.

"I'm sorry, Kylie. I gotta go and feed her, but have a great time tonight. Call me tomorrow, okay, hun?"

"Sure thing, Mom. Love you guys." I sigh, thinking about how every now and then, that feeling of homesickness sets in.

Chapter 26

Kylie

I decide to talk to Lisa after her party given it's her birthday, and I don't want to cause any conflict during the party. When I get to her apartment, most of my co-residents are already there, and there are a few other people I don't recognize. I spot Kara in the corner of the room talking to a few other girls, probably some of her and Lisa's mutual friends. Her iconic hair, those glossy locks masterfully styled, glow under the radiance of the lamplight above her. Lisa runs up and embraces me.

"Kylie, so excited you're here. Let me get you a drink!" I can tell she's a little tipsy already. She's wearing a short pink chiffon dress that draws attention to her statuesque legs. Her sleek, pin-straight hair shrouds the contours of her face. She pulls me towards the kitchen, where there's a bar-like setup. Space in the city is limited, but Lisa and Jeff have a pretty big apartment by Manhattan standards, mostly thanks to Jeff's salary. A large kitchen area with a counter that can double as a bar spilling into an even larger living room space makes it an ideal spot for hosting. Unfortunately, Lisa is going to be moving out in a few months when the lease is up because she can't afford to keep the apartment on her own.

"What can I get you?" she asks with a smile.

"I'll just take a Celsius, thanks."

As she hands me my drink, Hassan comes up and gives me a hug.

"Always nice to see you outside the hospital," he says. He's wearing a blue button-down shirt with khaki pants, and I realize I rarely see him out of his scrubs. I think about how even though I spend hours a day with these people, the most hours of my day, and they already feel like my family, we don't get to socialize as much as I'd like outside of work. Hassan and I join Bailey and Marta on the couch and per usual, our hospital-focused chatter starts. Anyone who regularly hangs out with a group of doctors knows that most of what they want to talk about is related to their jobs.

"I had the most depressing case today at the hospital, guys," Marta begins. "This fifty-five-year-old man came in with weakness in his hands. When I first got the consult, I was thinking this is going to be a waste of time. I got to his room and started asking him questions. I wasn't too intrigued by his story until I started examining him and noticed he had fasciculations randomly in his forearms. Then I thought, oh no, I hope this is not what I think it is." Fasciculations are involuntary muscle contractions or twitches that look like ripples under the skin. They can be subtle, but when an astute neurologist picks up on them in the context of muscle weakness, they can be indicative of ALS. I look around, and both Hassan and Bailey look perturbed. Sadly, we know what this is going to end up being. "I really dislike diagnosing ALS," says Marta. We all nod in agreement.

"Yeah, it's the worst. I never forget those patients," says Hassan.

We will always feel connected by the patients we see and the trauma of residency in general. As the night goes on and more neurology is discussed, it occurs to me how we will all be tethered together in some way forever. We've grown closer since Chloe's murder too. Witnessing death on a regular basis in the hospital for patients we care for is one thing, but now that sense of loss is compounded by losing one of our own. I don't think bearing death will ever get easier, but we just get better at accepting it as the tragic part of life.

"What's Omar up to?" I ask Bailey, surprised that he is not at the party.

"Well, he's a bag of nerves right now. His investigative piece is coming out today," Bailey says with a proud grin. A jolt of excitement runs through me. I wonder if Omar has found something groundbreaking, as he did with his previous piece. "I think he's worried that there might be backlash to some of the information he's discovered."

"Like what kind of information?" I ask, unable to mask my curiosity.

"You know how he is. He has literally told me nothing. He says I have a big mouth and can't be trusted with sensitive information. Can you believe that?"

Yes, I certainly can. Bailey does have a big mouth. We all nod in unison.

"You guys!" he stammers. "You think I can't keep a secret?"

"We *know* you can't keep a secret," says Hassan.

Bailey glares at him. "Anyway, Omar will meet us out wherever we go afterwards to celebrate. He just needs to wait out the initial shock period when it drops." He rests his drink on a side table as he pulls his fingers through his hair.

"Interesting, that makes me think there's a bombshell in there," I say, pondering what kind of information he could expose.

"I shouldn't say anything, but Omar is not so sure the right person is in jail," says Bailey. He furtively scans the room with his eyes as if checking to see if anyone heard him. My eyes widen at the thought.

Before I can pry for more details, Lisa plops down on the couch next to me and hands me a shot glass. "Time for birthday shots!" she yells. Feeling a bit nervous about what Bailey just said, I lay the shot glass down on the coffee table and excuse myself. I want to be clearheaded when this article comes out. If there is a question of whether Jeff is the actual murderer, though, I hope Lisa does not get a whiff of the piece, at least not for tonight, so she can enjoy her party.

The party gets crowded around 10:30 p.m., and people talk about making plans to go to the nearby bars. Something I've learned living in Manhattan is that people rarely go out until 11 p.m. In most cases, that's when the night starts. I feel my phone buzz in my pocket and see that Stratton just texted me something. Maybe he decided to come over after all. I open my text messages, and a surge of anxiety rushes through me as I see the link to the investigative piece that Omar wrote.

Before I can open the article, Stratton calls me. "Hello? Hey, are you coming?" I yell, trying to overcome the sound of Bad Bunny playing in the background.

"Hey, Kylie, I need to talk to you. Can you hear me?"

I step outside the apartment, closing the door behind me so I can hear him. "Hey, sorry about that—it's so loud in there."

"Did you read the article?" He asks, sounding hyped.

"No, I literally just tried to open it when you called me."

"Omar found some new information about Chloe's case. Detective Cranston just called and said they are looking into other suspects now."

My ears perk up at this, and now I'm glad I didn't have more than one drink. "Really? What did they find?" I ask. A wave of dread envelops me as I think back to Jeff's call from prison.

"Turns out one of Chloe's neighbors was on vacation the week they were doing the investigations and happened to have a Ring camera outside her apartment. Omar kept going back to the apartment building and talking to the neighbors and made sure to go speak to the one who happened to be away. The neighbor submitted her Ring camera footage, which Omar sifted through, and you won't believe what he found."

Chapter 27

Blake

Yesterday, I met Aunt Claire at the airport, and we took a cab to one of my favorite Thai restaurants on the Upper West Side. Over pad Thai and mango sticky rice, I told her about my most recent surgery and then the interesting party at Dr. Clark's. She's always been a great listener and made a conscious effort to support me in all my endeavors. When she learned I wanted to be a neurosurgeon, she started following my journey every step of the way. Her supportive nature was apparent even in small, simple ways. In college, when I told her what book I was reading, she'd start reading the same book and would later discuss it with me. In medical school, when I'd talk about a fascinating case report, she'd ask me to send it to her, and she would talk about it with me after she thoroughly read it. In residency, when I bragged about a surgery I got to partake in, she'd look up the type of surgery. Sometimes, she would even send me a document containing an outline of the article with questions that she wanted me to clarify about the surgery. Despite everything she's done for me, at times, I still feel emotionally stilted around her, trying to keep a safe distance, for fear she may also be taken away and I'd lose another person.

Bringing a mouthful of pad Thai to her lips, she asks, "So, anybody special in your life these days?" I knew this question was coming sooner or later. I never told her things got intimate with Chloe, but she always sort of knew there was someone I was smitten with, and I think she assumed it was her. She typically doesn't pry, so I never feel the need to elaborate.

"No, not really," I say, avoiding eye contact.

"Well, I know Chloe's murder was pretty traumatic. You two seemed to have a close relationship at one point." She raises her glass of water to the lips, holding it there, waiting for me to answer before taking a sip.

"Yeah, we did. She was a great girl," I say curtly, as I take a bite of my dish.

"How's Stratton and his family dealing with everything?" The server comes over and tops off our water glasses.

"I guess as best as they can. They definitely feel better knowing the murderer is off the streets, but I don't think they can ever feel whole again." As I utter those words, I think about whether I ever felt whole or what that might feel like—to feel whole. Neurosurgery gives me purpose. Chloe also gave me purpose and a sense of security. But what does it mean to feel whole? Is wholeness only achieved when others can fill the spaces of your life? Is wholeness something you're born with that slowly gets chipped at when trauma ensues? Each traumatic event eroding the wholeness until there's emptiness. And when people talk about others "completing" them, does that mean they were always incomplete until that one person came along and made them complete? That puts a lot of pressure on the other person, the pressure to make someone complete. I don't think I ever want to rely on someone else to make me complete.

After dinner, we walk to Lincoln Center. It's one of her favorite things to do when she visits me in the city—hanging outside the plaza and watching the well-dressed crowds filter out. The backdrop of the fountains and the faint sound of music emanating from inside create a unique serenity. We take a seat on the marble steps, and she turns to me. "Have I told you how proud I am of you?" Her eyes are radiating joy.

Feeling uncomfortable, I avert my eyes to the floor. "Yes, you have, many times," I say, almost coldly. "Well, I'm saying it again. I know you don't like to talk about feelings and things that have happened to you, but what you've been through and what you've managed to accomplish is really astounding." "Thanks," I mutter under my breath. She pats me on the knee and gets up, walking close to the center of the Plaza. She motions for me to follow her, and I do.

"I wish your mom could be here to see who you've become, what you've achieved. She would be oh so proud of you, Blake." She gives me a warm smile as we stroll side by side.

Whenever my aunt compliments me, I feel undeserving of it. If only she knew how disconnected I feel from others and how I often treat women poorly. It's not my intention to be a jerk, but it's just how things unfold for me. When I try to pursue relationships, ones I think will bring me happiness, something always gets in the way. Maybe I get in my own way. That's probably what a therapist would tell me. At times I think I do want to change. I really do want to be better, more human, but then other times, I think my lack of humanity is what makes me a great surgeon. Maybe being less human is the key to being a successful surgeon. I consider going back into therapy all the time. Maybe when I'm less busy, I will.

As she hums with the orchestra heard faintly from inside Lincoln

Center, I'm transported back to the operating room, reliving the surgery I just completed. The symphony playing in my head brings me a sense of solace. I've finally made it. That little boy—scared, alone, and angry—put his energy into doing something great, something he never thought possible.

The next day over breakfast, Aunt Claire shares details about her first marriage with me. This comes as a surprise to me, as she's never told me the story of how she met her ex-husband and why things fell apart. Assuming it was some big secret, I never asked, but I always wondered what happened and why she was alone.

"We were in different places in life," she says. "He decided he wanted children. I didn't think I was ready for children." I'm surprised to hear this because I think my aunt did a great job taking care of me. "That was really it, but then six years later, when I had no choice but to be ready for a child, it felt like perfect timing. I was in a dark place having lost my closest family member, your mom, but now I had a chance to get to know my sister again, through you, *and* to have a child."

Her eyes fill with tears, but I can tell she's trying to hold back and not cry. She looks down at her plate and takes a bite of her omelet. She always gets an omelet loaded with cheese and bacon, dripping in grease. When I was little, she would make me omelets on Saturday and Sunday mornings and ask me to pick ingredients from "the omelet bar." She'd have chopped onions, mushrooms, spinach, bacon, cheese, just like at a hotel omelet station. She was always good at creating experiences for me. She peers up at me after she takes a bite.

"Sometimes the timing of your life just works out, but other times, you have to pursue things that you want." She places her fork down on the table. "I thought after Dan and I got divorced, someone else would come along. Someone else who had all his great qualities but also matched my timing. That never happened. When I turned forty, I decided I wanted a baby. I looked into adopting on my own. I even went to a fertility clinic and looked at the possibility of sperm donors." She takes a sip of her coffee, the aroma hitting my nostrils. "The strangest thing happened, though. The night before I was supposed to go to the fertility clinic to get inseminated, I got the call that changed my life and your life. I was heartbroken and devastated for you and your mom, but I felt I had been given another chance."

I fidget in my chair. This weekend is bringing up a lot of emotions for me, so many things I had kept buried down that are resurfacing.

She continues, "The next morning, I canceled the appointment. Not because I didn't want a baby anymore, but because I felt I owed it to you to be fully invested and step in as both parents. You had been through something unimaginable, and I knew you would need me to be fully present. I figured I could always go back to the decision to have my own. You quickly became my own, though, eliminating any other need that I had for a baby. Our connection was almost instantaneous. Once the sadness of losing my sister began to feel less all-consuming, joyful moments with you replaced it bit by bit. You chipped away at my sadness. You brought joy into my life. I knew I didn't need anyone else after that." She's still holding her mug of coffee and peers up at me over the top.

"Well, you saved mine, Aunt Claire," I say somewhat stilted.

"No, Blake, you truly saved me." She lays her arm across the table, reaching out for me, and gives me a squeeze on the wrist. "Alright, enough reminiscing. Let's talk about what we're doing tonight!"

I was never good at talking about my emotions, and I don't think I ever will be, but Aunt Claire always treads lightly, making sure not to push me too much.

Later that night, we walk through Times Square to the Broadway show. Clutching a box of Milk Duds and flipping through the playbill, Aunt Claire exudes excitement. She looks like a child giddy with anticipation for the show to start. I realize in that moment that it brings me joy to see her happy about something. Perhaps I can one day have a meaningful relationship with someone else. Just as the lights dim and the show is about to start, she looks at me with hopeful eyes.

"Blake, you don't have to do anything on society's timeline. You don't have to get married or have kids or want kids or any of that. All I ask is that you be open to love and allow love to come in."

After the show ends, I take a cab with Aunt Claire to her hotel and drop her off. She's staying near my apartment, but given I live in a studio, she always stays in a hotel when she visits. It's also nice for her to make a trip of it, feel like she's on vacation. She makes a point to stop by my place, though, and survey the apartment, checking out how it looks. When I first moved into this place, she helped me decorate it. She's always had a knack for finding good deals on expensive furniture. She also gave me her antique bookcase, the one that was in my room back home. I have always cherished that bookcase because I remember it bringing me so much solace, especially in those first few weeks after my mother's murder. I would spend hours going through all the books in there, finding stories to fill my head, distracting me from the reality I was living in.

I have to work tomorrow morning, and Aunt Claire is taking a cab back to the airport. As I walk back to my apartment from her hotel, I open my phone to a text from Stratton—actually, multiple texts. An article entitled, "The Ring footage that saved the Chloe King case" glares back at me. I scan the article, and when I get to the part about how Jeff might not be the murderer, I'm stunned. I don't even finish it as I realize that Stratton has texted me several times after that, the last one fifteen minutes ago. His last text message asks me to meet him at an address on the Upper East Side, a few blocks away from where I live. Looking through his texts, my heart sinks.

I have a bad feeling that someone may be in danger.

Chapter 28

Kylie

"The Ring recorded someone entering Chloe's apartment after Jeff had left," Stratton says.

My breath catches in my throat, and a sound escapes my lips as I take in this information. So maybe it wasn't Jeff after all? Bailey alluded to Omar not being so sure that Jeff was the murderer. But how could that be? All the signs point to him. There's a visceral gnawing feeling in my stomach, repeatedly scratching away at my lining. An acidic taste fills my mouth.

"Yeah, I know. I was shocked too," says Stratton. "But get this. Jeff never even made it into her apartment, Kylie. He knocked a few times, and she presumably didn't open the door. It's hard to know if she was even aware he was outside her door. She could have been in the shower or something, but a few minutes later, another person appeared at her door."

So Jeff was telling the truth. He told the police he went to her apartment, but Chloe never came to the door. He must have thought it was because she felt guilty about the whole Lisa situation and didn't want to see him. Stratton continues, "The suspect was wearing a hoodie, so it was hard to see the face, but they were about five-foot-six and actually had the build of a woman. Kylie, I don't think Jeff did this."

Trying to get my bearings, I grasp onto the wall outside the door. "But they found the knife with his fingerprints on it," I stutter. I don't know what to think. My mind is racing, and I'm in a state of shock. I'm trying to make sense of all this. "There has to be a mistake. He was clearly there, and the murder weapon had his prints." There's a moment of silence on the other end.

"But what if he was set up?" says Stratton.

I try to think outside the box. The murderer is not always the most obvious suspect.

"There's more, Kylie," says Stratton. How could there be more? I don't think I can handle any more bombs. "They found Xanax in her system."

"Did she have a prescription for Xanax?" I ask, confused by this information, as I'm not sure how relevant it is.

"No, Chloe would never take Xanax. She never took any medication. In fact, she was averse to taking over-the-counter medicine even for a headache. Plus, the amount in her system was enough to kill someone." I am suddenly acutely aware that I am experiencing a headache, and the bright beam of light shining from the ceiling lamp in the hallway is making the pain worse. Ugh, not again.

Just as I'm spiraling, the door swings open and Bailey sticks his head out, a cheerful expression on his face. "We're going to the Lion's Den; are you coming with?"

"Just a second. I'm on the phone. I'll meet up with you guys." Suddenly, I feel like I need to use the bathroom. "I'll call you back in a second," I tell Stratton and go back inside the apartment.

As I enter the apartment, the loud sounds of the music paired with the information I've just received make my head spin and exacerbate the pain that is building at my forehead. I can't even process what Stratton just told me. Xanax? Why would there be Xanax in her system? The murderer used a knife. It had Chloe's blood on it, along with Jeff's fingerprints. What would be the point of the Xanax? I need to go somewhere quiet and dissect the article.

Someone is in the bathroom in the hallway. I wait for about ten minutes, and nobody comes out. Putting my ear to the door, I hear what sounds like someone hacking up a lung. Gross. I consider using the bathroom in the primary bedroom. Hopefully Lisa won't mind, but when my eyes search the room, I can't find her to ask. My phone, with the article open on it, is burning a hole in my hand, but I don't want to continue reading it until I'm alone.

I make my way to the primary bedroom, pushing past people who are now walking towards the front door, leaving the apartment. When I get to the bathroom, I close and lock the bathroom door behind me. Before I sit on the toilet, I notice there's no toilet paper. Great. Kneeling down in front of the sink, I shuffle through the bathroom cabinets below it. Spotting a roll of toilet paper in the back corner of the cabinet, I reach my hand in, and in the process, topple over several prescription bottles. Perhaps I can find some Advil or Excedrin in here. I remind myself to see a neurologist and get a prescription for migraine medication. I pick up a bottle, and right there on the front, I see it.

Xanax. Why is everyone on Xanax? I mean, I know residency is stressful and we probably all have anxiety, but is everyone in my program taking medication? Placing the bottle back in the cabinet, I stand up and use the toilet while studying the article. I get to the line in the investigative report that says there was Xanax in her system per the medical examiner. The police did not find any Xanax bottles in her apartment, although they speculate she could have taken some from a friend, or the more shocking scenario would be that she was drugged. The amount in her system was enough to kill someone, to make them stop breathing. It's unclear then whether the Xanax is what caused her to stop breathing or the stabbing did, but something tells Omar they are connected. This further reaffirms the suspicion that Chloe knew this person. It also hints at foul play. Could she have been drugged? But Xanax is such a common drug. Maybe she was dealing with a lot and started taking it. But then why wouldn't the police have found any in her apartment? Stratton also seemed convinced she would never take medication. Who knows, though? She was hiding her relationship with Blake and then later with Jeff, so what's to say she wouldn't hide this?

The article also states that the person who was seen at her apartment had the build of a woman. What woman would be at Chloe's apartment that night?

Suddenly it hits me like a ton of bricks.

My throat tightens, and my palms start to sweat.

There's only one woman who has a motive.

Lisa.

Hold on, Kylie. Just think about this.

There are tons of people everywhere taking Xanax. Perhaps Jeff even took some of Lisa's and used it to kill Chloe. Perhaps Chloe asked Jeff for some Xanax. Perhaps the police missed the bottle when they searched her apartment. But the article clearly states that a woman entered the apartment after Jeff, or rather someone with the build of a woman, whatever that means.

The weight of this discovery is heavy. Crouching next to the toilet, I stick my hand back in the cabinet and take out the bottle of Xanax again. I take a picture, my hand shaking, and send it to Stratton. My phone rings almost instantly. It's Stratton. I'm speechless. I don't know what to say. I feel like I'm in a pool of my own sweat now.

"Listen, Stratton, this is freaking me out, and I'm scared to even say this, but do you think it could be Lisa?" I ask, my voice tremulous.

He goes silent, and I can almost hear the wheels in his mind churning at this thought.

"I heard from a friend of hers today that Lisa has known about the burner phone and Jeff's relationship with Chloe for longer than she led me to believe. In fact, she's known about it since October. Why would she lie about the timing of when she found out? I think she's hiding something."

Stratton sighs. "You may be right. I didn't see the video footage, but Detective Cranston confirmed the suspect appeared to be a woman."

"I was going to confront Lisa about the discrepancy in her story after the party. I didn't want to ruin the party, but I don't think this can wait." A pang of anxiety surges through me as I imagine having to confront Lisa about this.

"If you think she could be involved, don't do it on your own; this could be dangerous. Wait there and I'll head over. I'll also call Detective Cranston."

I wonder how long I can wait it out in the bathroom until Stratton gets here, but I don't want to draw even more attention to myself. There doesn't appear to be much noise coming from outside the bathroom anymore, meaning most people have probably already left, and I am now in here alone. "Kylie, stay there. I'm on my way," Stratton says and then hangs up the phone.

Chapter 29

Kylie

When I leave the bathroom, most of the party has already filtered out of the living room to go to the Lion's Den. Several text messages from Bailey, Hassan, and Marta flood my phone asking where I am and if I'm going to meet them out. Lisa is sitting on the couch with her legs crossed in front of her. She's changed out of her dress and is wearing a pair of loose-fitting jeans with a comfy-looking hoodie on top. She has a pensive look on her face.

"Hey, are you going out too?" I ask nervously.

"No, I think I'm staying here." She says this with a devilish glimmer in her eye. She no longer seems tipsy. There's a glass of clear liquid on the end table next to her, presumably water. She takes a big gulp of it. "Did you hear they got some new information about Chloe's case?" I ask.

"Yes, Bailey sent the article to the group chat. So, sounds like people are doubting whether it was actually Jeff." She turns to me as she says this and looks me dead in the eyes. "Are you doubting it's Jeff?" Her gaze is heavy, boring into me.

I glance at the time on my phone, breaking eye contact with her. It's 11:05 p.m., and I wonder when Stratton is going to get here. The front door slams behind me as the last party guest leaves the apartment. It's just me and Lisa now.

"Lisa, earlier today, I went to see Kara to get my hair blown out.

She told me you had known about the cheating and Jeff's relationship with Chloe since Halloween."

I wait to see her reaction, but her face remains still, eyes locked on mine. She taps the top of the glass in her hand with her fingertips, each tap synchronizing with the pulsations in my ears.

"When you came over to my place that night that it snowed, you told me you had just found the burner phone. Did you know about it before that night?"

She still doesn't budge.

I continue, "Why would you lie to me about when you found out?" As I say this, I feel sweat collecting at the back of my neck, and my back feels like it's drenched too. A feeling of panic rises within me, and I have the urge to vomit to rid myself of it. Maybe I should have waited in the bathroom longer until Stratton got here. I may need reinforcements.

She stands up and walks towards me. "Well, Kylie, do you think I had a reason to lie? That's the real question here." She is now inches from my face.

Feeling suddenly brave, I ask, "Lisa, did you have something to do with Chloe's murder?"

To my surprise, she doesn't even blink or reel back defensively. She just stands there staring at me. "Right. So that's the question then? Did I have a reason to kill Chloe, the bitch sleeping with my boyfriend? Or is the question whether I had a reason to frame Jeff? The guy openly cheating on me with my co-worker, humiliating me, and not being smart enough to cover his tracks?"

Glancing at the front door, I consider bolting out and running down the steps, but something makes me stay, standing there, waiting to know the truth, wanting to know what she's capable of. Hoping I have this all wrong.

She backs away from me and walks towards the kitchen. She suddenly speaks. "It took me weeks to think through what I was going to do. I knew what I was not going to do, which was to allow another man to denigrate me and embarrass me. I had already dealt with a cheating boyfriend in medical school, and I was not going to let that happen again. I schemed for weeks. I wondered whether I should confront Jeff and make him beg to have me back, whether I should make a spectacle and publish their text messages to social media or send an email to his boss revealing his philandering ways. I even considered confronting them both. Making a plan to have them both show up at the same place. I'd invite our friends and co-workers, maybe some of his co-workers, and humiliate both of them at the same time in front of everyone. That seemed difficult to pull off, though, knowing our conflicting schedules. In the end, I decided I didn't want anyone to find out, and it was best not to tell him I knew either."

She paces back and forth in the kitchen. "After I found the burner phone, I compiled a list of the women he was talking to. There were a handful of women he never actually met up with and a few he had one-night stands with from what I could tell based on the messages, but there was only one that he kept going back to. At first, it didn't occur to me that this Chloe was our co-resident Chloe. That's when I realized he had met all these women on a dating app. I opened the Connections app on his phone, and there it was. His pseudonym—Clay Johnson."

She laughs to herself, an evil cackle. "What a stupid name," she cries, throwing her head back. I couldn't tell if she was still a little buzzed or just plain crazy.

"I searched through the people he had connected with and found Chloe King. I could not believe it. How could he have matched with someone I work closely with? The audacity to then continue the relationship after realizing we were connected! I know Chloe was the innocent one in this situation, as she immediately cut him off when she found out he was my boyfriend. Even so, I had to punish Jeff in a major way. Breaking things off with him was not punishment enough. At this point, I don't even think he would have cared if I broke up with him since he was fawning all over Chloe." As she says this, her face transforms into a look of disdain. "I had to come up with a different plan."

Lisa closes her eyes as she conjures up the steps of her plan in her mind. I can feel my heart beating faster and faster in my chest, thumping so loud that I fear she may hear it too.

Chapter 30

Lisa

It hasn't been easy being me. I hate to play the victim, but as a child, I never quite fit in. My clothes were never right, my hair never cooperated, my personality, tepid at best. That being said, my parents prioritized my education, placing me in a fancy private school, hoping it would ensure my success. But they never paid any attention to me apart from making sure I was focused on my studies and meeting their standards of academic success.

There wasn't any overt abuse, and my parents loved me to the best of their ability. Both being busy attorneys, they never really had much time to spare. I always suspected that I was a mistake because neither of them were particularly interested in having a child. When I was seven years old, I overheard them arguing about who was going to take me to gymnastics on a Saturday. In the end, they settled on calling the nanny to ask her to take me over the weekend. It was lonely growing up in that home, but it was even worse at school. My mother never really took the time to show me how to dress or how to do my hair, so I was always getting made fun of. I was also a chubby kid, so that didn't help. I remember in eighth grade when I overheard Deborah Shaw, who was snickering with her girlfriends in the hallway say, "Can you believe she still wears pigtails? She looks like a toddler." I pretended I didn't hear her, but I know she said it loud enough so that I would hear as I walked by her locker.

There was always an anger that simmered inside of me. Sometimes I had the urge to hurt others just so they could see what it felt like to be me for a day, but I never acted on it, suppressing it the best I could to maintain some sense of normalcy. My attempts were futile though because that urge only grew as I got older.

In high school, I got excellent grades and was at the top of my class. I was expecting to be valedictorian, but then perfect Deborah Shaw with her perfect hair and her perfect family stole the title right out from underneath me. I ended up in second place—salutatorian. Everything I had worked for, everything I had accomplished, was for naught. She even had the audacity to walk up to me with a smirk on her face and say, "Second place isn't so bad." That was when I started having dangerous thoughts, ones that made me consider hurting Deborah Shaw. I started daydreaming about how I would eliminate her. Sitting behind her in AP Calculus, I watched her take dainty sips of her hot tea and imagined poisoning it. In gym class, I watched her run a seven-minute mile as I envisioned a car driving onto the track and crushing her. For nights, I had nightmares that at graduation, I would be sitting in the seats of the auditorium watching as Deborah Shaw delivered her speech to all my classmates. My parents, probably disappointed in me for being second best, would be flashing me irritated looks. A week before graduation, it was as if the universe had answered my prayers. Deborah Shaw was killed in a car crash. She was driving home after a party when a drunk driver ran a red light and collided with her car. I remember that morning at school, our principal called an assembly and told us what happened. I was stunned and even momentarily sad, but then a thought occurred to me. The universe wanted me to win. It was fate. My future was about to look different. While Deborah was still honored at graduation, I ended up giving the valedictorian speech. It was then that I realized I could get what I want with a little luck, a little karma, a little patience and maybe sometimes, only when necessary, murder.

College was pretty uneventful. I stayed committed to my studies, knowing I had to get the grades to get into the best medical school. I kept to myself for the most part. I didn't date, I didn't get close to people, and all my relationships were strictly academic. In medical school though, I started getting attention from men, like nothing I had experienced before. I had slimmed down and started to gain a sense of what was fashionable, and when I looked in the mirror, I no longer felt disturbed by what I saw staring back at me. When I met Connor, I had found my person. I still had the darkness within me, the one that rose up every time I felt someone going after what I wanted or felt threatened.

Things didn't work out well with Connor though either. I wasn't going to let Jeff and Chloe get away with this. Just like I didn't let Connor get away.

When I first found out about Jeff and Chloe, I thought long and hard about the best way to deal with them. I started constructing my plan. I followed Jeff to her apartment that night. I knew he was up to something. We kept track of one another's schedules by using a shared calendar. I had caught on to the fact that he was slipping out and meeting up with women during the times I had indicated I'd be working on the calendar, so I decided to start putting in fake shifts for myself so that he'd think I was working when I wasn't. At this point, the only other person he was talking to was Chloe, so I knew if he was going to sneak around, it was likely with her. Before I headed to my "shift" that evening, I waited for Jeff to get into the shower and pulled out the burner phone. It was exactly where he always left it—in his underwear drawer. Guys can be such dummies.

Sure enough, he was desperately texting her like the loser he is, asking to come over and talk with her. She didn't respond, of course, but my stupid boyfriend was going to go anyway. I had prepared for this day, though. I had bought two steak knives exactly alike. Earlier that evening, I had asked Jeff to cut up some lemons for me when I was tossing a salad together. I then took the knife he used and placed it in a Ziploc bag while wearing gloves. That was going to be the murder weapon. I took the identical knife and placed it in my pocket. I put the burner phone back where it was. He got out of the shower, and I, trying to remain inconspicuous, left the room but watched through the crack in the door as he pulled out the phone. That idiot looked so desolate as he saw that she didn't text him back, but he was determined to make an ass out of himself.

He got dressed. I kissed him goodbye, and a few minutes later I left too, trying to keep a good distance between us. Of course, I had to be incognito, so I was wearing a hoodie and wrapped a scarf around the bottom half of my face. As we approached her apartment building, I snuck around to the side of the building and hid under the awning of the building next door. I watched as Jeff left the building not five minutes after he entered. I then covered the main security camera with a black sheet. Of course I had scoped out the premises a few days prior and identified any cameras. I then entered the building, walked up to the second floor, and knocked. When Chloe saw it was me, she opened the door. Dumb bitch. She was probably thinking we'd have a nice chat and then make up. I told her I knew about Jeff, and she probably felt guilty. When I walked in, she looked genuinely upset. She started off by apologizing and saying how she had been meaning to talk to me and confess but had given Jeff the chance to come clean first. When she realized he wasn't going to, she wanted to reach out to me herself.

It wasn't all about Jeff, though. Everything about Chloe got under my skin. When I first met her, I knew her type. She reminded me of perfect little Deborah Shaw. They were the type of people who went through life always getting their way, always coming out on top because everything was placed on a silver platter for them. Natural beauty, loving parents and wealth—the trifecta for success. I had worked hard to be at our residency program, and I resented Chloe always trying to upstage me. I remember we were both on the general neurology unit. We would gather around a table to present our patients on morning rounds to our program director, Dr. Mick. Chloe would shine during these presentations. She didn't miss a beat. She always went above and beyond to show what an overachiever she was. One night, I was covering the neurology consults, and I saw a young woman who came in for headache. She had a history of migraine headaches, and her current headache fit the diagnosis, so I asked the emergency room to order some intravenous medication for her and went to see another patient. The next morning, while I was running around seeing patients, Chloe had gone to see the woman with the headache. She told Chloe she was having vision changes and couldn't see well out of one eye so Chloe got an MRI of the brain. When the report came back, it revealed that she likely had Multiple Sclerosis. She gloated as she revealed this information to Dr. Mick during our morning rounds. Dr. Mick flashed me a disappointed look. I was seething. The patient never mentioned vision changes to me, but Chloe could also have given me the updated information. I knew then that I had a new rival. The affair with Jeff was just the catalyst for what needed to happen.

During intern year, I was prescribed Xanax. I started seeing a mental health counselor for my anxiety and depression, and she put me on Xanax. I took it only once, and while it made me feel numb, I didn't like that feeling. I hate not being in control, so I decided to just deal with my anxiety and hope it would go away. I'm glad I kept the pills, though, because they obviously came in handy. At the hospital, we get so many stroke alerts that end up being cases where elderly people accidentally overdose on their pills. Family members bring in Grandma or Grandpa, concerned they can't formulate a sentence because they accidentally took too many benzodiazepines. That's where I got my idea. Well, actually, I'm lying. I had the idea a long time ago because I used it to kill someone else.

Chapter 31

Kylie

My mouth is gaping as I listen to Lisa explain how she framed Jeff for Chloe's murder. I'm stunned that this is the person I confided in, the person I've considered a good friend. Completely unrecognizable to me, she seems like a total psychopath. As I'm processing her confession, she drops another bomb on me.

"Chloe wasn't my first kill," she says, her eyes watching me, waiting for me to react. "You must remember the Brandi Lyle case. I know how deeply embedded you get in these true crime cases. Well, here's a little secret about that case. I knew her intimately."

Brandi was a young college student whose body was found in the East River before I started my residency. I don't remember the details, but the police never found her murderer. Actually, they weren't even sure there was any foul play involved. It ended up being a case of a depressed college student who probably drank too much and flung herself into the river. Is Lisa about to tell me she had something to do with that poor girl's death? A wave of nausea comes over me. *When is Stratton going to get here? I don't think I can take many more surprises.*

"So, Brandi, also known as homewrecking whore, was the girl my ex cheated on me with. I've told you about Connor before. He was truly my first love. Jeff doesn't hold a candle to him. Connor really brought out the best and worst in me. The first day I met him, I knew he was the one. Everything was going pretty great until that slut came along."

I'm not sure I want to know anymore. The more I learn about the awful things Lisa's done, the bigger a liability I am. As she paces, I notice something bulging out of her back pocket. Fearing she has a weapon, I drift towards the front door.

"Where do you think you're going, Kylie?" She sneers at me. "Don't you want to hear the rest of the story? I figured you'd be dying to know. This is firsthand true crime gold." A slow grin spreads across her face as she speaks. She steps a few inches closer to me, and although I will them to move, my feet are planted, frozen. "So anyway, one night, Connor and I were in the library studying. He went to the bathroom, and I saw that someone had texted him, so I grabbed his phone, and there was a text message from a person with the initials *BL*. It said, *Hey, what are you up to?* With a smiley face. That looked suspicious to me. I unlocked his phone and started reading the string of text messages between Connor and this person and figured out within a few seconds he was cheating on me. The person he was texting with was named Brandi. I racked my brain, and then it came to me: his ex was named Brandi. Connor had gone home to New Jersey over break and likely reconnected with her. Well, you can imagine how devastated I was." Her gaze drifts towards the floor, and the corners of her mouth turn downward into a frown as she paces around the apartment, stopping short of the kitchen.

Trying to appease her, I chime in, "I'm so sorry that you had to find out that way. That must have been terrible."

She looks at me, a sinister glint in her eye. "They would both be sorry soon enough. How terribly unoriginal and trite, though, right? Going home for the holidays to rekindle a former flame? A former flame who is still in college? Guys can be such pigs. I knew she was in college in the city, too, so then I started to wonder if they had been seeing each other behind my back this whole time, but after going through her social media posts, it looked like she had a boyfriend for some time and they had recently broken up, so of course she had to take comfort with *my* boyfriend." The look on Lisa's face is frightening, and there's a fervor in her eyes, like nothing I've ever seen before. As she paces, walking in a circle in the kitchen, she's breathing heavily. She appears to be re-living the emotions associated with the story she's telling me. "My blood was boiling. I told myself that I would wait to confront Connor after our exams. I wanted to think about what to do."

As Lisa speaks, I can hear the sounds from the street level below getting louder. It's close to midnight, and the city is just coming to life. The apartment building also sounds loud. There are people walking in the hallways and running up and down the stairs. I wonder if anyone would hear me if I started screaming. My mind flits back to the Kitty Genovese case. Perhaps, no one would come this way if they heard the screaming, assuming that others would step up instead.

"A few days later, I came up with a plan. I was going to confront Connor but not reveal that I knew who the girl was in case I had to take care of her later. I told him I saw texts on his phone and that he had been acting strange. He confessed he was seeing someone and wanted to break up. I took it gracefully. I think it made him more nervous that I took it so well. I've realized that no matter how you react, it doesn't change the outcome. If someone is ready to move on, resisting or acting crazy will just come back to bite you later on. It's better to let them think you're fine without them and then pounce when it's the right time."

She leans into the kitchen counter and starts twirling her hair, keeping her gaze steadily on me. "So, here's where it gets really good. I told myself I'd wait a few months, see how things unfolded with Connor and Brandi. I'd be waiting in the wings if it fell apart, and if it didn't, I had a backup plan. Connor, being the brilliant guy he is, wasn't that brilliant after all. I had a key to his apartment, where he lived alone. A few times when I'd stayed over, I had caught a glimpse of where he stashed his Xanax. Connor couldn't sleep without Xanax. He was probably addicted to it. What a weakling. I mean, medical students often abuse Adderall, which makes sense, but Xanax? He was probably too soft for me anyway." Her face looks animated, like she's proud of the things she's done. It then occurs to me that she *is* proud. She's relishing the moment. I need to get out of here now.

Chapter 32

Lisa

As I recount what I did to Brandi, I get flashbacks of that time. When Connor and I broke up, and he was free to be with Brandi, he introduced her to all of our friends, and once again, I was an afterthought. I stopped going to social events because I knew Brandi and Connor would be at them. My attempt to remain inconspicuous during those months worked in my favor though, and played right into my plan.

There was an end-of-year party. The night of the party, I overheard my anatomy partner talking about how Connor was sick with the flu. He wasn't going to make it to the party. The whole dormitory was going. I thought that this was my chance. While everyone was at the party, I unlocked the door to his apartment. It was dark in there, and I could hear him snoring from the entryway. He was always a loud snorer. I'm sure the benzos knocked him out cold. I walked to his nightstand and pulled out the drawer, taking a bottle of his pills. His phone was resting on the nightstand where he always left it. I took it and pulled up his text messages with Brandi. Apparently, she was going to the party. God forbid she miss a party and hang out with her sick boyfriend, but he told her to go so she wouldn't get sick.

I wanted to make sure I got to the party when Brandi was already drunk. It would make my plan work better. The timing was incredibly tricky, though. Across the bar, I spotted her, chatting away without a care in the world with a few medical students who also looked inebriated. She had a glass she would take frequent sips from resting on the bar. I figured it was now or never. I slowly approached her. My back to hers. As she was caught up in the conversation, I slipped several crushed Xanax tablets into her drink. She continued to take sips. I thought I'd have maybe about twenty or thirty minutes to execute the rest of the plan. Just then, I texted her from Connor's phone. *Hey, hun, I'm feeling much better and decided a short walk to get some fresh air would really help me. Will you come meet me at the park entrance on East 84th?* When Connor and I were dating, we would often go on long runs along the East River and spent a lot of time at that park, so I knew he had likely spent time with Brandi there too. I watched as she looked down at her phone. At that point she had enough of her drink for me to feel confident she would be a complete log in no time. She said her goodbyes and left. I followed stealthily behind her.

The location of the bar couldn't be more ideal. I knew we were in close proximity to the park, and it would be easy to get her there. As she walked, she was stumbling all over the place. She tried calling Connor's phone a few times when she got to the entrance and couldn't spot him, but of course I didn't answer. She walked closer to the benches lining the river and started calling out for Connor. When she got close to the river, she plopped down on a bench and passed out. She couldn't keep her eyes open anymore. I stayed behind and watched, making sure no one else was standing nearby. There are always homeless people hanging about, so I didn't want one of them catching me. It was almost 1 a.m., though, so I was hopeful the park would be relatively empty.

So, the rest was really quite easy. She was already passed out on the bench. I just had to drag her over the railing and dump her in the water. And voila, mission accomplished.

Chapter 33

Kylie

Lisa seems possessed as she stands across from me, her eyes glassy and her voice cold and distant. The weight of her gaze makes me fearful, and I wonder if I can outrun her. "You know, timing is everything, Kylie. In Brandi's case, I had to wait several months before I could execute my plan, leaving just enough time for people to forget about the way things ended between me and Connor. That way, I could never be a suspect. With Chloe, the timing issue was much harder, but executing the plan was a little easier since I didn't have to force my way into her apartment." Her mouth curls into a satisfied grin. "The waiting period between discovering the burner phone and coming to you with the information was so hard. I knew I had made a mistake telling Kara what I had found on Halloween. At the time, I didn't think it would ever get back to you, but you just had to go to my friend to get your hair done." She rolls her eyes in an exaggerated fashion. "The worst part, though, was having to endure Jeff for several weeks after I knew. At first, I thought, well, maybe he and I can work things out. Maybe I wouldn't have to get rid of him. The police didn't suspect him at all, and then you seemed hell-bent on Blake being the murderer, so I just let you run with it. You were basically going to take care of the problem for me. But then, much to my chagrin, Jeff continued to talk to other girls. Can you believe the nerve of that asshole? It became clear that I had to make his life miserable." As Lisa continues to speak, the sounds outside her apartment are getting louder. Shouting heard out on the streets and the patter of feet running up and down the stairs of the apartment building compete with the pounding in my ears.

"On my way to Chloe's place that night, I stopped by Starbucks. You know how she loved tea? I crushed several Xanax pills into the tea and handed her the concoction as soon as I got in the door of the apartment. Not having to employ any fancy methods for getting inside her apartment made this kill way easier. She was so appreciative. Her perfect little smile got so wide, and she was practically giddy. I wanted to slap that grin off her face, but I had to play along for just a bit longer. I told her it was a peace offering, and that I had come to terms with it and was willing to move past it in our friendship. We talked as she sipped the tea. She was such a lightweight. She was fading fast, so I knew this was going to be a quick kill." The way Lisa is pacing and gesticulating reminds me of someone in the midst of a manic episode. As she speaks, she rings her hands together and takes heavy steps. Her expression fluctuates between one of satisfaction and anxiety. "Fifteen minutes into our conversation, she excused herself, and before I knew it, she was out cold on the carpet. She didn't even make it to her bed. I think I was pretty compassionate, stabbing her while she was basically asleep. I grabbed the knife I used and put it in the Ziploc bag that I brought with me, containing the clean knife with Jeff's fingerprints, and then switched them out. I grabbed a towel and cleaned off the actual knife that was used and laid the towel next to the fingerprint-covered knife so the police would think the killer had attempted to clean his knife. I then left through the fire escape, carefully closing the window so there was no sign of anyone leaving that way. I walked over to the East River and threw the murder weapon in. That river is so dirty, I figured no one would even bother searching. It already stinks of dead bodies anyway, so what's one more murder weapon?"

As she finishes her story, I stand there and consider my next move. I glance over at my phone to see if Stratton is near, hoping to see a text message pop up indicating he's close by. Lisa walks over to me, her eyes narrowing.

"So, what do you think, Kylie? Can you keep a secret? Or is it too late, and you've already started running your mouth to half the city?"

"I haven't told anyone," I lie.

"Hmm, I'm pretty sure I saw you sneak out to talk on the phone. I told Bailey to go get you, and he said you were on an important call. Are you sure you didn't tell anyone?"

Before I know it, Lisa is charging at me with a knife that she pulls from her back pocket. Her eyes look satanic, a darkness taking over, and she has a sinister grin on her face as if she's enjoying this. I think about how violently she stabbed Chloe and how she's fooled me this whole time. I think about Jeff sitting in a jail cell when the real murderer is right here in this room with me. I think about how he called me and how I should have listened to him or gone to see him. I clearly didn't see this coming.

She grabs hold of me and stabs at me with the knife, which gives me a superficial cut on my arm, but enough of a cut to cause some bleeding. The pain is excruciating, and I feel like I might pass out. Her aim is off, and she's wielding the knife in an erratic fashion, making me wonder whether she is fully aware or in a state of madness. I grab her arm, twisting it to get the knife to fall from her hand. She's gripping the handle so tightly, holding on for dear life. I get on top of her to try to stabilize her, but she is stronger than me and pushes me to the ground. A sharp pain tears through my back as I hit the floor. Apparently, those Pilates classes have paid off for her. Not so much for me, though.

She comes at me again, more ferociously this time, and slices through my arm. I let out a wail, one that is surely heard throughout the entire building. Suddenly, I feel like I might not make it. As she's hovering over me, an angry look on her face, I lose focus. I think she's struck me again, but I can't be sure anymore. My body feels numb.

I may not survive the night. I never imagined it would end this way. I'm no stranger to seeing blood, but seeing my own spout out of an orifice in my body is a surreal feeling. My eyes search as my hands feel around to locate where the blood is coming from. Hopefully the knife hasn't seared through a vital organ. The serrated edge comes towards me again, and I maneuver to avoid it, twisting my torso like a contortionist. I gasp as it misses my heart by two inches, slightly grazing my stomach. My heart, which must be going at a million beats per minute, the way it pounds in my chest, the thump-thump deafening in my ears. My instinct to survive, kicking in to protect my heart and my head, the control centers of the body.

Blood continues to spill onto the pleated rug beneath me as I'm pushed down hard and my head makes contact with the floor, sending tremors through the walls. I let out an anguished wail and come to terms with who is trying to hurt me, to kill me. Wincing in pain, I grab the back of my head, hoping it's not cracked open. A breath, trapped in my lungs, escapes my lips as I force myself to confront my attacker. How is this happening right now? How did I get here? I try to scream again, but my voice gets caught in my throat. I am paralyzed with fear. Willing myself to fight back, to escape, I bang my feet hard on the floor beneath me, my body thrashing as my movements reverberate through the floor. I hope someone below us will hear me and call the police. The knife hovers above me, threatening to strike again, but I manage to grab my attacker's wrist and twist it away from me.

Attempting to scramble to my feet, struggling to push my assailant off of me, I'm once again confronted by brute force, and my body slams into the coffee table. A glass vase falls to the floor, shattering, the broken pieces dispersing around us. I feel for my phone, but it's not on me. My eyes scan the room, and I think I see it by the doorway—likely tossed across the room amid the scuffle. I try to crawl my way towards it when I feel another swipe of the knife at my arm. I look fervently around the room for any object I can use to shield me from the blows and stabs.

But it's too late.

My vision is fading.

I hear…

And then darkness…

Chapter 34

Blake

When I get to the address Stratton gave me, Stratton is standing outside, trying to get a neighbor to buzz him in. He yells into the intercom that it's an emergency, but the door remains locked.

"Stratton, what's going on?" I yell as I approach him. He turns towards me, a frantic look in his eyes. "Thank God you're here, Blake. I'm pretty sure Kylie is in trouble. Chloe's murderer has to be Lisa."

"Wait, what? Lisa, the neurology resident?"

"Yes, this is her building. I'll explain later, but we need to get inside."

Thankfully, one of the neighbors walks out of the building just then, allowing us to run inside and rush up the stairs. We bang on the door, but nobody opens it. We can hear muffled sounds inside the apartment, like people arguing and tumbling around on the floor.

Stratton yells Kylie's name. Just then, a man wearing pajamas, who looks like he was woken up out of a deep sleep, comes up the stairs. "Hey, what's going on here?" He shouts to us, a stern expression on his face. "What's all this noise about?"

"Sorry, we really need to get inside. Our friend is in trouble, and the police are on their way," Stratton tells him. The man takes out a large key ring with multiple keys on it, his hands quickly searching for the one to the apartment. After a few anxiety-provoking seconds, he locates the key and unlocks the door.

Standing in the doorway, I am stunned by what I see. The man gasps behind me. Lisa is straddling Kylie, who is passed out on the floor. In her hand, a knife that's clearly been used hovers over Kylie's body. For a moment, I hesitate, as I am back in my childhood home, weighing the decision to descend the stairs and protect my mother against seeking my own safety. Standing there, anticipating my next move, my adrenaline suddenly kicks in, and I run into the apartment and push Lisa to the ground.

She drops the knife onto the carpet, soaking it with blood. I look over at Kylie—her lips pink, eyes gently closed, chest heaving up and down, signs of life present. Grabbing her wrist, I feel for a pulse, and while thready, it's definitely there. It wasn't too late—we got here in time. Paramedics pour into the room, and then police follow soon after. In the mayhem, I lose sight of Lisa but turn towards the kitchen and find her crouched in the corner, once again holding the knife, blade lowered to the floor. She must have grabbed it again when I was examining Kylie.

An officer stands over her and calmly asks her to hand over the knife. Her face is still, eyes staring straight ahead. Her hair is matted to her face. She has blood all over her hands, dripping onto the floor. She finally breaks her gaze and looks up at the officer, releasing the knife as it clashes to the floor. I move aside as paramedics take over and put Kylie on a stretcher.

Stratton, who is clearly shaken up, is standing over the paramedics with a fear-stricken look on his face. I think about how traumatic the last year has been for him. I know the feeling all too well. We walk down the stairs of the building and decide to ride with Kylie to the hospital. It crosses my mind that she probably doesn't want to see me, but I have an obligation to be there for Stratton. She would understand. Part of me also feels connected to her now in some indescribable way. A feeling of warmth rises in my chest as I think about Kylie being okay, and an image of my mother flashes before my eyes.

Chapter 35

Kylie

When I wake up, I'm in an ambulance. I open my eyes and wonder if I'm hallucinating because there he is, staring back at me, a lopsided smile taking shape on his face. Why is CNS here? Oh gosh, is this a nightmare or real life? Am I even alive?

Then, another voice: "Kylie?"

I shoot a glance to my right, and Stratton is sitting there, his face brimming with hope. "Are you okay?" He gets up and comes to me slowly, holding on to the sides of the ambulance transporting us. A sharp pain is going through my head, and I grab it with both hands, trying to quell the ache. The bumps and potholes in the road reverberate in my spine as the ambulance drives.

"What happened? And what is he doing here?" I ask, glaring at Blake.

Stratton moves closer to me. "I'm so glad you're awake. I'm so sorry I didn't get there sooner, Kylie."

"What happened? What's going on?" I ask again, this time louder. As I speak to Stratton, I feel the weight of Blake's gaze.

"I came as fast as I could. When you told me about your suspicions about Lisa, I called the police. They were already tipped off by Omar's findings and were planning on going by to arrest her. When we entered her apartment, you were bleeding out on the floor, passed out, and she was sitting on top of you." My mind flashes back to our confrontation. Stratton continues, "She looked like a total psycho, Kylie. When we walked in, she seemed to freeze, and Blake rushed in and pushed her off of you." My gaze turns to Blake, who is still sitting there, silently watching me.

"Blake got down on the floor and checked your pulse, so we knew you were still alive. Thankfully, the paramedics arrived quickly."

Blake chimes in, "Yeah, I think you'll be okay, but you might have a concussion."

"Ugh, I feel like I've been to war and back. My whole body aches. But wait, how did Blake end up at Lisa's?" I ask.

"Oh, I called Blake as soon as I suspected you might be right about Lisa. I told him to meet me at her apartment. I was worried she would hurt you or someone else, and I didn't know if the police would get there in time."

"I see." I nod. Still feeling uneasy about the circumstances, but grateful that I'm alive, I look from Stratton to Blake and say, "Well, thanks for coming, both of you." As the hum of the ambulance drones on, I think about my last few moments with Lisa. She was unrecognizable. While my chest is intact, a sharp pain goes through it as I recall how Lisa manipulated me.

I turn to Stratton. "What happened to Lisa?" I ask.

"She's in custody now."

"And Jeff?"

"We're not sure, but hopefully being released."

"I hope so. I feel awful."

We pull up to the hospital, and Blake and Stratton get out and walk to the side of my stretcher as I'm hauled inside. Good thing they thought to bring me here, to the hospital where I work. As if I don't already spend every waking moment in this place. The bandage on my left arm is coming loose, the corners detaching from my skin. I'm scared to lift it in its entirety and see how much blood I've lost soaked on the gauze. A searing pain goes through my abdomen, and I look down and see a bandage also at my left abdomen. My mind flashes back to Lisa stabbing me. I can't believe she could be the one to hurt me like this.

"Do I need to be here right now?" I ask Stratton. "I think I'm okay."

He looks at me dumbfounded. "You were stabbed, Kylie, several times. The paramedics said the wounds are superficial, but you need to get checked out."

I sigh as I plop my head back down on the stretcher. The back of my head feels sore as it hits the stretcher. Thankfully, it's not oozing with blood. I'll probably end up getting the standard head CT, as every patient who enters the emergency room ends up with one. Blake waits outside the emergency room while Stratton accompanies me inside. He watches us as we go inside, and I can't help but feel a sense of gratitude towards him, maybe even a longing to have him close.

The emergency room is packed to the brim as usual. The lights are blinding, prompting me to shield my eyes. The sound of loud voices and shuffling first responders makes it hard to think. As I'm being wheeled into the trauma bay, I hear several familiar voices. Bailey, Marta, and Hassan are rushing towards me with fearful expressions on their faces. Several nurses and doctors come in to assess my wounds and determine whether they need any intervention.

"Kylie, we were so worried!" screeches Bailey. He grabs my hand and gives me a squeeze.

"I'm okay, guys. Thanks for coming, but truly, I'm fine."

"Can you believe we've been working with a full-blown psychopath this whole time?" asks Bailey.

"No, I can't," I mutter, still feeling the sting of my best friend in residency trying to kill me.

"Yeah, did you have any idea she was this deranged?" asks Hassan.

I shake my head no. Just then, I'm wheeled into another room, and an emergency room physician I recognize comes rushing into the room.

"Dr. Saunders, sorry to see you here in this state. You've been through an ordeal, haven't you?" he says with sympathy in his eyes. His glasses are perched on top of his head, pushing his sandy brown curls back.

"Hi, Dr. Klein. Definitely didn't expect to be here like this. Do you need me to see a consult while I'm here?" I say, trying to bring some levity to the situation.

"Hah, we are so busy tonight that I might just ask you for one." I wouldn't be surprised if the emergency room physicians did try to get curbside consults while I'm lying here practically bleeding out. He lays a stethoscope on my chest, and I remember how fast my heart was beating as I was fighting for my life. "Thankfully, stab wounds are superficial, but your pulse was thready when you came in. We're just going to keep you overnight to make sure your vitals stabilize."

"Sounds good. Thanks."

As he's wrapping up his examination of me, another physician enters the room. "Klein, remember that girl from last night, the one who was found in the river? Her urine toxicology came back positive for benzos."

My ears burn up, like they're on fire. Did he just say a girl was found in the river with benzodiazepines in her system? Is everyone in this city taking prescription drugs?

"There was a girl found in a river?" I ask Dr. Klein.

He puts his glasses on his face, and I can see smudges from his fingers on the lenses.

"Yeah, crazy story. A homeless man who was passed out on one of those benches near the East River heard a commotion coming from the water. He looked down and thought he saw a human limb, so he ran out onto the street and alerted someone, who then called the police. When they pulled the person out, she was barely hanging on. She was unconscious, and they couldn't get a pulse. After CPR, though, she was able to be resuscitated. She was also hypothermic, as you can imagine. We don't know how long she was in there, but she's in the ICU now."

My breath catches as I stare at Dr. Klein wide-eyed. "And they found benzos in her system?" I stutter.

"Yeah, apparently. Who knows? Sounds like she was troubled. Maybe trying to end her life?" He shrugs his shoulders.

This doesn't sit right with me. I'm not going to be able to rest until I figure out who this girl is. I think back to what Lisa confessed to me about Brandi Lyle. My head is still pounding as I try to remember the details of the case again. I consider telling my friends about my conversation with her, but my mind is so jumbled, I don't want to come across as unreliable. Plus, I probably do have a concussion.

"When am I going up to my room?" I ask.

"You're lucky you work here because they have a bed ready for you." He smiles warmly. Typically it takes forever for patients in the emergency room to get a bed on the hospital floor, but I guess a perk of being a much-needed resident at the hospital is getting a bed quickly when you're sick. They need to make sure we recover to be back at work as fast as possible.

After pleading with my watch party to go home and get some rest, Bailey, Hassan, and Marta finally leave. Stratton waits until I get up to my hospital bed. He promises to return the next day. I feel lucky to have so many great friends in my life. While things have been awkward with Blake, I'm grateful he was there to provide support for Stratton when they found me.

Now that I'm alone in my hospital room, I can do some investigating. I need to find out who this girl is that was found in the East River. I have a strong hunch Lisa is connected. I start frantically checking the hospital bed for my purse, which contains my phone and hospital ID badge. Stratton said the paramedics placed it in a plastic bag and sent it with me to the hospital. If I find my badge, I can log into the computers and find out what room she's in.

A redheaded nurse with a disgruntled expression steps into my room. "Dr. Saunders, correct?"

"Yes," I answer.

"I'm Sandy. I'll be taking care of you tonight. Seems like you're doing okay, though, considering what you've been through, so I expect you'll be out of here tomorrow." She slaps a blood pressure cuff on me and pumps the cuff to check my blood pressure. She writes down a few notes on a post-it, and I chuckle to myself as I remember Sean and his post-it story.

The clock on the wall reads 1:45 a.m.

"Excuse me, do you know where my purse is? I was told it would be sent to my hospital room with me." Sandy's gaze drifts to the corner of the room where my purse rests on an armchair. The overcoat I wore to Lisa's apartment is draped over the chair. I breathe a sigh of relief.

She grabs my purse and hands it to me. "I know it's really late, but your parents have been contacted, and they are getting on the first flight out here."

A sense of calm rushes over me. I was dreading having to explain what happened to my parents. As I open my phone, I see a barrage of text messages from various people—my mom, my dad, my older sister, Bailey, Hassan, Marta, Anaya. Feeling overwhelmed by the fact that so many people are looking out for me, tears come to my eyes, and a single teardrop falls on my phone screen.

"Is everything okay?" asks Sandy.

"Oh, yes. I'm sorry. It's just been a rough few weeks."

She nods her head in understanding. "If you need anything, just press the button at the side of your bed," she says as she exits the room. Relieved that she's not a talker and I can finally go look for this Jane Doe, I put my phone away and carefully get out of the bed, making sure to detach all the wires I'm hooked up to. Thankfully, she didn't put my bed alarm on.

I step out of my room and look around, making sure none of the nurses are around to reprimand me and force me back into bed. There's a computer sitting right outside my room where a nurse typically sits, but thankfully the night shift is quiet, and they're likely understaffed tonight.

I swipe my ID card, and it logs me into the computer. Pulling up the ICU patient list, I search the profiles for a twenty-eight-year-old woman. *ICU bed 8. Lacey Jones.* That name doesn't sound familiar to me. I open the chart and start perusing it. The emergency room physician who saw her when she initially came in is Dr. Klein. His note basically states what I already know— *28-year-old woman found in the East River at 2:30 a.m., pulseless.* There's no other information as to what the circumstances were other than that a homeless man is the one who found her.

I scroll through the other notes in her chart written by the ICU physicians. She's still unconscious and intubated. I throw on my overcoat to mask the hospital gown I'm wearing and stroll into the ICU, trying not to bring attention to myself. It's eerily quiet in here, the silence only punctuated by incessant beeping sounds coming from monitors in patient rooms. There's a nurse sitting at the nurse's station in the center of the ICU, scrolling aimlessly through her phone, but no one else in sight.

Casually walking to ICU 8, I peer inside through the glass window. No one is inside except for the figure on the bed. Sliding the glass door open, I tiptoe inside to get a closer look of her face, checking over my shoulder to make sure no one is coming in. An IV pole at the side of her bed delivers medication through various tubes connected to her body. The ventilator at her bedside monitors her breathing, and she appears to be breathing at least partially on her own. The breathing tube obstructs her face, which is swollen, and her hair is matted to the pillow propping her up.

The sound of her breathing gets louder as I inch closer to her face. Whoever she is, she seems to have a fighting chance. Suddenly, like a lightning bolt shocking through me, I realize who this woman is. Stunned, I almost fall back and topple over the IV pole at her bedside. My whole body starts to quiver. Scurrying out of the room, I take one last look at her from the doorway and walk hurriedly back to my room.

This is the woman I saw with Jeff outside that restaurant that night, the night of my date with Mateo.

Pangs of guilt hit my chest as I realize I may have played a part in her assault. Lisa did this. I have no doubt in my mind, and I'm the one who told her about Lacey.

I realize that I've been working alongside not only a psychopath, but a serial killer. I wonder if there are more victims. When Lisa was telling me about what she did to Brandi and Chloe, it was almost like she was gloating—proud to share how stealthy and calculating she was. How she managed to fool everyone—her friends, her co-workers, her boyfriends, the police—is incomprehensible, but I guess that's how killers become serial killers. They know how to get away with murder.

Epilogue

Blake and I sit on the bench watching as joggers pass by, others strolling with lattes in one hand and a dog's leash in another. The atmosphere feels light this afternoon, not the usual heaviness of the East River smog. There's a slight breeze in the air; the clouds hang low, darkness enveloping the skies over the river, portending impending rain perhaps. A pigeon sits perched on the railing lining the river, its head cocked to the side as it watches a woman take a bite of her bagel. I envision Lisa pushing Brandi and Lacey over that same railing, and I feel an acidic churn at the base of my stomach, but I'm glad that Lisa is paying for all of it.

We're looking out onto the water, avoiding eye contact. There's a silence hanging between us now, but an auspicious one, not foreboding. A silence that brings us peace, a shared moment bringing us closer together. A trust has been established. My right palm, feeling clammy, rests on the bench. Blake's pinky lightly brushes up against mine, sending a rush of warmth through my body. My left hand, holding a coffee, grips the cup more tightly, creating a tension that combats the warmth emanating from Blake's touch. I'm having a hard time processing what he just told me.

Blake just finished telling me about his mother's murder. He spoke as if it were the most mundane event of his life, a nonchalance, even levity given to a horrific situation. Perhaps he's told this story many times before. Perhaps he's desensitized to the trauma. There are no words, though. I stare straight ahead because it's too painful to meet his eyes. What he endured as a child is unimaginable, something I can never fathom. I surreptitiously steal a glance at his face. He appears to be in deep thought, but there's a sense of relief visible on his face. The lines on his face seem to soften, his taut lips loosen. Maybe relief at getting this off his chest.

Since leaving the hospital, since putting Lisa's case to rest, since putting the pieces of my life back together, I've found comfort in Blake's presence. I am reminded that he was there, possibly in time to save my life. What I know now doesn't change the past between us, the behavior that was so off-putting before, but it gives me a window into his struggles. Maybe the trauma of his past has helped him cope with the trauma of his present. He sprang into action when I needed him most, and for that, I'll always be grateful.

Blake turns to me, a focused look on his face, and seems to fixate on a spot on my neck.

"What are you looking at?" I ask.

"Just admiring your carotid artery," he says as if it's the most normal thing to say. A sly grin takes hold on his face as I look back at him with curiosity mixed with a little concern. He momentarily breaks my gaze and asks, "So, want to get dinner later this week?" His grin widens, crinkling the corners of his eyes, that cryptic expression lingering on his face. This man is baffling, but something about him keeps me intrigued.

"I'll have to think about it," I reply, giving him a playful nudge.

Note from the author

Thank you for reading my debut novel. This book was a labor of love, an ode to the city that trained me to be the physician I am today and the wonderful colleagues I've met along the way.

Being in the field of medicine can be arduous, exhausting and at times demoralizing, but oh so, fulfilling. I will be forever in awe of those who dedicate their lives to the service of helping others and contributing to scientific progress and innovation. Science makes all things possible, and I am grateful to be in the presence of inspiring, compassionate and brilliant people every day.

I am forever indebted to those who've worked alongside me, those who've trained me, made me the best doctor I could be and the patients who've given me the privilege of allowing me to serve them. I also owe my parents everything for their hard work and sacrifice to make my dreams a reality.

To my husband, thank you for supporting me in everything I set my mind to and always being my #1 fan. Please look out for the sequel to The Resident Murder, a continuation of Dr. Kylie Saunders and Dr. Blake Weathers' journeys.

If you enjoyed this book, please consider leaving me a review on Amazon and/or Goodreads:

Amazon: geni.us/theresidentmurder
goodreads.com/book/show/240723135-the-resident-murder

Read on about Kylie in book 2: The Socialite Murder

To buy: geni.us/Qp0JA

Sign up here for updates on the release: jessikroft.com

About the Author

Jessi Kroft is a native New Yorker and physician. This is her debut thriller.

Social media links: Follow me on Instagram, Facebook, Tiktok, Goodreads

instagram.com/jessi_kroft

facebook.com/profile.php?id=61578259437593

tiktok.com/@jessi_kroft_author

goodreads.com/author/show/58714652.Jessi_Kroft

Website link: jessikroft.com

9 798218 767204